D1084594

YOU
ALWAYS
COME BACK

YOU ALWAYS COME BACK

A NOVEL

EMILY SMITH

CROOKED
LANE

NEW YORK

Published in the United States by Crooked Lane Books, an imprint of The Quick Brown Fox & Company LLC.

Crooked Lane Books and its logo are trademarks of The Quick Brown Fox & Company LLC.

Library of Congress Catalog-in-Publication data available upon request.

ISBN (hardcover): 978-1-63910-586-1
ISBN (ebook): 978-1-63910-587-8

Cover design by Nebojsa Zoric

Printed in the United States.

www.crookedlanebooks.com

Crooked Lane Books
34 West 27th St., 10th Floor
New York, NY 10001

First Edition: October 2023

10 9 8 7 6 5 4 3 2 1

For my parents, Dave and Mary

I can't sleep 'cause my bed's on fire
Don't touch me, I'm a real live wire

—Talking Heads, "Psycho Killer"

PROLOGUE

M Y FIRST MEMORY is of a beautiful violence—a Southern summer storm.

It haunts me in my dreams, whirling and echoing across the lake, but it's really *his* voice I hear in every bellow. My father, my birthright—they're calling me home.

I hear that clap of thunder, reminiscent of a deep drum, the rapid plinking of rain droplets on our beaten tin roof like the high-pitched notes of woodwinds. If I really let myself in it, I'm back in my bed, that spitfire kid, and I already think I understand the universe.

It's a symphony this night. I know it in my five-year-old bones as I swing my legs over onto the worn oak floorboards. My straw hair's tied up in uneven pigtails, sweat soaking my white nightgown as it has every night this summer, even with the box fan. I don't put on shoes. If I own a pair yet, I don't wear them. Besides, I like the feel of mud between my toes, the smooth stones clipping my heels whenever I run across our gravel drive.

I glide down the hall, past my three brothers asleep in their rooms, then sidle right on by Kathy's, where her door stands cracked. I know better than to wake any of them, especially not my mama. The one time I tried, she cuffed me clean across the ear in the way she reserved exclusively for her children back in those saner days. "Those storms are too frequent. If I woke for every lightning blast or hurricane breezing by, I'd never sleep in this Georgia heat."

My siblings feel much the same way. Auggie, my only ally, is a deep sleeper, and Kathy always says it's a sin to wake the dead. Mark never cares none for staying up, Deck's too little, and the twins won't take seed in Kathy's womb for another half a decade yet.

So I leave her and the others be, run on down the recently renovated stairs, past the receiving rooms dominated by flora and garden construction equipment in every shape and kind, and slide on past Father Time dominating the center of the foyer. I hardly pause when I reach the porch outside and see fog.

I've always been a night owl—even as a baby Harry swears I didn't sleep, and tonight I'm determined to watch the August tempest roll in across the lake. Something in me has been waiting for it.

I step out in the haze. Down the hill I saunter like a ghost, possessed to see what all the fuss is about. To me the coming storm is a conversation between lake and sky.

Next thing I know, I'm sitting on the edge of the dock, the onyx water before me, when another telltale crack sounds overhead. It's a concerto of anger and joy and the Almighty, though I don't have words like this yet. The atmosphere paints gray as the clouds encroach on a perfect moon.

Then I see something across the water: my daddy, Harry.

He works the night shift at the factory in Hazel one town over. He's the type of man who would rather work two jobs sixteen hours a day than see his wife work one. I often wait for him on nights like this to come back home. He always appears on the lake like a speck of dust, slowly growing into sight. As an adult, I still fantasize about his form floating toward me, the sound of his troller's motor cutting out as he reaches the dock like he is right now.

"Livewire," his bass voice says to me as he secures a rope to a dock cleat beside me. "What're you doing out here? It's about to storm."

My feet dangle over the edge, still too short to hit the water. "No, it ain't."

Storms have been passing through all night, but I've always been good at fibbing to keep out of trouble.

"Isn't, not ain't," Harry corrects, as he evaluates me with suspicion. "And how do you know that?"

I grin. "Just a feeling. It's in the wind if you listen. Can't you tell?"

He makes a move to crane his neck, as if in that gesture alone, he can communicate with Summer herself. "Yeah. I can hear it. It's telling me it's gonna be a big one."

He sits down beside me, crossing his legs on the wood like I hear they do in school. His ankles would be in the water if he draped them over the edge like I do.

"I want to teach you something, if you're gonna be out here like this," he says. "Now, listen good."

He holds his finger up toward the sky and waits. I bunch up my gown to my knees and stare at him, feeling funny, impatient. He shakes his head. "Just wait."

I do as I'm told, the wind wrestling my hair as it begins to pick up. Murky clouds block out the stars. A clap comes overhead, though there's no visible streak of white to accompany it.

"One Mississippi," Harry speaks slowly. "Two Mississippi. Three Mississippi. Four Mississippi . . ." He keeps going, gets to sixteen.

The sky roars. A deafening crack.

"You hear that?" he asks.

I nod.

"That means the storm's three miles out. Every five seconds you count equals one mile."

"A whole mile?" I say. "Well, that's ages away!"

"No, it isn't. You try it." Another clap.

I hold up my finger, like I am conducting the heavens. "One Mississippi." I pause.

Harry counts with me. "Two Mississippi." Pause. "Three Mississippi." We reach ten.

Clap. This time the clouds over the east end of the lake flash.

My mouth drops and I look to him in amazement. "Two miles."

He nods. "We better head back up. Storms like this move in quick."

"Do we have to? It won't hurt us," I insist, believing the encroaching mist is my friend.

Harry runs his hand over the back of his neck. He's covered in sweat from his shift, probably tired to the bone. But he never has been able to say no to me. Of all his children, I'm his favorite, and I know it. Probably because I'm the only girl.

"Come on back here, then," he says, gesturing to the shed behind the dock. "Your mama will cook me alive if I let you get struck by lightning."

He takes my small hand in his and I can feel the rough calluses. No one would guess by the look of Harry that he's a high school science teacher by day. He has the body of a foreman, a farmer's tan, and gray eyes that light up when he's excited. He and Kathy had us young. I think it's part of the reason they've always preferred for us kids to call them by their first names.

I follow him down the dock, our feet clanking along the rickety beams. I know these planks like I know my own freckles, every wobbly inch and loose nail sticking out. Auggie and I spend most of our days running down these stilts into the flat world of the lake. I've scraped my knees on them more times than I can count.

Harry opens the door to the shed and leads me just inside. It smells of mold in here, the balsam walls damp black and rotting. Harry uses the eight-by-ten-foot hovel as a graveyard for tackle and boating equipment. It's a spider's paradise, so Mark never wants to come in, but Auggie and I like to imagine it's our personal treasure trove.

Harry stops me just within the doorframe and places his hands on my shoulders from behind. It's from here that we stare out the door at our own private wonderland.

It's coming. I hear it. The rapidly gaining wind skids across lake. It sways the pines, who cast their bows to and fro as if to brace themselves. The sounds of the birds cease, the frogs and bats end in a screeching hush.

Clap. Another flash to the air, this time closer.

"One Mississippi. Two Mississippi," I find myself counting out loud.

Clap. That last one's jarring. I lean back against Harry, nestling into his sweaty shirt, then turn to a whisper. "One Mississippi." *Clap*. "One Mississippi." *Clap*.

That's when the universe opens up and a thing of beauty takes hold, the harmonies of the dark coming together as the rain pounds down in sudden thick ribbons. It's fierce, violent, but it's also stunning, the water returning to the earth from which it came and running down our hill in delta formations.

I hold my breath as the crashing overhead becomes frightening, booming, and I feel Harry's palms tighten on my shoulders in reassurance. A thick sliver of lightning strikes the center of the lake, a cascade of white zigzag cutting through the surface. A great wall of water, like a mine going off, propels an upsurge of tide in all directions. I see an entire lifetime in that singular strike.

"That's why your mama and I make you get out of the water when a storm's coming," Harry calls over my head. "If you wait around, and it strikes while you're in there, it could electrocute you. It could kill you, July. Do you hear me?"

I nod, too captivated by the image and the rhythm of the night air to fully take his words for what they are. A warning. I will remember them later, though, after everything.

PART I

1

Now

> They say the past don't define you
> But I never put much stock in that
> They say she's no better than her mama
> Daddy's little girl gonna follow in his tracks
>   —"Daddy's Little Girl," written by Jules Thomas

I'M STANDING OUTSIDE, the atmosphere crackling, when my producer Scott slides open the glass door behind me, and calls out, "Jules, you think you'd be willing to grace us with your presence anytime soon?"

"They here yet?" I ask, without moving my gaze from the clouds rolling in overhead.

"About to be," the producer says.

He takes in my stance: my arms spread at my sides, my head tilted back to take in the heavens, and my sneakers kicked off to squish my toes between the studio lawn's grass blades. Maybe someone else would offer up a comment right about now, but Scott's an old friend and used to my eccentricities. Instead, he only pauses long enough to stare up at the ominous air too. I wonder if he can feel the spark to it like I can. I don't think so.

"You should get in, anyway," he says. "Looks like it's about to storm."

The door whooshes closed behind him. There's a bellowing thump overhead and I count in my head out of habit. Nine Mississippi.

"No, it ain't," I whisper, then hate myself just a bit for reliving that memory.

Nine years in Nashville and I still feel no more at home walking into a recording studio than the day I got here in 1997. It's the same with Music City in general. Sure, the people are familiar, and some have even become friends, but it's not like any of them really know me. My reputation is almost entirely by song credit—Jules Thomas: songwriter, guitarist, notorious recluse. I like to keep it that way.

"What are y'all watching?" I ask, entering the control room. Scott and the sound engineer have their eyes glued to live footage on one of the computer monitors above the sound boards.

"That woman in Alabama," says the engineer. "Adrian Bennet. They're calling off the search."

I cringe, sorry I asked. I try to avoid all news coverage on the abductions and murders of young women. As the older sister of a girl who went missing long ago, it's healthier that way. Still, even I know about Adrian Bennet: middle-aged mom of two, disappeared from the back parking lot of a Piggly Wiggly. Two months later and national news coverage is still going crazy over her. As I stare up at the photo of her holding one of her kids, I hope for her sake she's already dead.

I'm mercifully saved from further comment when the singer we're meeting tonight enters the control room. "JT, how you doing, darling?"

Like every other time I've worked with him, Kade Daniels is late. He touches the small of my back before shaking hands with both Scott and the sound engineer. I resent the difference.

He's missing the hat, but everything else about his getup is straight off the ranch. Most singers in this city are country, with a few pop and folk bands mixed in.

"Hey, thanks so much for filling in." Kade follows me out of the control room and into the live room. The rest of his band of four are already setting up their instruments. "Speaking of which, what's your summer schedule looking like, JT?"

"Why?" I ask, mockingly batting my eyelashes. "You want to make me an offer?"

"You laugh, but I think it would be a great opportunity for you. The current album's done after this. You could play nights with the band, spend days co-writing my next album with me. Could be a whole lot of fun."

I've had "a whole lot of fun" with musicians like him before, and it's never ended well for me.' "Yeah, well, you know I don't perform in public."

I pick up my guitar and nod to the other guys in the band. Kade shakes his head, amused but undeterred. "That's a damn waste of talent and you know it. I'll have my agent send you a contract anyways. Think about it."

I sit on a stool, bring my fingers to the strings. They hum; this act feels more like home than anyplace I've ever been. "We gonna record this damn love song or not?"

The storm's full raging by the time I get back to my cramped house in West End Park. It's humble, falling apart, but it suits me just fine. The walls are coated in their original 1970s limes and lemons, the backsplash in the bathrooms and kitchen a grimy subway tile. I don't have decorations on the walls, only enough furniture to be useful, and over my dead body will you find a living plant in this house aside from weeds on the front lawn. I like to live what I call a transient lifestyle, with the ability to pick up and move at a moment's notice. Only thing is, despite the décor and my Jack Kerouac philosophy, I've been in this same house, alone, for the last seven years, ever since the royalty checks began rolling in from my first hit single.

After my keys drop to the kitchen counter, my next move is to the fridge to crack open one of my non-alcoholic beers. I need the taste before I can crash. I unclasp my bra beneath my shirt one-handed, drop my jeans to the floor, and check my answering machine on my way to my bedroom—all while balancing the bottle. It's a talent.

The receiver's flashing angry, announcing twelve missed calls and four voice mails. I checked the thing this morning, so this comes as a surprise.

First message:

"July, It's Mark. You need to call me."

My body goes rigid. I play the next one, already knowing all four messages will be from him.

"Jesus, July. Don't you ever pick up your phone? I'm serious. Call me back now."

Next message:

"If I wasn't clear, it's Mark."

Final message:

"Goddamn it, July. Answer your phone!"

It's the first time I've heard my middle brother's voice in nine years, and if he's called twelve times in the span of two hours, it means nothing good. I suck in a deep breath, will myself to redial, and almost talk myself out of it altogether.

He answers on the second ring, his voice breathy. "It's about time."

"Hello to you too, *March*," I emphasize the name he was born with, knowing it will needle him.

"Don't you ever answer your phone?" he asks.

Nine years, and that's what he says.

"It's my landline. I don't own a cell phone. How'd you even get this number?"

I never give anyone non-industry my number. This goes especially for those who share my DNA. There's only one exception to this, and that person certainly isn't this brother.

"So what? I'm not allowed to call my own sister then? Sorry to have bothered your very important life as a country hick."

"Don't pretend you don't know why. You're lucky I picked up your call at all."

"I wouldn't begin to know what you're referring to."

I roll my eyes, because why would someone as profoundly selfish as Mark acknowledge the damage that he's caused in someone else's life? I realize that, even after all this time, I still haven't forgiven him. "I'm going to need you to get on with whatever the hell it is you want, or I'm going to hang up now."

"I'm booking a flight out of JFK for Friday, right now," he says. "You're going to want to get in a car or on a plane and head home around then, too."

I already know where this is leading and am determined not to follow. "And why the hell would I do that?" I ask.

"There's been an accident."

Of course. There'd been an accident every week in my childhood house of horrors for as long as I could remember. Only once in an eclipsed moon did one actually warrant a response—and I'll be honest, I hadn't given one in a long time. Not since that summer after our sister May went missing.

"Forget it. I'm not coming back. I told you all that a long time ago."

"This isn't about our mother," he says. "It's Deck."

Deck, our youngest brother; the constant screwup; my greatest failure. Mark doesn't have to tell me what I already know. The pit in my stomach makes me realize I've been waiting on this call for a long time. I think I'm going to be sick.

"He OD'd again?"

My brother is silent for a long second on the other line, then lets out a haggard breath. "No, it's worse. He had some sort of episode, got high as a kite and ditched his clothes, then went to jump off the goddamn Hazel Bridge."

At first this doesn't register, but then my body reacts before my mind, the air squeezing from my lungs as I grasp the back of one of my kitchen chairs. "What do you mean, he jumped?"

"I mean, he decided to end it all or was hallucinating or God knows what and drove a stolen Chevy up to the highest place he could find, and went to throw himself over the edge. The son of a bitch." He says it almost enviously, like Deck's stolen his brilliant idea.

I choke back a sob. *This is your fault,* glides through my mind. *You did this to him.*

"Deck's dead?" I try saying the words out loud. They still don't sound right.

"What?" Mark says in surprise. "Jesus, no. Sorry. My head's spinning from all this. He isn't dead . . . the cops tackled him off the railing."

None of this is making any sense, but I breathe again and try to recalibrate. More than anything, I'm pissed. "You couldn't have led with that?"

"Sorry."

I look out my window. The storm has picked up significantly, rain smacking the windowpanes. "How is he?"

"He's detoxing in the psych ward at Hazel General for the next few days. Apparently, he was substituting his anti-psychotics for harder stuff for a few weeks at least. Auggie and April are home with Kathy now. The docs won't let them visit until seventy-two hours pass."

I chug what remains of my beer, then wish like hell it was a real one, but stamp down the thought. "So you're going?" I'm surprised by this.

"The great August was rather insistent." He pauses. "Aren't you?"

I can't even see outside anymore, the atmosphere is so at war with itself. I know the feeling. Every other time my youngest brother has fallen apart, it's been in Nashville, San Francisco, Atlanta. Not one town away from home, which brings me to another person I'm not quite ready to face.

"Auggie told you to call me, didn't he? What? He didn't think I'd pick up the phone if he was the one to do it? Still can't stand the sound of my voice?"

"Forget it. Whatever's going on between the golden pair, I'm not getting involved," he says. "I did what I was supposed to do. I'm getting on a plane to Atlanta, and I called you." His tone switches to impatience. "So, am I telling Auggie you're coming, or not?"

I pinch the bridge of my nose. "Deck's OD'd before, Mark. Twice. You never bothered to fly down from New York then."

"He's never intentionally tried to kill himself before."

That is true, at least not directly. But I know the statistic. Twenty to forty percent of schizophrenics attempt suicide at some point in their lives. I'm sure that number's even higher among those who are also drug users.

I search around me, needing to find the right words. An excuse. If Deck was any other place in the world, I would be on my way already. "I can't. I have things going on here. Gigs."

"Right," Mark snorts. "How convenient. Your brother tries to throw himself off a bridge, but you have gigs." He clears his throat. "You think I want to go back to this piece-of-shit town any more than you do? I haven't been back in eight years, either."

"It wasn't the same for you. You weren't directly a part of everything that happened."

His voice goes icy. "We were all directly a part of everything that happened, July. It wasn't confined to just you and Harry. We *all* had to live with this."

"No."

I can't. I can't bring myself to so much as think about returning to that place. To that town where everyone knows my name. My father. My family. I can't face that lake that killed my baby sister.

"Fine," Mark snaps. "It's not like I give a shit if you show up or not." He pauses. "Auggie did ask me to tell you one thing."

"Yeah, and what's that?"

"He said to remember your deal."

It is the equivalent to a knife wound. Only Auggie could have the ability to gut me from two hundred and fifty miles away.

"I'll email you my arrival details." Mark ends our call.

I am at a loss. My knees go out from under me and I push my back against the wall, the windowsill being smacked by the receding storm over my head. My heart floods—overwhelmed by history and all the things I have spent the last nine years of my life desperately trying to keep at bay.

But this is the one thing I cannot fight: Auggie and my deal. Made clutching one another teary-eyed at the end of that last summer—that Auggie would take care of April and Kathy if I would take care of Deck.

In the span of five minutes, the world I have so carefully constructed here in Nashville has collapsed. I have to go back.

For Deck, but also for Auggie. I owe them both.

I trace my fingers over the knots in my floorboards, making out faces of screaming ghosts. I can't help but think back to that final summer in Pacific, now. About Harry and the dead girls. There's no use pretending they don't exist anymore, or that I wasn't almost one of them.

2

Then

A T THE START of the summer after my sister May disappeared, I had a siphon in my mouth and my body in a
handstand over a keg, when my buzzkill of a brother ripped
me off.

The crowd of drunken teenagers around us booed and
began to disperse at his nasty look. I, in turn, straightened
myself and shoved my eldest brother.

"What the fuck, Auggie?"

My body rocked from the onrush of blood to my head,
or maybe it was the cheap beer. The surroundings felt fuzzy
in general, the flames of the bonfire behind me popping red
and gold as Third Eye Blind blasted from the stereo of one
of the dozen trucks parked at sharp angles along the grass.
The field buzzed, crammed with the bodies of three-quarters
of the upperclassmen of Pacific High—maybe two to three
hundred people total. We were celebrating: the senior class of
1997 had graduated that afternoon, Auggie included.

"I think you've had enough," he said, taking my shoulder
to guide me through the crowd.

This alone earned us looks. My brother was breathtak-
ingly beautiful and shy. That, along with serving as our

school's star wide receiver for the past four years, had left him with a line of girls constantly staring after him with wistful expressions—not that he ever noticed.

I wrenched my arm from his grasp. "I can take care of myself."

A tired frown formed along my brother's face. "Yeah. What about anyone else? Where's Deck?"

"Is he here?" I hadn't seen Deck since Auggie's graduation ceremony that afternoon. It had just been the five of us siblings.

"Don't play dumb," Auggie said. "I know you brought him."

I propped my fists on my hips, annoyed then. "Auggie Weaver, do you really think so low of me that I would bring our fourteen-year-old brother to a keg party?"

"You expect me to believe Mark brought him?"

That was when I noticed the uptick of anxiety in my brother's expression. Auggie was worried, growing more so by the second.

I sobered up faster than if someone had shot me with an IV full of caffeine. My immediate panic matched his, our protective older sibling instincts going into simultaneous hyperdrive. "He wasn't with April and the sitter when you left them?"

Auggie shook his head. "Linda Breyer said she thought she saw him here when I pulled up. That's why I thought he was with you."

"We need to find him. Now."

For any other set of siblings, a missing teenage brother wouldn't cause such an immediate upstir. But those siblings weren't Weavers. They hadn't had their younger sister vanish without a trace four months ago.

Auggie followed me around the bonfire, and we split up to search for Deck, each taking half the crowd. As I wove between my classmates, I was struck again with the overwhelming stares and what I assumed were whispered questions as to why I was there, *after everything that had happened.*

As if evidence to that fact, I overheard Kelly Anders gossiping to Nicole Sheridan at a keg up ahead of me. "Oh, please. An eight-year-old girl just doesn't walk out of her bed and disappear in the middle of the night. *Somebody* in that family killed her."

My mind was still on Deck, but no one had ever accused me of having a long fuse. I slammed myself into Nicole's back, cascading her beer so it drenched both her and Kelly's shirts. They screamed and whipped to face me.

"Are you freaking kidding me?" Kelly yelled.

Nicole's face went crimson.

"Whoops," I said, moving to shove past them.

I stopped when Mark appeared to snake his arm around Nicole's waist. His eyes bore into mine accusingly. "Everything all right over here?"

"Oh, we just ran into each other was all," said Nicole, a new layer of sugar to her voice. She shot me a nervous look. "Total accident."

My middle brother was sixteen and the darker shadow to Auggie's light. Where the rest of us Weaver children had accepted the label of oddballs that our unconventional parents had forced upon us, Mark had resisted from the start. Each of us had been named after the month we were born— August, July, March, December, April, and May (May being the exception, as she and April were twins, and our mother was forced to concede a month). Where the twins and I had never been bothered by our given names, and the oldest and youngest boys imperceptibly shifted to Auggie and Deck, our middle brother had been emphatic from the time he was very young that his name was Mark, and only Mark.

He finally obtained the approval he so desperately sought in high school, through baseball and football. This secured his coveted position in the popular crowd. Even in this, though, Mark was overshadowed by our loner older brother.

Whereas Mark trained nonstop all summer and season long, Auggie had the ability to walk onto a football field and catch the pass of the season. It caused perpetual tension between the two. I would have had more sympathy had Auggie not been so inherently good and Mark so inherently dick-ish.

"Don't you have anything better to do than harass my girl-friend?" He offered the scowl he reserved specifically for me.

"Don't you have anything better to do than act like a prick?" I yanked his beer from him and took a sip. "Did you bring Deck here?"

Mark frowned tighter. "No. Why? He here?"

"According to Auggie. You gonna come help us find him or what?"

Mark's gaze cut to where Auggie was questioning people over by the pickups. "You two are so fucking neurotic. He's about to be a sophomore. Let him live."

I chugged what remained of his drink and crushed the red Solo cup against his chest. "Thanks for nothing."

He scowled, and I left them, catching Auggie heading for the woods.

"Dan said he saw him over with the stoners," he told me. Dan was Auggie's childhood best friend and the son of Pacific's chief of police.

"You can't be serious?"

I kept pace with him toward the edge of the tree line.

I had had a dalliance with the stoner crowd for a hot min-ute during my sophomore year, so I knew most of its current members. Auggie and I headed over to that section of the field, which was surprisingly crowded, the usual twenty regulars joined by ten or so letterman jackets and pom poms, all proba-bly looking to score. One in particular noticed me immediately.

"Well, hello, July Weaver."

"Colton."

Colton's father, Clarence Davidson, was the mayor of Pacific and owned half the county. His son was the resident hotshot of our grade, and up until a few months ago had

never so much as looked at me. Not that I ever wanted him
to—he was trouble, to say the least.

He had surprised me, though, a week after May disappeared, when he ran into me in the stacks of the library and
told me how sorry he was. I had been taken aback in the
moment. I didn't even think he knew my name and I for sure
didn't expect to find him in the library. From that point on,
though, whenever we saw each other, he greeted me in that
same way, "Well, hello, July Weaver," my name rolling off his
tongue like honey. Whether it was said with kindness or flir-
tation, I couldn't tell you. What I did know was that summer
I kept a close intimacy with danger, chasing after anything
and everything to make me feel alive again. Colton seemed
like a number one opportunity.

He flashed me an arrogant smirk. "Didn't take you for
one to hang out in burnout land."

I stared down at the dime bags in his palm, which he
quickly pocketed. "I'm not surprised to see you."

"Yeah, well. What can I say? I'm celebrating. We're
seniors now."

My brother cleared his throat beside me. "Davidson. You
seen our brother Deck?"

"That's the freshman one, right? Yeah." Colton nodded
his head back behind him. "He was sitting on the back of
that red truck last I saw him."

Auggie nodded and headed in that direction.

Colton moved on, too, but then stopped to flip his head
back around. "Hey, Weaver."

"Yeah?"

"I'm picking you up Friday night. We'll go to the
drive-in."

"Will we, now?" I couldn't help but grin.

It was a bad idea, I told myself. Colton Davidson had a
reputation for running through girls like a river does rocks.

He smiled wider, taking that for a yes. "I'll pick you up
at seven."

I didn't bother to ask if he knew where I lived. My house was infamous in those days.

Colton moved on when Auggie came charging back toward me, tugging a wide-eyed Deck by the back of the shirt. Deck looked mortified, his curls and gangly disproportionate limbs flopping all over the place. He was in the middle of another growth spurt.

"Jesus. I get it. You're so fucking embarrassing." He yanked himself out of Auggie's grasp.

"Not as embarrassing as what I'm gonna do to you if you were back there smoking anything other than weed," I growled. My mind jumped to the ever-growing population of heroin addicts in town.

"What? You think I'm crazy?"

Auggie and I stared at our youngest brother pointedly.

"You're too young to get mixed up in any of that stuff," I said. "You should be at the movies or playing Dungeons & Dragons in one of your geeky friends' basements."

Deck threw up his hands. "You're such a hypocrite, July. I'm not too young to remember when you used to come home reeking."

Auggie clasped Deck by his back again. "You clearly don't remember when Harry went into her room and confiscated her stash, threatening to kick her out if she did it again." He shoved his brother forward. "Now, come on. We're taking you home."

I leaned into my oldest brother's ear and whispered. "You're conveniently forgetting the rest of that story."

Our father had made a show of confiscating my weed when I was fifteen. But the next morning, Auggie and I had gone out on our dock and found our parents asleep in a naked embrace on the floor of the tied-up speedboat, a bong that wasn't mine on the carpet beside them.

Auggie shook his head and we followed Deck back toward the bonfire. I waved to my best friend Zoey in a group on my way by, signaling with my hands that I was leaving. She nodded and I gestured that I would call her tomorrow.

Auggie and Deck stopped before Mark, who was in his usual huddle with Nicole on his lap, and a group of five other lettermen and pom poms, soon to be seniors, around a fire. Our parents started Auggie and me in school a year late, which put Mark and me in the same grade.

"You need a ride?" Auggie asked.

Mark frowned. "It's only eleven."

"We're taking Deck home. You coming or not?"

Mark looked to Nicole, who puckered her lip and laced her grip tighter through his arm. Mark turned back to our brother. "Can't you come back in, like, an hour?"

"Don't be a dick, Mark," I said. "Either get a ride from one of your groupies, or come now."

He rolled his eyes at me, then twisted to Nicole. I turned my back on them as their faces fought to swallow each other whole, then nodded to our other brothers. We all silently agreed—Romeo would catch up.

When the three of us reached Auggie's truck at the end of the line, Deck hurried ahead and pulled the tailgate down, before springing up into the bed. He held his hand out to me and bowed. "Milady."

"Who you calling lady?" I laughed, taking his hand and climbing up after him.

As expected, Mark hurried to catch us.

"You riding in the back?" I asked.

He threw the tailgate up and circled over to the passenger's door. Auggie was already at the wheel. "Hell, no. I'm too old for that shit."

Deck and I traded mocking eye rolls and sat down, side by side, our backs to the hood.

I leaned my head up in the window between my two brothers and looked to Mark. "Your girlfriend's a bitch, by the way."

"Fuck off, July."

He slammed the window closed and I caught a hint of a smile on Auggie's face as he pulled the truck into drive.

The night was late spring in Georgia at its finest. The air weighed dense, as if our town was sucking in all the humidity from the state that night. I could feel it pulsating—its own tenor specific to me, as I propped myself up to squat in the bed. I wanted to be a part of it all—needed it, to forget.

I knocked on the glass divider. Mark stared at me but ignored it. Auggie was the one whose hand pulled the thing open.

"I'm gonna do it," I said.

Auggie shot a glance back. "No. You're not sober enough."

"Just turn up the damn radio."

Auggie sighed, knowing better than to argue with me, and rolled the dial up. No Doubt took on a deafening tone in the cabin and my brothers rolled down their windows to take in the night air.

"You're going to get yourself killed," Mark muttered. "And I'm not gonna go to your funeral. Hell, I'll throw an anti-funeral to celebrate."

I turned back around and winked to Deck before slowly taking hold of the hood's roof behind me and staggering to my feet. My stance was shaky at best, the ridges of the truck bed sliding beneath my Converse. But I caught my groove, then spread my arms out like Christ the Redeemer. The wind rushed past me, and I stared back at the road behind us.

The pine and sweet gum enveloped me. I closed my eyes and threw back my head, feeling like I was rushing through a tunnel, feeling the wind whip my hair and the sound of Gwen Stefani's voice flood my eardrums. This is what it meant to be free. This was alive.

My siblings and I had taken part in this ritual since Auggie was old enough to drive three years ago. Now it was an intoxicating habit, one I enjoyed most of all our siblings. Mark believed he had outgrown it, and Auggie and I deemed Deck and the twins too young, so that left me, and Auggie when he wasn't driving. I liked to pretend in these moments that I was a bird; I could feel the air kick up with every jolt of a turn.

"I want in," Deck said, propping up on his heels.

"Just because she's an idiot doesn't mean you have to be, too," Mark yelled back.

"Come on!" Deck begged, looking up to me.

I pivoted, and caught sight of Auggie staring back at me through his rearview mirror. *You got him?* His look asked. I nodded. *Yeah, I got him.*

"Take it slow, kid," I said, as Auggie decelerated the truck.

Deck grabbed onto my arms, and I helped him up.

"The trick is to stay close to the top of the truck and hold it with one hand. It breaks some of the force of the air if you're directly behind it. You go back toward the tailgate, you're going to get whipped right off. Grab hold with both hands if you feel yourself falling."

Deck nodded. Pure bliss lit his eyes. It was his first time up—an acceptance into the older half of our clan. He howled like a wild dog.

CHAPTER

3

Then

GONE. LOST. DEAD. None of us knew the right word for what happened to May.

What we did know: Kathy had tucked her and April into their beds at eight PM on February 5 and sometime before morning, May had either walked or been taken out of their room without a trace.

The town of Pacific had rallied in the first month around us Weavers, despite how crazy my parents were deemed to be. A police investigation was launched the day after May went missing. Local sex offenders' houses were searched, the heroin squatters down in Dewey Meadow dispersed and picked up for intel. Search parties of volunteers combed the fields and woods of both Pacific and the neighboring towns of Hazel and Montgomery, while a patrol of boats and divers went out on Pacific Lake. But with nothing turning up after two weeks, the search parties began to slow and the town remembered who my family was. With that, the search came to a crashing halt.

Little eight-year-old May was gone, and the busybodies of town would "be damned if that sweet child wasn't murdered by one of her own kinfolk." The leading suspects: Harry, who had been at a teaching conference in Atlanta that night, but may have driven back; Kathy, who was likely off her meds and unstable; and any of my three brothers, who could have harbored perverse fantasies. Every theory was sicker than the last and made me want to scream.

I sat down in the bed of the truck as the lake came into view, then tugged on my younger brother to do the same. Deck came down, and we watched as the reflection of the moon crescented the lake, the water's ripples being brought on by a gentle wind. I couldn't help but remember the fairytale of the Swan Princess when I looked out, of the swan that transformed back into the girl in moon's light. I imagined it as my eight-year-old sister's fate. I wanted to believe in that better ending.

Auggie's truck wove around the dirt and gravel shoreline. The pines and oak towered above us and the woods hemmed us in to the lake as we reached the hill that led up to our house. I would never not be in awe of this place, my home.

My father Harry had moved us all here when I was two years old. I had never known any other home than Pacific Lake. He was hired as the high school biology teacher by day, and a foreman at Hazel's tire factory by night, but he had bigger dreams when moving to this sleepy Georgia lake town. The house he and Kathy purchased was a run-down mansion in such dismal shape that the bank let it go for half of what it was worth in 1982. No one had lived in the house since it'd been an all-boys boarding school in the forties. When my family bought it, it had massive cracks fissuring across every wall, a grand staircase that had collapsed in on itself, and a foundation that was sinking into the hill. With a three-man crew, Harry spent the larger part of the following decade renovating it on weekends and holidays, starting with the essential rooms before moving outward.

My father's aim in purchasing an old boarding school was not just to live in it. He hoped that his burgeoning family would come to take up only about half the residence.

The remainder, he intended to turn into a fully functional arboretum.

"Just think of it, kids," I heard more times than I could recount in my childhood. "This place makes a nickel or two, I can retire from both jobs early. Then your mama and I can just host tours. People'll come from all over the state to see this arboretum."

Harry was known locally for his grand schemes—most of which never resulted in the nickel or two he insisted they would make. Auggie and I remembered his ventures more than the younger kids did. In addition to the arboretum, there had been the idea for an unlicensed gambling ferry that would ride up and down the lake; a Siegfried & Roy knockoff show where Auggie and I held up hoops for Kathy's army of chinchillas to jump through (they never did, and had since all passed away); and even his own church service on the water that asked for donations to our arboretum that he was certain God had ordained him to build (that one lasted only two months, before our town's selectmen slapped him with a fine larger than all the donations combined).

The arboretum was much like the rest of these undertakings. My father never quite finished it. My mother Kathy at least had the foresight to make her husband complete the residence section first, leaving us all with a place to sleep, two working bathrooms, and a kitchen. As for the rest of the rooms, after fifteen years, they were a mix. Where the back patio had been converted into a fully functioning, temperature-controlled greenhouse, the formal living room that was meant to serve as a desert climate, and the mud room as a tropical rainforest, only had a few shelves built into their walls, tubing purchased and forgotten on the unswept floors, and plants of all different varieties cascading across every surface in various states of growth and rot.

The manor might as well have been a jungle. My father lined every room with his beloved plants of all sizes. I couldn't walk into the bathroom without staring into the mouth of vibrant purple bougainvillea snaking up the walls along the vanity. I couldn't lean over the window of our kitchen sink without dangling hair over waiting Venus fly traps that wished me ill. I couldn't walk down the main hall without tripping over the vines of *Heliconia*, orchids, and pitcher plants that wove along the floor and climbed up the walls and ceilings.

Harry's greatest pride stood in the center of the house, in the massive three-story foyer: a fifty-foot Douglas fir we called Father Time. It was why my father had purchased this house in this town in the first place. The century-old boarding school had been built around the then-smaller tree to honor their headmaster. The roof of the foyer had been cut out in one thick square so that the top of the tree could meet sky. Beautiful, but a bitch when it rained. The entire foyer would have flooded had it not been for Harry's complex drainage system that snaked around the base and emptied back and out down to the lake.

As Auggie pulled his truck in front of the manor, I couldn't help but narrow my eyes at the house I grew up in. With night it took on the color of coal, but even in daylight the house's shingles appeared faded with dust and mold. The window trim was a peeled white and the glass within each pane warped and crooked. I could see Father Time's top bulging out of the roof like a lopsided propeller hat.

"Home sweet home," said Deck, hopping out of the truck.

"Yeah," I whispered. "Home sweet home."

Mark was already out and following Deck through the kitchen door that opened out of the side of the house, but Auggie lingered to pull the tailgate down for me.

"You all right?" he asked.

I turned my gaze from the house and offered him a small smile. "Sure. You?"

"Sure."

Neither of us meant it. He helped me down.

* * *

A few hours later, I woke to a bang. My first instinct was to grab my sister. Ever since May disappeared, April had slept in my bed every night. Now I studied the waves of her hair across her pillow. She looked so peaceful. It was nice to see. Since May's disappearance, my once bubbly chatterbox sister had been reduced to a shell, never lingering in a room without the presence of an adult. I didn't blame her.

I left her after a second bang sounded. I was fairly certain it was coming from the first-floor kitchen, but checked my brothers' rooms just to be sure. Mark and Deck were both passed out in their room, Auggie in his own. I crept across the hall to my parents' room and their door was open. The bed, empty.

I found my mother in the backyard off the kitchen. Kathy could have been mistaken for an apparition in the moonlight. She wore a gray nightgown, her braid tight down her back. She had been beautiful once, with blue eyes to match Auggie's and April's, a spattering of red freckles bending across her luminous skin.

"Kathy, what are you doing?"

My mother bowed over the grass, her hands moving objects around. There had to be twenty crystals scattered about, intermixed with every item from our kitchen cabinets and drawers. I spotted the toaster and convection oven over on the rock wall. Plates and cups were strewn along the walkway. The silverware looked as if it had been ricocheted across the lawn in combat.

"Mama."

She looked up. Her pupils were dilated. She looked straight through me. "I'm charging my crystals. You know you can order them online now? I bought three cases and did rush delivery. I figured there's no such thing as too many, right? They have to be out in the moonlight to charge, and I thought, well, if the crystals need to charge in the moonlight, then shouldn't the silverware, too? I mean, all those chemicals we put in our bodies. The moon's got to charge and neutralize all that, too. I mean I don't want my babies putting all that in their mouths. Little April can't be putting those chemicals in her mouth . . ."

I stared at my mother. This was the worst she'd been in a while. I knew better after seventeen years than to argue with her during an episode. For once, I put my snark away.

"Okay," I said, taking on a gentle tone. "That's a real smart idea. Why don't we leave it all out here then, to charge up tonight? No use in you staying up. Why don't we get you to bed?"

My mother's attention remained fixed on her project. "I . . . I don't know. I should stay. Make sure it works."

I nodded. "I'll come back down and keep watch. Here, come with me."

I led my mother inside and up the stairs to her bedroom. She didn't fight back, only continued to mumble. In the hall, Mark came out of the bathroom and stared at us, hands in his pockets. He took one look at our mother and shook his head in exasperation, before returning to his and Deck's room.

"It's important they charge all night . . ." my mother babbled on as I helped her into bed and took off her slippers.

"I know."

I tucked her in and walked to the bathroom to get her some water and her meds. There was no sign of them. She must have flushed them again—at least a week ago, based on where she was mentally. I opened the linen closet and pulled out my father's toiletry bag where we kept spare prescription bottles of my mother's antipsychotic pills for occasions such as these. I measured out the medications, in addition to a sleeping pill, and filled a glass in the sink. I returned to my mother with a smile plastered on my face. "Here, take these, Kathy."

She leveled her eyes at me in tiredness. "I don't want them."

"They'll make you feel better."

"They make me fuzzy."

"Will you do it for me?"

My mother arrowed her eyes like I was asking for the world.

"Please," I added. "There's a sleeping pill here for you, too. It'll help you get some rest."

My mother sat up on her elbows and held open her mouth. I popped the pills in and tilted the water back like she was a small child.

"There you go," I said.

She scooted down in the bed. "Those crystals will do wonders for all of us. They'll keep us safe. You wait."

"I bet they will."

I waited for a while until I heard her breathing hitch and drift into a state of sleep, then waited even longer to be sure. Harry was due to come home tomorrow. I kept telling myself that. I didn't know what good it would do, but Harry would be home.

4

Now

I SPEND MY FIRST twenty minutes back on Georgia land vomiting in the airport bathroom. It's been a visceral reaction since the moment we began descending into Atlanta airspace, as if my body wants to expel my very homeland from me. My fingers are trembling. I haven't craved a drink this bad in I don't know how long, maybe since right after I got sober. All I want to do is turn around and get back on the plane to Nashville. Forget about all of this.

It is the curse of my promise that leads me to clean myself up in the bathroom mirror, rubbing the mascara smudges from beneath my eyes and gargling water, before rejoining the school of commuters in the terminal.

Auggie's waiting exactly where Mark said he would be beneath the arrivals and departures board, his hands in his pockets. It's been six months since I've seen my eldest brother and his hair has just reached his shoulders, his beard grown in. He's gone full lumberjack in plaid and boots, but I'm not going to tease him about it. I've lost that right after our last encounter.

I drop my duffel down between us, along with my guitar.

"Hey, Aug."

"Flight all right?"

"Flight attendants were too chipper for their own good."

He nods without so much as cracking a smile. Same old Auggie. He could wait out a Trappist monk. This is going to be more awkward than I thought.

To my relief, Mark appears from the direction of the baggage carousels. The 2006 version of my middle brother is dressed as Auggie's opposite: rumpled dress pants and shiny loafers, a jacket over his shoulder, followed by a rolling suitcase and briefcase on top.

"It's funny," says Mark, frowning at me. "When someone agrees to meet you in baggage claim, you typically expect them not to make you wait thirty minutes to show up."

"You just stumble off Wall Street in that getup?" I retort, because it's easier than explaining why I'm late.

Mark in turn scans the two of us. "That's funny considering the two of you look like a hick and a homeless person. I'll let you figure out which is which."

Our half-hostile banter is the equivalent of a hug for us. We aren't touchy-feely people and lord knows we have enough history between the three of us to resent one another. All I feel when I look at the two of them is anger in Mark's case and guilt in Auggie's.

We walk out of the terminal in silence. When we reach Auggie's truck in the parking lot, it takes both of them to sling Mark's bag into the bed. The three of us slide into the truck's cabin.

"What? You moving home?" I ask Mark.

Auggie reverses the truck back and out of the lot.

"I made the mistake of letting Lindsay pack."

"Is Lindsay some girl you tricked into dating you?" I ask.

"My wife, actually."

I scoff as Auggie stops at the parking booth and pays. "Someone actually agreed to marry you? Willingly?"

Mark smiles at me with acid. "As of five months ago. Let me guess, your country songs last longer than your relationships."

"That's the way I like them," I say.

I turn to Auggie, as he rolls his window back up. "You know about these nuptials?"

"Yup." There's still ice from him.

"What? You didn't want to invite your long-estranged sister to the ceremony?" I ask Mark. "I mean, I wouldn't have come, but hell, I might have sent a gift."

Mark rolls his eyes. "We eloped. I purposely didn't invite any of you horrible people."

"Oh, I've missed you, too."

"Can we not start this already?" Auggie asks, his voice grated as he enters onto I-285. It's the middle of the day so the Atlanta interstate is only highly congested as opposed to stop-and-go traffic.

Mark and I simmer down, scolded.

"Well, when's your big day, Auggie?" Mark asks.

I feel as if I've been slapped, my attention whipping back to my older brother. "Excuse me?"

"Oh, you haven't heard?" This clearly brings Mark too much joy. He's downright sunny. "Your soul twin over here is engaged to the girl next door. They're getting married this summer."

"Bridget Cane?" I ask, because that's the only girl Mark can mean.

A townie who lived down the road from us growing up, Bridget was quiet and a grade above Auggie's. She also happened to be one of the many girls who had worshipped him from the moment he hit puberty. Hurt gushes out of me like a fountain. Mark's life is one thing; I don't give a damn. But Auggie? Had our fight really been that bad that he wouldn't tell me he was getting married?

Auggie nods, sheepish. "At the end of August."

"You weren't with her when I saw you in January," I say.

"It happened fast," he mumbles.

I'll say. I can't help but wonder if what I said during that final fight was exactly what led Auggie to make this impulsive life decision. I'll have to grill him on it later, whenever he gets around to forgiving me.

"What do you do, Mark?" I ask, because I need time to wrap my head around what I've just learned.

"I'm a broker . . . on Wall Street."

I laugh and he curses. "You can laugh all you want, but I make six fucking figures. My gross income could probably rival even you, *Jules Thomas.* And I don't have to do something I hate to get there, either."

"Hey, I like songwriting."

Mark raises an eyebrow at me dubiously. "The July Weaver I grew up with wouldn't go near a country song with a six-foot pole. You wanted to write folk, rock, this alternative indie shit that's popping up. Instead every one of your hits is about beer, pick-up trucks, and hicks falling in love."

"It's nice to see you've followed my career."

"You're singing about nothing. Less than nothing."

I feel more crushed by this than I should. Mark knows all the nerves. "Fuck you."

"Fuck you right back."

Auggie flips his blinker on and darts across two lanes, causing several frantic honks.

"Are you insane?" Mark shrieks as I yelp, "What the hell?"

Auggie gets over onto the highway shoulder, brings the truck to an abrupt stop, and hits his hazard button. He takes a deep steadying breath as if searching for patience before he looks at us. Then he is silent.

"What are you doing?" I ask.

"Waiting," he says.

"For what?" demands Mark.

"For one of you to ask how our brother is. You know, the one who tried to kill himself, that's in the hospital."

It's a directness from my older brother that I don't often see.

"Give us a break, Auggie," Mark says, "It's been like five minutes. We're here, aren't we?"

"Yeah, for what? Because it looks to me like you two are just picking up where you left off nine years ago, blaming each other for what happened and wanting to tear each other's throats out."

He's not wrong. Mark and I have always had this way of starting out joking, only to devolve into full-hostile screaming. If I don't curb my part in this trajectory now, I will go off on him. Not that he doesn't deserve it, after what he did that final summer, how he ruined any future for me and Gabe. It's not something I'm capable of forgiving him for. It's why he was the first one I cut out when I left Pacific for good.

"How is Deck?" I ask. "When can we get him?"

"Tomorrow morning," says Auggie.

"What the hell happened? How long has he been back in Pacific?"

Auggie's eyebrows knit in confusion. "He wasn't back in Pacific. I hadn't seen Deck in two years. Not since I came to spend that New Year's with you both in Nashville."

"What are you talking about?" Mark asks, because clearly this is news to him too. "You didn't know he was here?"

Auggie shakes his head. "The first I heard about Deck was when he was in transit to the hospital after the bridge last week. And the only reason I knew then was because one of the cops recognized him and called me."

I see the color drain from Mark's face, and I'm sure it's a reflection of what's occurring on my own. We don't need to say the words out loud, our conclusion is the same: *Deck came home to die.*

"Did you see him?" I ask.

Auggie nods. "That night, before they admitted him on suicide watch. He was . . ." Auggie pauses to run a hand through his hair. I watch the cars whoosh past us and rattle the truck while he finds his words. "He wasn't right. Not like I've ever seen him. On something, hallucinating. As bad as . . ."

"Kathy at her worst?" I ask.

He nods.

"He's been that way before," I say. "Right before the last two times he went really off the rails and OD'd." I look down at my hands. I've clamped my palms to my jeans to steady them. "He was never suicidal those times, though, only off his meds and using the drugs to dull the psychosis instead." I see the judgment in both my brothers' eyes when I look back up. "What? You two blame me for this?"

Auggie doesn't say anything, but Mark snorts. "Well, if you knew he was capable of this, where the hell have you been? Wasn't Deck supposed to be in Nashville with you?"

They have no idea what Deck and I have been through together over the last nine years. I haven't arrived at this point of detachment willingly, I've been pushed to it. If I learned anything from my brief stint in Alcoholics Anonymous (AA) when I first got sober, it's that drunks and addicts have to want to get help. Deck would always come around preaching that he wanted to change, then would disappear into a crack den, claiming it was the only way to keep his schizophrenia at bay.

"How's New York, Mark?" I hit back.

My middle brother clamps his jaw. "I'm just saying. Weren't you supposed to help him? He's sick, for Christ sake."

"Yeah?" I say. "Well, sick in this family sometimes translates to lost cause."

I regret the words as soon as they escape my mouth. That's teenage July talking, not me. The teenager who didn't bother to try to understand Kathy and her mental illness—only resented her for it. Not the twenty-six-year-old woman I've become, who's lived and cared for someone with the same disease. Even now, after everything that happened with the bridge, I could never actually view Deck as a lost cause.

"What's wrong with you?" asks Mark.

"I'm a fucking Weaver. That's what's wrong with me."

This statement hangs in the air for a moment, haunting all of us.

"Enough," Auggie barks. He flips off his hazards and merges back onto the interstate, his point made. "No one's to blame for this. What matters now is that we get him help."

"What was he saying that night when you saw him?" I ask because I want to know if they are the standard delusions: paranoia about the FBI trying to kill him, the world (including me) conspiring to lock him up.

Auggie hesitates. "You know that woman on the news? The one who went missing in Alabama?"

The news report in the studio control room flashes in my mind.

"Adrian Bennet," Mark supplies, because of course all of us know the story.

Auggie nods. "Deck was rambling on. He thinks her disappearance—he thinks it's related to what happened with Harry."

I try to wrap my brain around this. Whatever this delusion is, it's a new one for Deck. "What exactly did he say?"

"He thinks they're the same killer," says Auggie.

I still, flash to the memory of Detective Rafael walking into my hospital room to handcuff our father. To charge him for the murders because of the evidence I found.

Mark scoffs. "That's not possible. Harry's been in prison for almost a decade. This woman went missing a couple months ago, and they don't even have a body."

Auggie takes a deep breath. "Deck thinks the cops got it all wrong back then. That Harry was innocent. That it's starting to happen again."

*   *   *

The bones of our childhood home are the same, rotten, cursed; of that I am certain. But the façade has all been redone, the old shingles ripped off, new ones installed in their place. The shutters are restored, the same unvarnished wood, the porch we had spent summer night after night on rebuilt. The windowpanes sport new glass. The fact that this was always Harry's vision isn't lost on me.

The kitchen is renovated, the same as the exterior of the house, rustic but new. I knew Auggie was good with his hands, had been running his own building company for a while, but to see the place rebuilt is living proof. The appliances all shine, the countertop replaced with oak. There are still hints of Harry all over, however, vines crawling across the walls, potted plants stuffed into all nooks and corners.

"I haven't touched your rooms," Auggie explains, holding open the door to the foyer.

We enter wilderness, only it is thicker, denser, more suffocating than I remember. The hall is endless and smells of chlorophyll. I can't help but wonder who maintains the plants now: Auggie or April?

"You didn't think to maybe bring a weed whacker up in here?" Mark asks.

"April wants to be a botanist."

This makes me cringe. A vestige of Harry left over in my youngest sibling that survived despite his absence.

"How often do you still get death threat mail and phone calls?" I ask.

This is the price Auggie has paid by choosing to keep the family name and remain in Pacific. Wackos across the country extend their hate for a serial killer to their family as well, no matter how oblivious they may have been.

"Less every year. The tenth anniversary next summer might stir them up again, though."

He stops us in the foyer in front of Father Time. The Douglas fir looks bad up close. The tree is most definitely dead, the leaves gone and the bark stripped to white. A great crack fissures from parted limps to near root, a dark singe signifying its split. The center piece of the mansion now reminds me of antlers; how both halves of the tree have managed to keep from cascading to the floor is a testament to the ancient roots. Still, I wouldn't want to stand beneath it.

"Kathy," Mark breathes and I turn my head.

I hadn't noticed her at first but there she is. Our mother, on a couch by the far window with a book in her hands. Ethereal—there is no other way I can describe Kathy Weaver, other than to liken her to a spirit. She's bonier than the last time I saw her, age having hallowed out her cheeks and turned what was once a long gold mane into a near bleach chop. It is her hands that cause me to linger. They knuckle the armrests of her chair, veiny, with fingers that should belong to a body ten years its senior. I'm not happy to see her to begin with, but this outward sign of aging in the woman that created me bothers me almost as much.

Beside me, Mark seems as taken aback as I am. He is immobilized. Auggie steps around Father Time and the forest that is our foyer and stops before her.

"Kathy, July and Mark have come home. Remember I told you they were coming?"

It takes her a prolonged moment to look up from the book. Her gaze wanders between her second- and third-born children and suddenly the ten feet between us feels like a canyon. Her expression is clouded, like she isn't entirely aware of her surroundings.

"You shouldn't have come," she says. Then she is pushing herself off the couch and away from Auggie. She circumnavigates the Douglas fir, then us. Touches Mark only briefly on the shoulder before ascending the staircase at a sluggish speed.

The three of us watch and wait until she is out of sight. Only then do Mark and I turn back to study our own puzzlement reflected in each other's expressions.

"That's . . ." says Mark, ". . . different."

Auggie had warned me about this change in our mother's state over the years, but it is another thing to actually witness it in person. The Kathy I remember, when she was regulated on her meds, was tender toward her children, if not slightly spacey and unreliable at times. Unregulated, she was nonsensical, prone to biblical ramblings and paranoia. I had never seen this version of my mother: subdued, vacant even. It's a surprise that after all the anguish of my childhood, it's mostly pity I feel toward her now—pity, and anger that she seems this drugged up.

"Her meds do that to her?" I ask. Because clearly that needs to be revisited.

Auggie nods. "I make sure she takes them every night."

"Does she call Harry in prison?" Mark asks.

Auggie shakes his head. "No. I think it would upset her too much."

"How is it with her, actually?" Mark asks. "Because that's not any Kathy I recognize."

Clearly, we've had the same thought. "Or the Kathy I last saw the day before I left," I say. I try to hide the accusation from my tone. "She was doing fine. More lucid than I've ever seen her." Granted, that was nine years ago.

"She's devolved since then. We had to play around with her medications. Sometimes the cure can be worse than the disease with this stuff," says Auggie. "She's stable now, though. No danger to us or herself." He emphasizes this last bit. "But don't take anything she says too seriously. She still has her moments."

Mark and I exchange looks, then listen. We can faintly hear her moving around on the floor above. Humming.

*   *   *

I don't see April until early evening. I'm standing on the dock at the end, my arms crossed, breathing deeply as I stare out at the reflection on the lake, wishing I could be like Alice and jump into its depths into any world other than the one I'm currently occupying.

Pacific Lake is a contradiction—calm and alive and glorious and a horrible nightmare I don't want to relive all at once. It overwhelms my body in the same way as the smell of mucky sand that won't leave my nostrils does, following me around like a spell. I wonder how I ever forgot about any of this. The lake water may as well run through my veins, for all the ecstasy and horror it has wrought my family and me.

It's the speedboat that disturbs this thought, the rippling of a boisterous motor as it moves too fast for these shallows. It's lucky it doesn't hit debris, as the engine cuts and I hear laughter heading for me. Six teenagers, more than weight capacity should allow, wobble at various angles on the decent-sized boat—not a single life vest on one of them. I can't judge them. It wasn't that long ago that I was doing the same, Auggie and I being pulled over by lake patrol for speeding too fast or trolling in spots along private property we knew were off limits.

I spot a head of pure red sunshine and I know without seeing her in almost a decade that it belongs to my sister. April is sitting quietly portside in the midst of it all, certainly the demurest of her rowdy companions, in a one-piece bathing suit with sunglasses in her hair. Her friends yell goodbye to her as she slowly stands and jumps into the lake's depths without hesitation. It is a sloppy jump, lacking grace, and it gives me an inkling of who my sister is as a seventeen-year-old woman.

I don't know how she can bear being in this lake. I haven't been able to so much as stick a toe into its weeded depths since we found May. It feels as though she is a part of it now.

I wait anxiously until April's head breaks through the barrier and then she is butterflying her way to the dock. This too demonstrates poor form. She doesn't look at me when she reaches and climbs up the ladder. It is only after she lifts her waiting towel from the planks and wraps it conservatively around her torso that the eyes of my baby sister meet mine.

I know she recognizes me. The only part of my physical appearance that has altered in nine years is an added inch.

"How's it going?" I know it's a lame start, but I don't begin to know how to go about this family reunion.

"Have you seen Deck?" she asks.

Apparently we aren't going to make pleasantries. "No. They won't let us in until morning."

She nods, goes to move past me.

"Nine years, and that's all you want to say to me?"

I don't know why I've spoken. It's stupid, but something about my little sister turning her back on me cuts me more than I thought it would.

April stops at the foot of the hill, whips her head around. "What do you want from me? I don't even know you."

It would hurt less if there was anger in her tone, but there's nothing but indifference. The look in her eyes says she couldn't care less about rectifying this situation.

I'm about to come back with an "I deserve that," but she's already turned away again and is strutting up toward the house. *I don't even know you,* her words repeat in my head. After years of being absent, I somehow expected to find the same eight-year-old kid I left behind, ready to jump into my arms despite the fact I've never so much as given her a phone call.

*   *   *

Dinner is awkward, to say the least, the five of us crowded around two pizza boxes at the kitchen table, the lighting dim, and the ghosts of Harry and May present in every breath. I do my best not to stare at the head of the table, where I sense Kathy's hollow eyes on me.

I don't even notice that I am anxiously tapping my fingers on the table surface until April turns beside me, utensils mid-cut in her pizza slice, and asks, "Can you stop doing that?"

"Sorry."

Auggie offers a pointed look across from me. His response earlier when I told him about my chilly reunion with April had only been a *What did you expect?*

Mark clears his throat. "So, how's school, Apes?"

He says it like they're on a nickname basis, but Mark hasn't had contact with our sister since leaving town either.

"Fine," she says.

"Auggie says you want to be a biologist," he continues, marinara dripping down his chin.

"Botanist," she corrects.

"Isn't that the same thing?" Mark asks.

That shows how much he paid attention to Harry's lessons when we were kids.

"Really? Growing up around all of this . . ." he gestures to the hanging flora around us, ". . . inspired you to want to be around more plants? I won't even buy my wife flowers for our house."

"That sounds like a marriage that will last," I mumble, and Auggie shoots me a warning look.

But apparently I'm not the one he should be worried about, because Mark blabbers on, his attention turning to our mother. "What about you, Kathy? How've you been?"

Kathy doesn't respond, simply bites into her slice of pizza.

"Hello?" Mark asks and waves a hand in front of her face. "Anyone home?"

Auggie grabs his hand and smacks it down. "Stop. Now."

Mark recoils. "What? I'm just making conversation."

"Leave her alone," Auggie says.

I'm glad he says it. I have my issues with our mother, the same as everyone else at this table, but getting her upset feels unnecessary our first night back.

"I'm fine," Kathy mumbles after heavy seconds of silence. "And I'm well aware of my surroundings. Thank you, Mark."

* * *

I offer to take the pizza box out to the recycling after dinner. Considering the five us sat in practical silence for the remainder of the meal, it is a relief to step away. The cool, dry air feels good in my lungs as I scissor closed the screen door to the kitchen and make my way out into the night.

I don't linger on the patio and I certainly don't allow myself to look over at Harry's greenhouse, the bright lights of the fountain inside illuminating it blue. Even the thought of it gives me the chills. Why hasn't Auggie knocked that hothouse down? It seems a crime against nature, worse even than the tree, that the site of our sister's murder should still be up.

I drop the box into the recycling bin and flip around, only to have someone grip my arm in a vise. It's Kathy. We're against the garage, so there are no windows for someone to witness this exchange. I realize this has been her plan all along—to corner me alone.

"You shouldn't have come back here, July."

Her voice is deeper now, sure.

I rip my arm from her grasp. "Nice to see you, too."

"I mean it," she lowers her voice to a conspiratorial level. It reminds me of all the times she used to confide her secrets in me as a child—typically about the demon she believed was haunting her, out to murder all of us children, then one did. She can't help it, I remind myself.

"This town isn't safe for you," she whispers.

I'm immediately stilled. I must be mistaken about the whole clarity thing. This obviously is what Auggie meant by flashes of her illness popping up. I want to laugh at the absurdity of it, at what I would have said had someone told me a week ago that I'd be standing here, back in Pacific, listening to the ramblings of my mother again—I would have told them to get the hell away from me.

"No place is safe for me, Kathy. That's what happens when your father's a serial killer."

"No. No. No. No." She's getting hysterical, shaking her head violently. "You need to go. Now."

"Don't worry." I rip my arm from her grasp. "The moment the hospital releases Deck, I'm taking him and getting the hell out of this town. You won't have to see me again."

My mother leans in closer and I can smell her breath. It's pepperoni, but also something staler, like she hasn't brushed her teeth in a few days. She whispers, completely somber now.

"Good. Take your brother and go. Don't come back."

5

Then

"SON OF A bitch."

My eyes snapped open and I looked out the window just in time to catch Mark tripping over the toaster in the backyard. I couldn't help but chuckle, as he kicked the thing across the patio.

"Those wide receivers got nothing on you," I yelled out the window.

He threw me the bird without looking up and grabbed his football gear from the ground. Then mumbled curses all the way to Auggie's truck and until he pulled out of the drive. It was the little things that gave me joy.

I flipped over, expecting to find a sound asleep eight-year-old, but the sheets beside me had already been ripped off and their nightly occupant nowhere to be found. How long had April been gone? I darted up, a bubble of anxiety settling in my gut. Not again. No. I was on my feet and rushing down the hall before my brain had a chance to fully wake. Black-and-white static fireworked across my vision as I stumbled down the rotting staircase, past Father Time, down the jungle wing—Brazil nut tree leaves smacking me along the way, before I rammed straight through the vine-entangled kitchen door.

There, standing on a rickety stool against the stove, was April. I let out a hoarse breath I hadn't known I'd been clutching, only to freak out again once I realized what she was doing. She had a saucepan on the stovetop going full blast, the blue and gold flames creeping up its sides, ominously close to her polka-dot shirtsleeves.

"What the hell are you doing?"

I ripped the spatula out of her hand and turned down the heat. What lay in the pan looked like some foreign amalgamation of maple syrup and vomit. Whatever it was, three quarters of it had burnt to an uneven crisp.

"I wanted to make everyone pancakes." Her face instantly teared up from my reprimand. "It was supposed to be a surprise."

I sighed and lifted her off the stool and away from the stove, my arms still clinging to her too-thin waist as I squatted to face her, eye to eye. It was how I'd always had important conversations with her and May. Harry had taught me to get on their level.

I softened my tone, realizing what an ass I'd been. "That's real sweet of you, Apes. But the stove's super dangerous. You can't use it without one of us older kids. Okay? We'll all help you with whatever you want to make. Just ask."

"Even Deck?" she asked, wiping her tears with her knuckles. This was always a question, Deck being the next oldest after the twins. Even though he was six years older, April felt the constant need to rope him into her and May's class of disallowed tasks. A younger kid's effort to level the playing field.

"Well, maybe not Deck. But not because he's young. He's just a little stupid."

That made her giggle.

"I heard that," Deck said, coming in with squinted eyes and half his hair up as if electrocuted. "Where's the coffee?"

"Where it always is," I quipped. "In the coffeepot?" I turned back to our younger sister. "Why don't we whip up a new batch of pancake batter, huh?"

She nodded and I hoisted her up onto one of the bar-stools. I shouldn't have still been able to do this, but April had always been small—May the sturdier of the two by three or four pounds, despite their identical bodies. I began assembling the ingredients out on the island in front of her.

"Only one cup," I barked at Deck as he swiped the milk carton from my hand.

"Thanks, Kathy. I think I can regulate myself."

I smiled tightly. "I thought so, too, until last night."

He rolled his eyes and poured the milk into his coffee. "You're one to talk. How's your head today?"

It was pounding actually. But my worry for April had trampled the urgent need to lock myself in a dark closet with a garbage can.

"Big sisters don't have to answer questions from younger siblings, do they, April?"

April shook her head. "Nope. That's July's one rule."

"Convenient." Deck pulled out the silverware drawer. "Where are all the spoons?"

"Have you checked the grass?"

I pointed out the backyard. He, in turn, shrugged like this was the most reasonable explanation in the world and stepped outside. I watched him rummage through the pots and pans, until he came up with a fork, triumphant.

"Is Kathy sick again?" April asked.

I cut my gaze back to her. "What makes you ask that?"

"She's been talking funny lately."

"About what?" I handed her the whisk and she rolled her sleeves to her elbows with the commitment of a surgeon.

"That Satan kidnapped May, or an alien." She knit her eyebrows together, like she was really trying to evaluate the possibility of this. "Am I going to get kidnapped by an alien, too?"

"What? No. No." *Damn Kathy.* I grabbed April's free hand across the marble surface. "No one's taking you any-where, Satan or E.T. or otherwise. All right? I promise you.

I'll kick their asses first, and you know I don't let people mess with me, right?"

She nodded. *God.* If there was anyone I wished I could suck all the fear and sadness from, and put it in myself, it would've been this little girl. Between her tears and nerves, I hardly recognized her anymore.

May had always been the quiet, withdrawn one, the one who preferred to read a picture book in the corner than play a board game with the rest of the family. April had been the butterfly of the two, the one to pull her sister along and force her to play with other kids. But when May disappeared, it was like April had swallowed her sister's personality whole in an unconscious attempt to keep her memory alive. It wasn't for the better.

Deck came back in and I was grateful for the change of subject. I'd chide my mother about opening her mouth in front of April later. Not that it would do any good, given her current state of mind. I made a mental note to go check on her after breakfast, but I wasn't worried. It was unusual for Kathy to wake before noon.

"No spoons?" I asked.

"Garden's fresh out," Deck remarked as he washed his utensil off in the sink. "In other news, Harold's home." He pointed in the direction of the greenhouse that ran along the opposing side of the patio.

My interest immediately piqued. Thank the sweet Lord. Daddy was home.

"Hey, Deck, do me a favor? Help April fry up the pancakes?"

My brother groaned. I knew he wanted to go play his PS1, where he spent every waking moment when he wasn't getting high in the woods.

"You can play *Final Fantasy* later," I added sweetly, for April's sake. But my eyes stabbed him with daggers. *Don't make me kick your growing ass,* I warned.

He groaned. "Fine."

I kissed April on the top of the head and went out the side door.

The early summer morning was cloudy, the hills of the manor bogged down in pockets of fog. I couldn't even see the lake. There was something gothic to the look of the house on mornings like these. Eerie didn't come close to describing it. No wonder we never had people over.

"House of Freaks, Island of Misfit Toys," I muttered as I opened the door to the greenhouse.

I had to hand it to my father. He may have had projects sit about the house for months, if not years on end, but once they were completed, they had the potential to be breathtaking. His greenhouse was a prime example.

The length and width of a football field, with a door on either end, the building was constructed entirely of glass, the copper edgings that connected the old, warped windowpanes having greened like a weather-worn penny. The structure ridged up into one elaborate dome at the top, with various dips and grooves angling downward in waved elegant points. A glass cathedral.

Stepping inside felt like entering into my father's personal fairyland. Where the house appeared as if Demeter, the goddess of the harvest, had sneezed all of her flora creations into one intermixed monstrosity, the greenhouse had order, structure. Not a mischievous leaf bent out of place or a dried-up petal having hit the floor.

All plants were in multicolored pots or flower boxes, some as big as Auggie and others as small as my fist. Color greeted me from end to end—from the limes to emeralds to seaweeds of the stalks to the golds to magentas to sapphires of the blooms. There were ten-foot palm trees in the back corner, a row of bamboo stalks that lined the opposing side. But what centered it all was the double fountain in the middle of the room, its Nile blue tiles sparkling beneath the cherub fountain head. A collection of tangerine, black, and white koi fish puttered up and down the breezeway at glacial speeds.

The biggest one, so white his scales were almost translucent, had been christened Melville by Kathy long ago.

But I didn't look at him or his kindred now as I stepped inside the hotbox of a room. I was after my father, who was kneeling in front of his box of chrysalids to see which of his little friends had broken out in his absence. Flapping, multicolored insects fluttered every few feet, ready to land on my shoulders or hair if I stood still long enough. Harry had of course also thought to make the greenhouse a butterfly conservatory.

My father had his back to me when I approached.

"Harry."

He rotated his head around, a tired smile scrunching the crow's feet at the corners of his eyes. "Livewire, there you are. Come have a look."

He turned back to his chrysalis box and urged me forward with his hand. I rolled my fingers into fists and squatted down next to him, clamping down my frustration. It wasn't anything I hadn't seen before. A blue morpho in its final stages of branching out of its cocoon. Its wings were still drying, and would be for several hours still, so the little guy's wingspan looked wet and pathetic. Only the dark outer wings showed, but once it took to air, its lustrous sky-blue backside would be on display. Not that the bugger would stop flapping long enough for us to catch a glimpse. Of all the butterfly species my father kept in this room, the morpho was the one that never seemed to stop trying to escape. It wanted out. I could relate.

"She's going to be a pretty one. I'll have to bring April out here."

I was losing patience fast. "Harry."

"Hmm?"

"I need to talk to you. About Kathy."

He pulled down a few abandoned cocoons from the wood panel. "What about your mother?"

"Have you seen her yet?"

He dropped the cocoons into the wastebasket he kept beside the box for this exact purpose, then stood. I came up with him. It was the first time he'd fully looked at me, his expression unconcerned. "Not yet. I just got in. She all right?"

I crossed my arms. "No. She's going batshit again."

He frowned. "Don't talk about your mother that way."

Typical Harry. Kathy could be trying to pull a Virginia Woolf in the lake and he'd insist she just wanted to go for a swim. Mental illness wasn't something my parents historically believed in. My mother hadn't ever taken more than an Advil until three years ago, when Auggie, Mark, and I had forced her into the office of a psychiatrist when Harry was out of town. Even then, it had taken six more months of Kathy's devolving delusions and a threat from child services before Harry was forced to acquiesce to the fact that Kathy "might need a little help from the pharmaceutical industry."

"It's true." I said. "I caught her last night out on the patio trying to charge the good silver. She thinks the moon will take all the toxins out, and she ordered about a hundred crystals online, to do God knows what with."

He walked over to the garden hose and cranked the valve. "Well, can't hurt, can it?"

"Yeah. Actually it can," I said following him around as he watered his creations. "She's been worse these last two weeks than usual. She's telling April that May got abducted by aliens. I've got an eight-year-old sleeping in my bed thinking she's about to be probed. Kathy's walking around like a zombie. And Mark caught her talking to herself the other night, making the sign of the cross repeatedly in the air. When he asked what she was doing, you want to know what she said? She was blessing the devil away."

"I'll have a talk with her." It was a dismissal, but I was undeterred.

"You need to do more than talk with her," I said. "She's off her goddamn meds."

He shook his head. "Your mother's not off her meds. I see her take her meds every night."

"What night? It's been months since you've been home for more than three nights in a row. How the hell would you know?"

My father dropped the hose into the nearest planter. His face was ash when he turned to me, a mix of torment and pride fighting across it. "I'm doing the best I can, July. Don't you want your sister back?"

I was so tired of this line. May had been gone for months. Whatever happened to her, I was confident she was either dead or never coming back. I knew it in my bones, even if no one else in this family was willing to admit it. Kathy had been on and off the ledge our whole lives, but since May, she was most decidedly off. Harry, on the other hand, was on a wild-goose chase, traipsing across the country from police station to police station trying to track down any remotely similar case, no matter how old, in search of a connection. So, my hackles went up. I had had it. I was seventeen and I was sick and tired of waiting for my father to show up.

"May is gone. You have five living, breathing children right here who are raising themselves. Which, let's be honest, is nothing new—God knows Auggie and I are used to it—but we can't take care of the other three, and ourselves too, when Kathy isn't staying on her pills. We can handle the rest of the crazy, but she's your one job. You're the one who's supposed to keep her regulated, not us."

My father's face turned beet red. He clenched his jaw and fists in a simultaneous fury I had never seen from him before, especially not directed at me. If I had been one of the boys, I'm confident he would have hit me. When he finally spoke, his voice was quiet, but there was heat to it. "I'm still your father, July. Show respect and watch your mouth. I appreciate you and your brother stepping up during all of this. But I am doing everything I can to keep this family together. Don't you understand that? The best I can, kid."

"Tell that to the colander in the grass."

We both shook. I was the only one with the nerve to confront him like this. Auggie was capable of only a verbal punch or two before he'd revert into his quiet simmer, while Mark ignored our father altogether. I, Harry's Livewire, was the only one with the capacity to wound him. I acted as his prism, refracting back every failure he saw within himself.

We stood like that, neither willing to acquiesce or apologize, until Auggie burst through the door, a stray zebra moth darting out behind him.

"You need to come," he barked at us, before backing out.

Harry and I didn't pause. We sprinted out of the greenhouse, across the patio, and into the kitchen after my brother. Auggie was already grabbing the remote from beside April and flipping on the TV that hung from the wall.

"What's wrong?" I asked.

I knew that look on my brother. It meant nothing good. Auggie switched to the local news station.

Harry turned to our youngest brother, who was mid pancake flip at the stove. "Deck, take April out to feed the koi, please."

"Why?" Deck asked.

"Now," our father said, a sternness to his tone.

"But, my pancakes," April insisted.

"I'll call you when they're ready," I said.

My eyes were already trained on the screen before my youngest two siblings left out the backdoor. A red ticker tape ran across the bottom of the display. *Second Girl Reported Missing in Montgomery County.* The image of a blue rowhouse appeared above it, the only suggestion of anything out of the ordinary: the yellow strip that repeated the word CAUTION zigzagging across the front lawn.

"How did you . . ." I started, but was unable to continue. I had to sit on the barstool April left behind. My legs would have gone out from under me if I hadn't.

"Dan," Auggie answered, his eyes equally glued to the screen. "His dad got called to the scene."

"Another little girl?" I asked.

Auggie shook his head just as the house was replaced by a photo. A teenager. Blonde. Small. A gap-toothed smile that would draw a second glance.

Scotty MacGyver, the local news reporter, appeared at his anchor desk beside the image, a somber look to his face.

"Authorities are asking the public to be on the lookout for missing sixteen-year-old Laurel Dillon. She was last seen in her home on Douglas Trail in Hazel, Georgia, two nights ago. The Hazel Police Department have reason to believe that she may have been kidnapped from her backyard while letting out her dog in the middle of the night. The police have not commented on whether her disappearance is suspected to be related to that of May Weaver, the eight-year-old who disappeared from her home in neighboring Pacific, Georgia, in February earlier this year under similar circumstances. Anyone with any information relating to either case is asked to . . ."

I couldn't retain anything else the reporter said. My eyes fixed on Laurel Dillon's face again, at the possibility of what this meant for my family. Of what this meant for May. That the two cases could be related—two kidnappings or two murders.

I barely made it to the sink before hurling up bile. I wished more than ever that I had given in to throwing up earlier that morning, because this proved so much worse. I gagged over and over again, my fingers clutching hold of the basin so tightly my knuckles went white. *She's not just dead. She was murdered. Someone murdered my baby sister.* I had never allowed this possibility fully in until now. It was so much easier to think May drowned or had lost her way out in the woods. But this might prove she hadn't. There was someone else, now.

I don't know at what point Auggie reached around me and pulled back my hair, but I found myself leaning against him, my strength depleted. He clutched me long after I stopped dry heaving, and shushed me soothingly.

When I regained my composure, I stepped back from him and looked over at our father.

Harry had hardly noticed us. His eyes were still on the screen as MacGyver's report concluded. His posture set rigid, but I swear I caught hope on my father's face. This enlivened him as much as it sickened me.

When the TV switched to commercial, Harry grabbed his keys.

"Where're you going?" I asked. As if I didn't already know.

"The police station. I have to talk to them."

"You . . . you just got back . . ." I tried. There was still Kathy. There was still all of us. "They'll call you if they want to . . ."

"We'll talk later," he said, waving me off, not having heard a word I said. He was already halfway out the door. "This is a lead, Livewire."

6

Then

I DIDN'T KNOW WHERE to begin reconciling what I'd witnessed on the news that morning. I waited around all day for Harry to come home, to report back what he had learned from the police, but it was almost nightfall and there was still no sign of him. No doubt he was currently in an interrogation room at the station, preaching his conspiracy theories to a group of disinterested cops. That, or they had grown so annoyed with him that they locked him in a cell. "One could only hope," Deck muttered when I voiced the joke, as we carried the kitchenware back into the house. I don't know why we bothered. At the rate she was flying, Kathy would have the silver back in the grass by morning.

It was five PM before I remembered that Colton Davidson was picking me up in two hours. I cursed and scrambled up to my room, April giggling in a chair as I dumped half the contents of my closet onto my bed. I should have canceled, I realized, but it felt like too short notice and, frankly, I was ready to give an arm and a kidney to think about anything other than Laurel Dillon and her connection to May's disappearance for the next few hours.

I stepped out onto the porch at five to seven, before I had the chance to rethink the floral dress and leather jacket I'd chosen. I was only starting to dress to accentuate my femininity that summer. I had grown up a tomboy, through and through.

Auggie was nursing a beer in one of the Adirondack chairs. He took one look at me and his eyes widened. "Where you going?"

"I've got a date."

His expression was dumbfounded. "You're going out tonight? After what we saw on the news?"

I grabbed the beer out of his hand and downed half of it, more nervous than I thought I'd be. "There is no news. We don't even know that missing girl is related to May."

"You sure changed your tune since this morning."

I glared at him. "What do you want from me? This whole family's been on pause for four months." I chugged what was left of the beer. "I need to live my life."

"No. What you *want* is to drink and act out, until you forget about it all."

"I'm not acting out."

"You want to explain Davidson, then? I assume that's who it is."

"What about him?"

Auggie studied my dress again, this time his eyes tracing it from my chest to where the skirt ended halfway up my thigh. "He's got a reputation." He looked back up to me pointedly. "For virgins."

My face flamed, partially because I already knew this and had chosen not to care. "We're just going to the drive-in with his buddies. Chill out."

"Do me a favor," he said. "Watch yourself. You're prettier than you think you are."

Something about his words cut me to the bone—a deep insecurity maybe I didn't even realize was fully there until then. I had spent my whole life a Weaver. The stares that had accompanied that had somehow always left me feeling undesirable.

Colton mercifully pulled his Jaguar up the drive then. Auggie muttered under his breath, "Of course, that's what he drives." It cost more than what Harry made in a year—with both jobs.

Colton's face lit as he turned off the engine beside the porch. "July."

"Colton," I said, climbing in beside him.

I was surprised that my brother followed me over and leaned his arms across my open window. His gaze fixed on my date. "Davidson."

"Weaver." Colton said, his eyes matching Auggie's slits. "Nice night."

"She needs to be home by eleven."

I scowled at my brother. Was he playing Harry, now? "No, *she* doesn't." I pushed Auggie off the door. "Drive," I said to Colton.

I caught the reflection of my brother in the rear-view mirror. He remained perfectly still in the center of the drive, his deep frown dwindling as we pulled away. I turned back to Colton. He was beaming, like he'd just won a standoff.

"Do all your dates have to go through your babysitter?"

I didn't exactly have dates lining up, but I wasn't going to mention that. "He's overprotective."

"I'll say." He scanned me up and down. "You look nice. I like that dress a lot."

"Thanks," I said, sinking back into my seat. I all of a sudden didn't feel quite as fearless about all this as I had before. *A reputation for virgins.* Damn Auggie for getting in my head. "I didn't ask you what movie we're seeing."

He smirked. "Hell if I know. But it's a Saturday night. What else is there to do in this town?"

* * *

The movie was *The Lost World: Jurassic Park:*, and how Colton hadn't seen the first one, I didn't rightly know. The sequel premiered the night before, so the drive-in was packed, cars lining every spot in the field as Johnny Edgar, who owned the computer store downtown, hooked up the projector to screen against the thirty-year-old slab of concrete the town had constructed for this exact purpose. Most of my classmates were present, along with a large portion of the rest of the town. Drive-ins weren't common anywhere anymore, but this was part of Pacific's character. We lived in the South, but we also lived in a time capsule. Nothing much ever changed around there and that's the way Pacific's residents liked it.

Colton's black Jag was swallowed by a sea of pick-up trucks and vans, parked dead center to the screen. We had picked up his friends Pete and Charlotte at Bobby's Diner, but they hadn't done much more than utter a hello before they'd taken up residency in the back seat, conjoined at the mouth. I did my best to ignore them from the front seat and sip what remained of my shake. Colton put his arm around me and chugged a beer as we watched the movie. Julianne Moore and Vince Vaughn had just freed the captured dinosaurs when Colton's hand slipped down along my side. His fingers began to trace up my bare thigh without removing his eyes from the screen.

My pulse spiked and I felt blood rush to my cheeks. The truth was I had gone there that night because I wanted to feel wanted. Like I said, I was dancing across a tightrope that summer, daring something to tip me off into the abyss, almost craving it. To help me make sense of May, or to forget about her altogether—whichever proved easier.

Still, basic nature's hard to fight. The instant Colton cupped my face and kissed me, I realized what a mistake it had been coming there. Auggie was right. I didn't even really like Colton Davidson, and it was plain as his fingers shot up my skirt without preamble and dug into my underwear that he only really liked me for one thing. I pushed him back so fast, his back smacked against his seat.

"I'm not into that," I said.

"I get it," he said. "Sorry if I made you feel uncomfortable." He made a show of sitting back, dropping his hands to his thighs. "You know I like you, July. You're not like those other girls. You're tough. I mean hell, look at everything that's happened to your family. Can't have been easy."

The last person I found myself wanting to talk to about May was this guy. "Sure."

I tried to look back at the screen. We were halfway through the movie. I figured the second half I'd just make a show of sipping my shake and watching until it was time for him to take me home.

"You know I really respect you," he went on. "I just think you're so damn cool." He brought his fingers up to tuck a stray strand of hair behind my ear. "Pretty, too."

He leaned toward me again, brought his lips up to press my cheek. I let him. I even let him kiss me again on the mouth, half buying his sweetness and realization that he'd moved too fast, but that all went to shit the moment his head ducked down to my cleavage. He bit the top of one of my breasts. Hard.

"What the hell?" I shoved him away.

"Hey, it's all good," he said. He looked so innocent, his eyes shining in the same way they had every other moment tonight. That was when I realized "no" was a starting point for Colton, not an end, and he intended to get what he wanted.

I shot a look back to Charlotte and Pete, but they were so absorbed in their own making out, they paid us no attention. Either that, or they were used to Colton's escapades. *Shit*. I was in this alone. Good thing I was pissed. I'm always braver when pissed.

"I'm not going to fuck you in a car with your buddies in the backseat, if that's what you were looking for."

Colton squared his jaw, not even having the decency to look offended. If anything, he was confident. "Who said anything about fucking? I think you're assuming things here, July. You need to relax. Have another beer." He grabbed one from the case at my feet and held it up to me.

"Nah. I'm good."

I was out my door in a flash. I wasn't going to wait around for him to lock me in.

I weaved my way around the trucks, most attendees making out or engrossed in the film. Moore and Vaughn were treating a baby T-rex with a broken leg on the projection. I scanned the cars for Mark, assuming he was here somewhere, but then I caught sight of Nicole sprawled out in the bed of a Ford watching with a group of pom poms. My brother was nowhere in sight. Damn. The one time I actually needed him.

"July, hold up."

I turned back to Colton. His brows were knitted. He looked irritated, surprised.

"I'm going home," I announced.

"I think we had a misunderstanding." It came out charming, but with a tight smile. "Why don't you come on back to the car?"

"No. I'm good. My brother is around here somewhere."

He grabbed my arm when I tried to walk. "Hey, let me give you a ride home at least."

I tried to yank my elbow back, but his grip clenched. A warning. His eyes told me not to make a scene. A few curious looks were starting to turn from the projection.

"Let go of me," I said with a newfound firmness. I felt panic seep in, but also fury. It was like my world went into slow motion, then. All I saw was me and Colton, his finger pads digging into my skin. I felt rage. "Get. Your. Hand. Off. Me."

"July."

I didn't wait for him to finish his response. I swung my fist and knuckled him clean across the jaw. He lurched back, his hand releasing me, his expression one of pure disbelief. He rubbed his face, then laughed.

There was a new voltage to his expression when he looked back at me, and I saw the entitled asshole, a dangerous one. He looked like he wanted to hit me right back. Maybe he would have if we didn't have an audience. "Don't you know who I am?"

"I don't care who your daddy is, Colton Davidson. You follow me one more step and I'll give that pretty face of yours a black eye." I clenched my fist at my side to prove my point and turned from him.

"July," Colton called after me, but he didn't dare follow. There were lines even he knew he couldn't cross in public.

I was halfway out of the parking lot, so raging mad I could spit, when I ran head first into someone coming from the snack stand. Popcorn rained down onto blacktop.

"Shit," I said, rubbing my face tiredly. "Sorry. I'll buy you another . . ." I patted my jacket pocket. "And I left my purse in his car. Motherfucker. This night can't get much better."

"Don't worry about it."

The familiar deep voice made my head pop up. I hadn't seen Gabe Santana in seven years, and back then he'd been a scrawny teenager. Not the bulked-up twenty-something with a buzzed head standing before me now.

"July, is that you?" Gabe asked, registering me too. His maple-colored eyes took in my expression. "What's wrong?"

"You're back."

He squinted at me like I had two heads. "Yeah, I'm back." I watched him scan around us, clearly attempting to locate the source of my distress, then my intended destination. I could have answered that last part: I didn't have one. We were at the entrance to the drive-in. The only thing past us was miles of dark, abandoned road, until you hit town. I was going to have to hitchhike or rough it on foot. Probably the latter.

"You're walking home," he said, reading my mind.

"Well, it's a beautiful night." I went to sidle past him. "Nice seeing you, Gabe. I owe you one for the popcorn."

"July," he said behind me, "Let me give you a ride. You clearly need one."

I stopped, took a deep breath, then thought about the fact that it was going to take me half the night to walk home. The nearest pay phone to call Auggie was outside the Kroger's in town.

I glanced back to the screen behind us. "The movie's not over. Aren't you here with friends or on a date or something?"

"It's a dumb movie," Gabe said. I watched him register what was undoubtedly desperation in my eyes. "Come on. I mean it."

He didn't wait for me to follow him back to the trucks, as if he already knew I would.

When we reached his navy Dodge Ram a few cars in, he popped open the back door and waited until I climbed in before shutting it. There was a pretty brunette in the front seat who swung her head around like an owl in surprise. I wanted to say she was a few years older than me. I recognized her from the boutique in the center of town, not that I'd ever been inside it.

"Hi, there," I said.

"Who're you?" She whipped back around as Gabe climbed into the driver's seat. "I thought you were bringing back popcorn, not a stray kid." She said it laughing, but the underlying annoyance was there.

Gabe stiffened. "She's a family friend. I've got to take her home."

"Are you kidding?"

"You didn't even want to see this movie."

I cut in, "If you just drive me to the center of town, I can walk the rest of the way or call my brother for a ride." Then again, the look on the girl's face had me going for the door.

"Hell, I can actually walk. It's fine. Really, Santana. I don't want to intrude."

"July, stop," Gabe said, his eyes boring into mine with an intensity I had forgotten him capable of. "I'm taking you home." He turned back to his date, an added layer of irritation to his tone for her. "It'll take twenty minutes. I'll take you wherever you want to go after."

The woman pursed her lips. "Drop me at McNeil's on the way."

Gabe groaned in defeat, and backed out of his spot, causing a series of honks as the trucks behind were forced to let him out.

The three of us rode in silence for the ten minutes it took to reach downtown, where McNeil's, Pacific's one dive bar— more reminiscent of a shack—sat on a deserted crossroad. The woman was out of the truck before Gabe had a chance to put it into park.

"Give me a minute," he said to me, then followed her out.

I pretended not to watch from the back window, as he called after her and they exchanged words. I couldn't tell what they were saying, his back was to me, but his shoulders were stiff and she was yelling. The woman eventually turned, and stormed into the bar, and I pivoted back around before Gabe caught me watching.

"You want to climb in front?" he asked once he got in, his voice tired.

I did as I was asked, and went over the console, my foot smacking one of the air conditioning vents as I went. The passenger seat was still warm.

"Sorry I ruined your date."

He pulled the truck back onto the road. "There wasn't going to be another one, anyway."

I thought back seven years to when I'd last seen Gabe Santana. He'd once been a passing fixture in the Weaver children's lives. His sister Daniela had been our babysitter until Auggie was eleven and deemed "mature enough" to watch the rest of us on the weekends our parents left town. Daniela didn't drive, so Gabe was the one who always picked her up. I knew him back then, but not well. I was eleven when he'd gone off to basic training, him a skin-and-bones eighteen-year-old with shaggy hair. If he'd been back since, I hadn't known about it.

"I'm guessing you don't need directions to where I live."

He smiled. "No."

I took in the familiar evergreens ticking away in the dark on either side of the two-lane road, the only light emanating from the golden line that ran down the dried tar's center. The truck's interior smelled of pine from the tree-shaped air freshener that dangled from the mirror.

"You want to talk about what made you willing to walk three miles home alone in the dark?" he asked.

"Nope."

He looked over at me, maybe for the first time actually seeing me since our chance run-in. It was the third time I'd felt my appearance blatantly inspected in one night, but it was the first where I didn't feel like I was being ogled or shamed. "You were a kid when I left. What are you now, sixteen?"

Older people telling me how big I'd grown was a pet peeve of mine, especially when they were older people I suddenly found attractive. "Seventeen. What does that make you? Thirty?"

He pretended to flinch. "Watch it. I'm only twenty-five."

Like I hadn't known that already. "How long you been back?"

"Two weeks."

I wondered where he was back from. A base? A port? A tour? I was assuming those were the only places he could have come from, but what the hell did I know about the military.

"What were you again? Navy?"

"Army. 101st."

I sat back in my seat, amused. "You know, I've never understood the armed forces' need to say what number y'all are in. Like I'm supposed to know what the 72nd or 98th even mean."

"Those divisions don't exist."

"Of course they don't."

That made him laugh. I liked the sound of it, coarse and effortless. He looked so different silhouetted in the truck's dashboard lights. He wore a crewcut and had the start of a goatee. It aged him, but I suspected its purpose was to cover the trace of a scar I caught peeking out at the base of his jawline. I tried to remember if he'd always had it. I didn't think so.

"How long you back for?"

"I don't know," he admitted.

"And you chose to come back to Pacific in your time off?"

"Why wouldn't I?"

"Ummm, because it sucks here?"

He squinted at me curiously. "You hate Pacific that much?"

"I think Pacific hates people like you and me that much."

The Santanas were one of the only Latino families in town. Gabe's mom ran a cleaning crew that serviced all the mansions, including the one owned by Colton's family. I had seen Daniela and his other sisters treated like the help by townies on more than one passing occasion. They didn't deserve to be roped into the same category as my family of freaks by the people of Pacific and its neighboring towns, but somehow they always were.

Gabe shrugged. "People are the same wherever you go."

"Where were you stationed, then?"

"You always ask this many questions?"

I held up my hands innocently. "Just trying to make conversation over here."

"How's your family holding up?"

"You're right. Questions are overrated."

He frowned, genuine concern lighting his face. "You been okay?"

I gulped, willing myself not to vomit for the second time
that day. "Fine."

His palm came down over my fist and he squeezed lightly.
It was only meant to be comforting, a friend, but more than
anything it took me off guard. Mostly because of how he
looked at me in that moment. Not with pity, but understanding. I had forgotten; his dad had died of a heart attack a few
years back. It wasn't the same situation, but loss was loss.

He pulled his hand away just as quickly as it appeared.
We rode the final five minutes in silence until the dark lake
rounded over the tree line. Gabe pulled his truck up and
paused to look at the house.

"I know. Spectacular isn't it?" I quipped. *Architectural
Digest* should be calling us any day now."

"It's always had character," was his response, his eyes
fixed on the hat of Father Time.

I opened my door, but hesitated before I climbed out.
"Thank you. Seriously."

He nodded, "See you around, July."

I watched him back his car out without looking back.
God, I hoped that wasn't the last time I'd see him before he
left again.

When I turned my head, Mark was waiting on the porch.

"Was that Daniela's brother?" he asked.

"Yup." I climbed up the steps to him. "Missed you at
the drive-in tonight." I meant it for once. It would have been
nice to have had my little brother there for backup, not that
I was confident he would have intervened if it came to it. It
depended on how many people were watching—that, and
his mood.

Mark frowned, gunned what was left of his beer. "I heard
all about it. Nicole called me from someone's car phone. Tell me
you weren't stupid enough to clock the richest kid in school?"

I smiled tightly and held up my already bruising fist.
"What can I say? I go out every weekend looking to start a
fight."

Auggie came out the door and caught sight of my hand. His eyes instantly went wide. Clearly he had not heard. "What happened?"

"Well, you were right about Davidson."

Auggie looked homicidal. He barely could bite out his next words. "Did he hurt you?"

"No." I put my hand down. "I handled it. Gabe gave me a ride home."

"Gabe Santana?" he asked, now even more confused.

I nodded.

"Is Davidson going to press charges for you fucking up his face?" Mark asked.

I shrugged. "Oh, one could hope. Lord knows we don't have enough excitement going on around here as it is."

My middle brother stood, appearing genuinely mad. "Goddamn it, July. As if this town doesn't think we're all nutjobs enough, you had to go and punch the mayor's son in front of half our school?"

"He was trying to assault me, Mark. In a car at the drive-in *in front of half our school*. What do you want from me?"

He looked venomous. "Maybe if you didn't act and dress like a whore, he wouldn't treat you like one."

I would have said something, but Auggie sprang at Mark, pinning him by the throat to the wall. I had never seen my eldest brother look so ready to kill.

"Take that back," he hissed. "Now."

"What are you doing?" Mark croaked.

"Auggie, stop," I said, going to pull on his arms. He was close to choking Mark, whose face had drained in fear. "What are you doing? He didn't mean it."

"Oh, yes, he did," Auggie said, but released our brother, and shoved him back hard.

Mark stroked his neck in disbelief. He was red-faced and furious, but I knew beneath that, he felt shamed. "You're as fucking obsessed with her as she is herself. You know that?" He ripped open the screen door. "I can't wait to get the fuck out of this town and away from all of you." He slammed it on his way in.

I turned back to Auggie. He was still flushed. "What the hell is wrong with you?"

"He was acting like a prick."

"That's not an excuse to choke him."

Auggie punched his hand into the shingles on the side of the house. The impact snapped one off at a jagged angle and I jumped back. This wasn't my brother. He wasn't violent. He was supposed to be the cool, reasonable one.

"You need to calm down."

He visibly shuddered, took a deep breath, clenched then unclenched his fists with his back to me. When he finally spoke, his words were a whisper. "I told you not to go out with him."

Then he disappeared back into the house, leaving me alone on the porch. How had this day gone from bad to nuclear? I felt the urge to rip my clothes off. To rip my own skin off. I couldn't deal with any of this. I needed an escape. An immediate one.

I beelined for the kitchen, went for the liquor cabinet, and came down with a bottle of vodka. It was still a quarter full. I threw the cap in the sink and ripped through the door down the jungle hall. I hadn't even had a chance to ask my brothers if Harry had come home. I hadn't seen his Jeep on the way in. But that, along with whatever our father had learned, could wait for morning.

Now, I had one objective. Curl up in my bed beside April, drink my booze, and let my personal oblivion blur into sleep. It had become my routine one too many nights these days, but tonight especially, I needed it. *Better watch that,* I warned myself. The darker part of me answered by tipping a shot's worth into my mouth as I walked.

My immediate plans were thwarted by the sight of Kathy sitting crisscross on the floor of the foyer in front of Father Time. She had Deck beside her with April coiled in her lap.

All three stared up past the Douglas Fir's branches through the open ceiling. It was a clear night. You could see the square patch's worth of stars.

I couldn't help myself. I sat down beside my mother and looked up, too. "What are we doing?"

"Stargazing," responded Deck.

"That's Orion," April said, pointing up at an indistinct cluster.

I knew for a fact that wasn't true. Georgia only saw Orion's constellation in the winter months. Harry had taught us that.

"Your father's home." Kathy drew her arm around me and leaned me in close. I let her, because I wanted my mother in that moment, even if it was just an illusion.

"Everything will be all right," she whispered in my ear. "Your father keeps the devil at bay when he's home."

I nodded. I hoped she was right about that. Just in case she wasn't, I chugged what remained of the bottle.

Now

THE THREE OF us are outside when visiting hours begin the next morning at Hazel General. We agree to leave April home, because of her age and not wanting to overwhelm Deck, so it's just Auggie, Mark, and me. It's déjà vu.

How many times during our adolescent years had the three of us waited until Harry was at work to sneak Kathy here to have her admitted to the psychiatric ward, to get her stabilized, to burn through the short list of doctors still willing to see and write her scripts? Too many to count. Only two or three of these outings had actually resulted in her being admitted through the ER to the psych ward, and even then, within a few hours, if Kathy wasn't already checked in past the point of no return, Harry would appear at the end of the hall, our mother's defiant liberator. He'd whisk her out of there, claiming she wasn't actually a danger to others or herself, and the three of us would slide back into Auggie's truck to ride home in defeated silence. We never talked about it after, and eventually Mark stopped coming at all.

We are ushered through the various security points now, the nurse punching in safety codes at each door. Mark grumbles beside me. "What is this? Alcatraz?"

We end in a stark, plain hospital room, where an old man is watching *Jeopardy* reruns. The nurse points for us to go around the curtain divider.

Deck is waiting for us on the other side. He has a cafeteria tray laid over his lap and is knifing a cup of green Jell-O like it's a foreign object with his plastic spoon. He's gaunter than the last time I saw him, his eyes hollow and his skin pale. He looks like he's been through hell.

"It's about damn time you worthless bitches showed up. If I'm forced to eat another tray of this crap, I'm going to throw it along with myself out the bloody window." He puts his hands on either side of his mouth and calls through the curtain to the room's other occupant. "That was me being facetious, Topher. If you call Nurse Ratchet back in here, I'll take you with me out the damn window." He screws his attention back to the three of us. "That's Topher, my roommate. He's taken it upon himself to be my around-the-clock suicide watch and can't take a joke to save his life. Ha, get it? Save his life?"

"You're an idiot," I say, because unlike our other brothers, I know this twenty-four-year-old version of Deck. His tortured mind doesn't scare me.

"That's not very kind of you to say to a man who just tried to throw himself off a bridge, July." But then a wide smile rushes across his face and the look of bliss in his eyes is infectious.

I can't help but grin wide too, climb onto his bed to hug him, and release a deep breath I haven't known I've been holding. Then I sit back and whack him across the face.

Auggie and Mark's eyes go wide.

"July!" Auggie cries.

But I ignore him. Deck breaks out laughing.

"Don't you ever scare us like that again, you selfish bastard," I say, but I can't hide the relief in my tone.

"Don't worry, boys," Deck assures them. "That's just how the ole Livewire and I say hello." He turns to our middle brother. "Marky, boy. It's been a minute. How's your last decade been?" He scans Mark's slacks and polo. "Want to loan me fifty bucks when I get out of here? Looks like you can spare it."

"Not on your life," Mark says. "From everything I've heard, you'll just circle back for more."

Deck claps his hands together. "Well, it's your turn. These two have each basically sold a kidney for me at this point."

"And a couple of ribs and a spleen, in my case," I mumble.

"How you feeling?" Auggie asks.

"Physically, like I ran a marathon. Mentally, like everyone in here thinks I'm batty. I sure could use a burger. Can we get out of here?"

"We need to check with your doctors first," Auggie says.

"They're going to tell you the same thing I am," says Deck. "They've dug around in my noggin and no surprise, I'm an addict, I'm also schizophrenic—thanks for that one, mother dearest, and as our lovely sister pointed out, also an idiot. What I'm not, is suicidal. They're just going to give you the usual bullshit spiel, throw some brochures at you, and tell you to cart me off to rehab and make sure I take my little blue pills." He jumps up from the bed. "Shall we go?"

"Sit your ass down," I command.

Deck plops himself back on the bed. "You're no fun, Kathy."

He says this to irk me, and it works, but these are familiar roles for the two of us—me busting him out of the hospital, half the time dropping him off at expensive rehabs or outpatient centers across the country he's lucky I can afford, half the time taking him home with me and forcing him into AA/NA meetings and back on his meds. I also can't help but think about that shameful last time, where I drove him straight to the airport and didn't look back.

"He's right," I say to Auggie and Mark. "They can't keep him if they don't think he's a danger to other people or himself."

Deck crosses his arms, validated. "See?"

Auggie cups his shoulder. "Give us a minute to talk to the doctors, Jack Nicholson."

I am of course right. Deck has done a particularly good job of convincing his psychiatrists that his attempted plummet into the Hazel River was due to a delusion, rather than an attempt on his own life. The doctors then proceed to reassure us that he is restabilized on his meds, even though it's only been a week. We don't have a choice to leave him. The insurance company won't pay for any longer and they're pushing him out. That's mental illness healthcare in America for you.

Mark chucks the handful of brochures into the first garbage can we pass in the parking lot. When Deck sees Auggie's old Ford, his eyes light.

"Just like I remember it. Come to Papa." He takes off at a sprint across the parking deck, jumps up a tire, and launches himself over into the bed, giddy.

"No wonder the cops thought he was trying to end it. The kid's got a fucking death wish," Mark says, then looks at me. "Are you sure he's not still hallucinating?"

I shake my head. "He'll still be off for a few weeks, but that's mostly just Deck."

"I guess I shouldn't be surprised, considering he was raised by you."

I grimace internally, but don't show that he's hit me. I've been thinking the same thing since the moment I saw April—raised the last nine years by Auggie and the normal picture-perfect student. Meanwhile, Deck, occasionally housed by me in Nashville, is an addict, fuckup, and overall lost boy. Guilt suffocates me, the feeling that I should have done more for him. He definitely got the shorter end of that stick.

"Who wants to fly?" Deck asks when we reach him. He's standing up in the bed, facing us, his arms raised out in the way we used to do.

"No way," Auggie says. "You just got out of the hospital."

"Come on." Deck stamps his foot like a small child. "It'll be fun, like old times."

"Get your ass in the front," Mark urges, seizing our youngest brother by the collar and yanking him down and into the truck.

Auggie gives me a look, and I nod, boosting myself into the bed. If somebody has to ride in the back, it's going to be me.

"Promise me we're doing the right thing by pulling him out," he asks once Mark has closed the passenger door.

"Keeping him in there longer would have made no difference anyway," I say. "As for the drugs . . ." I shoot a look to the front where Deck is already fighting with Mark over the stereo.

Auggie closes the tailgate and circles over to the driver's door. "I have an idea for that."

From his middle seat, Deck yanks open the back window so I can hear everything my three brothers say, as Auggie reverses the truck.

"Can we go to Pickens?" he asks. "I'm not kidding. I'm starving."

Mark and Auggie stare across him at each other, then back at me. We all nod. Pickens is the one thing we can agree on.

*　*　*

Pickens is much the same as when I left town. There are minor differences, of course: the forest green wallpaper is peeling to reveal plaster now, many of the old mounted fish and painted landscape saws have been rearranged on the walls in a decorative upheaval. The kitchen is no longer in a separate room, but open diner-style for patrons to watch their greasy eggs and pancakes being cooked. The hostess stand is polished and new, the menus in a different font, and the booths reupholstered in a sludge brown.

I'm on edge. Being out in public in this town has that effect on me. People are staring—all townies. I recognize most of their faces from back in the day. They cluster within the small café booths like a mutinous mob.

The four of us are jammed into one of the booths in the back corner on purpose. None of us want to put the town's serial killer family on display.

"You know, I don't think there's a single person in this whole universe that makes coconut cream pie quite like Daniela does," Deck says stuffing his face with a plate of it. "Where is she anyway? She still own the place?"

The rest of us have ordered actual food—burgers and club sandwiches, but Deck's stacking up on the sweets in addition to his burger and fries. It's an alcoholic/addict thing: a lot of us replace the high with sugar.

"She's off on Mondays," Auggie says.

The mention of Daniela has my stomach in knots. I'm grateful she isn't here. If she were, I wouldn't be able to keep myself from asking about her brother. It's been hard enough not bringing him up to Auggie since I got back to town.

I catch the eye of an elderly woman at the counter beneath the TV. She's glaring at us with open disgust. I glare back. Seventeen-year-old July would have flicked a fry at her.

"We need to talk about what happened," says Auggie.

I down my sweet tea, needing the shot of caffeine in my veins for this conversation.

Deck sighs, and his fork clatters onto his empty pie plate. His earlier joking tone has evaporated. "Do we have to do this now?"

"Yes," I say. This should be the moment I grab his hand, but I'm not that kind of sister. "We're not going to bring you back to the hospital either way. So, out with it. Were you trying to kill yourself or not?"

"Keep your voice down," Mark urges.

Sure, a few people like that woman are staring periodically, but it's the lunch shift. The clatter of plates and the conversations among the thirty or so patrons mostly drown us out.

Deck looks at me with genuine hurt. "How can you of all people ask me that? You who knows me better than anybody?"

I shake my head. "I haven't seen you in months, Deck. The last time I saw you . . ."

". . . you put me on a plane and told me to fuck off," he finishes.

His words are a cord around my throat. I feel all three brothers stare at me, the oldest two accusingly.

"I didn't tell you to fuck off," I say. "I paid for your plane ticket to go wherever you wanted to go."

"You did what?" Mark asks, nearly knocking over the maple syrup bottle.

I scowl at him. "And we're back to the part where you don't get to talk."

"Stop," Auggie commands.

"You gave up on me," Deck repeats.

I keep my voice down, but I'm pissed. "I busted your ass out of jail, the hospital, and drug dens more times than I can count. Nursed you through two ODs. Paid for private rehab three times, two of which you checked yourself out from early. Also an outpatient center to help you get restabilized on your meds. Paid off dealers, bookies, your loan shark. Got you job after job in Nashville that you quit or got fired from, always within two months. Then the second to last time I saw you, you stole my TV and five hundred bucks from my wallet that I needed for sound equipment. So don't you dare give me shit that I gave up on you. I'm the only person in this goddamn family that's been there for you these past nine years."

Deck has fallen silent, his mouth clamped shut, and he sinks into the bench. Tears swell at the corners of his eyes and he wipes them with his jacket sleeve. Our brothers glare at me and I instantly feel like the worst sister in the world. I push away my plate in disgust.

The chatter of the diner seems to up a level and the door chimes, a growing line of patrons gathering around the hostess stand up front. Plates and silverware clatter. The two busboys scramble about the room to turn over tables.

"I didn't mean that," I say. "I'm sorry."

Deck pushes his empty plates away and hugs his arms to his chest. "I'm sorry I've never been able to get a handle on my childhood shit like you have, July. You just make it all look so easy. You quit drinking six years ago and never looked back. Hell, you don't even need the meetings."

"You're sober?" Mark asks.

I can see the wheels turning in his head—the July who Mark knew that final summer was a burgeoning drunk. That was fine. He could judge me all he wanted; at least I never intentionally hurt anyone.

I turn back to our youngest brother. "It isn't easy, Deck. I've got a lot of the same demons as you, not the chemical ones, but sure as hell all the rest." I hold up my hand, show them all just how unsteady it is. "All I've wanted to do since I landed back in this goddamn state is drink." I put my hand down. "So, tell the truth. If you weren't trying to kill yourself, why were you on that bridge?"

"I don't know," Deck says.

"Did it have to do with Harry?" I press.

Deck looks confused. "What?"

"The night you were admitted," Auggie explains. "You said that he was innocent."

Deck thinks hard, swiping a french fry from Mark's plate. "Huh? Did I?"

Auggie nods. I appreciate that he leaves out the Adrian Bennet part. There's no need to share more than necessary.

Deck laughs and spins the maple syrup bottle between his palms. "Sounds whack. I don't know why you even listen to me when I'm high like that."

The waitress appears and Mark plops his credit card down on top of the check before she even puts it on the table. "Speaking of which," he addresses Deck when she leaves, "Don't you think we ought to talk about what to do about your little problem? I know a really great place in Arizona my buddy swears by . . ."

Deck cuts him off. "No more rehab. I can do it on my own."

"Can you?" Mark asks doubtful.

"Yeah," Deck says, "I can. I made it eight months last time."

"You did?" Auggie asks.

All three of us are surprised.

Deck pulls a blue coin from his pocket and tosses it onto the table. It's a NA chip. "They don't give you one after six months until you hit nine, but yeah, I made it eight."

"Well, what happened, then?" Mark asks.

Decks shrugs. "Hell if I know. After July put me on that plane, I went to Atlanta and started going to meetings." He looks at me. "I wanted to show you that I could get it together. So I got work as a janitor cleaning warehouses. I . . ." He looks down at his hands. "I'm not proud of this, but I needed the extra cash to pay off an old debt. So I started selling some of my buddy's pills, just a few bottles here and there." His eyes meet mine again, begging me to believe him. "I wasn't taking them though, I swear. But I went to do an exchange one night, and next thing I know, I wake up in an alley with a needle in my arm. I don't remember shooting up, honest, but that was two weeks ago." He looks to all of us. "Honestly, I don't know what the hell I was doing on that bridge—if in my delirious state I thought it would be cool to come home and jump off it, or just wanted it all to stop, or was half out of my mind and hallucinating between the drugs I was taking and antipsychotics I was supposed to be. Nothing gets clear until I'm in the hospital."

The rest of us are silent, because what is there to say?

Of course it is our eldest brother who speaks first. "You kicked it once, you can do it again."

"I won't go back to rehab," Deck insists. "It doesn't work for me."

"We've got to do something with you," Mark says.

"You'll come back to Nashville with me," I say, voicing to all three of my brothers for the first time what my plan has been all along.

"Sounds like the move to me," Mark agrees. "Auggie's got his business here and his hands full with Kathy and April. And I've got to get back to New York, to Lindsay and work."

"No," says Auggie.

There is a set firmness to his tone that reminds me of Harry.

"Mark is right," I say. "You have your hands full. Deck belongs with me, always has."

"No," Auggie repeats again. "The formula of the two of you in Nashville doesn't work. You need help. Besides, this family's been apart for too long." He searches the faces of the three of us. "We need to make a better effort to be in each other's lives, starting now."

"Look," says Mark, "this little reunion's been fun and I'm glad Deck's still breathing and not totally batshit, but I have no intention of staying in this town past tomorrow morning. I like being on my own."

The waitress returns with the check and Mark flashes her a too-wide smile.

"Oh yeah?" asks Auggie when she's gone. "You put yourself through college and business school all on your own?"

Mark looks mutinous. "Hey, I worked every day of my life from the time I was fourteen years old."

"And you still owe me," says Auggie. "You wanted no part of this family for years, and I respected that, but I was still there whenever you needed me financially, no strings attached. You can do me this favor now and take a role in our younger siblings' lives." He flipped to me. "And April needs her family as much as Deck does."

"And how would you suggest we be that for either one of them?" Mark asks. "You expect us all just to move in? Braid each other's hair beneath the freaking tree? July and I can't go more than an hour without wanting to wring each other's necks." He laughs without humor. "And that's me not even considering the Kathy variable."

"No," Auggie says. "You've got to work in New York. You want to keep your wife separate from all of us, fine. But I would appreciate it if you made a few trips down here this summer to check in every once and a while. As for you two," He looks again to me and Deck. "Nashville is not the right call. You two need to stay the summer."

"Oh, are you telling me what I *need* to do now, Auggie Weaver?" I ask.

"Someone should," he says.

"Screw you," I say back.

"I like the idea," Deck says.

I pivot my head around. "What happened to 'I wouldn't move back to that town unless the world was on fire?'"

Deck shrugs. "My world is on fire. Besides, being around this much family might help. It wouldn't all be on you, Jules. Auggie would be here, and April. I don't even know our sister."

"This is blackmail," says Mark.

"Call it what you want," Auggie says, "just instead of driving to the Hamptons for weekends, fly to Atlanta while you're bitching about it."

Mark grumbles, but I can tell by his reaction that Auggie has won. Our middle brother hates owing anyone anything. The noise in the diner ticks up again, or maybe that's just my anxiety. Is every patron in here staring at us, or is that just me?

"I have to work, too," I say.

"You can write songs remotely," Auggie insists.

"No. I can't actually," I assert. "And that's not my only work opportunity. I've been offered a spot on Kade Daniels' tour this summer."

"Kade Daniels?" Mark asks. "You know him?"

"You'll never say yes to that tour," Auggie says. "You hate performing in public, the exposure it will bring you."

I clench my teeth. "I'm not staying in this town."

The busboy clears our plates. The staff's clearly trying to get us out of here, to turn over the table, but we Weavers aren't done. Especially not the eldest.

"Oh, yes, you are, July," says Auggie, "because you know how to help Deck with this better than I can, and the best place for Deck is here. Besides, is it too much to ask for all my siblings to be at my wedding at the end of the summer? Can't you all do this one thing for me? After everything I've done to support all of you?"

Who is this man in the body of my eldest brother, because I sure don't recognize him. Auggie has never been assertive, never domineering, nor tyrannical. I stand up and push Mark to let me out of the booth, not giving a damn if I cause a scene at this point. We're the talk of this town already.

"Who the hell do you think you are to tell us how to live our lives?" I spit down at Auggie. "I've built something for myself back in Nashville. I know that might be hard for you to comprehend, seeing as you never wanted to leave this town, and pitched yourself to be a martyr, but some of us *actually* got out. Some of us *actually* tried to forget that our father was a monster. I have a job I like, and a name that doesn't make people cringe or feel sorry for me every time they hear it. I appreciate everything you've done to take care of April and Kathy, but don't pretend you wouldn't have stayed in Pacific anyway. I know you better than either one of these two. You were never gonna leave and I won't let you trap me here, too."

The diner has turned silent. I can feel it without looking that every person in here has frozen mid-bite or gab to stare at the crazy Weaver girl, *yes that one,* who has raised her voice three decibels. I look over to our youngest brother, desperate. "Deck?"

He shakes his whole body. "I want to stay, July. It might not be as bad as you think it's gonna be."

I look to Mark, but his head is down between his palms. No one can say no to Auggie.

"Fine," I say, bearing into my oldest brother's eyes. "I'm gonna walk home."

I'm out the door of the diner, passing the front glass window where the line is beginning to recede. But the door chimes, and I know it's him coming after me.

"July."

"No," I yell back.

Auggie reaches me along the side brick of the building. We're in the alley facing each other, out of sight of the main street. Probably for the better.

"Please," he begs and I can't look in his eyes, because he's the only person I've never been able to say no to either. "Please, July. I'm not trying to tell you what to do. I'm just . . ." He runs a hand through his hair in exhaustion. "I just don't know how to keep this family going anymore alone. I've been falling apart the last few years, between Kathy and April. I need you. I need it to be the two of us again."

"You know what this town does to me."

"Yeah. It does the same thing to me. I live in it every day. I live with the fact that Harry murdered those girls every day."

"You weren't almost one of them, Aug. I was this close." I hold my thumb and pointer finger together. "My own father tried to kill me."

"I know," he says and takes me into his arms, wrapping me into him. I don't want to let him at first, but I relent.

It's the greatest comfort of my life, being embraced by my eldest brother. He pulls back and stares at me long and hard. "You keep running away from it, July. You've been running away all your life and what good has it done you so far? Maybe for once, if you walk into it, it won't have that power over you anymore."

I close my eyes, exhale sharply. I want to say no. Every bone in my body is screaming at me to say no.

Then he repeats the only words that can bind me here. "We made a promise nine years ago on the side of that road. I'd take care of April and Kathy if . . ."

". . . I'd take care of Deck," I finish for him. I open my eyes. "Goddamn you and your promise, Auggie Weaver."

"It will just be for the summer. Just help me get him through the worst of it over the next two and a half months. At the end of August, you and I can reevaluate. It'll give you a chance to help me and Bridget with the wedding and you can get to know April again, too."

I tap my fists at my sides, internally cursing eighteen-year-old July for a promise I don't want to keep. Still, I nod, because what choice do I have?

"I'll give you until the end of summer. But September first, Deck or no Deck, I'm gone."

8

Then

Pickens smelled sweet and salty between the crispy bacon frying on the stovetop and maple syrup on the tables. I walked right on past the regulars lined up in front of the hostess stand and gave my usual wave to the other waitresses on my way through the kitchen door. It was the Sunday morning brunch hour, we were packed, and as usual, I was ten minutes late.

"I swear, girl. The day you show up on time, I'm checking the sky for cracks," Daniela called from where she and Hector were busying themselves behind the stove and prep counter.

Daniela was the oldest of the Santana siblings, and the only other young person in this town who seemed as keen on staying as Auggie. She had a solid decade on me, near pushing thirty, and had three kids all under the age of five she frequently let me babysit. It was a role reversal from the days when she'd been the only teenager within five miles willing to watch the Weaver children—what with our crazy mama and *that house*.

"Sorry," I said, coming up to kiss her cheek. "Crazy night."

"Uh-huh." She would have fired anyone else by now, and we both knew it, but for me there was a soft glint to her eye. "Ain't it always?"

"I saw Gabe last night," I said, pulling my apron from the hook and shoving napkins in the front. "He looks good."

"Yeah, he's back for a bit. Debating whether to stick around or reenlist." Daniela shoved two plates into my hands, all business.

I stacked the one on the back of my forearm the way she taught me, and grabbed a third. I was still surprised it didn't actually burn.

"Hey," she called out to me right before I pushed my back to the swinging door. "You reminded me. What are y'all doing for the Fourth?"

If I was being honest, the Fourth of July had hardly crossed my mind. Only a few weeks away, yet the idea of celebrating any holiday without May seemed wrong.

"That's what I thought," said Daniela, reading my face. "Well, you know you and your siblings are all more than welcome at my place." She hurried to add, "Kathy and Harry too, of course." That last part felt like a weak offer. Daniela was a good mom and never much liked parents who weren't.

"I appreciate it, but I think this year we're . . . I think Aug and I'll just take the younger ones out on the water."

Daniela nodded her head. "That's fine, too, just know the offer's there. I'm making a ton of food and, whether you show up or not, you best expect trays at your front door the morning of."

I nodded my thanks and headed into the restaurant. The other waitresses shot me dirty looks that they were in the weeds because I dallied. I gave them both a shameless shrug and sashayed my hips with deliberate slowness to table eight where the plates I was holding were destined to end up.

The remainder of my morning shift was spent in a blur. That's the beautiful thing about busy work like waitressing or bartending. Your hands move ahead of your mind. The job becomes mechanical. Get customers in, get customers out. A constant machine.

We finally had a lull around three PM and I wasn't surprised to find Deck twirling on one of stools at the counter. He often came in with his friends for a milkshake on Sundays, then lingered behind the extra hour to hitch a ride home in Auggie's borrowed truck with me.

"You see this?" he asked, gesturing up to the TV screen.

It was further news coverage of Laurel Dillon's disappearance—missing over forty-eight hours. Scotty MacGyver was at his anchor desk once again, this time announcing that the Hazel Police Department had no further leads than when they'd first announced her disappearance yesterday morning. That wasn't good. I knew from our experience with May that if the missing person wasn't found in the first two days, there was a high possibility they were already dead.

"I saw it," I said, wiping down the counter with a bar mop.

"You think they'll look at Harry again?" he asked.

Harry was still the police's most likely suspect in the disappearance of our sister. His alibi about being out of town at that teaching convention in Atlanta was considered shaky at best. No one had seen him after nine PM that night when he'd left his colleagues to turn into his room, and he hadn't appeared again until that following morning at breakfast. Plenty of time, the detectives hypothesized, for him to drive the hour and a half back to Pacific, commit whatever act had been committed against my baby sister, then return to the conference to seal his alibi by morning. The thought of it disgusted me. Harry was a lot of things, but a killer?

I'd watched him fall apart along with the rest of us after May disappeared. Would a guilty man be so hell-bent on tracking down every lead across the country to find his daughter's murderer if all he had to do was look in the mirror? No. Harry didn't check out. I'd suspect Kathy before him any day, and even that seemed absurd.

I relayed to Deck what I'd heard second hand from Auggie that morning—the information I had failed to obtain last night. "No. Harry went down to the station yesterday, and they questioned him, but they let him go. Dan told Auggie the chief practically threw Harry out of the office to stop him from playing detective with his wild conspiracy theories again."

"That's a relief, I guess," Deck said.

None of us wanted to see our father in jail.

My brother gestured back to the screen. "I just talked to Nick Ryder. They've been doing search parties through the woods. Switching to Dewey Meadow right about now. Can we go?"

I sighed, the knot in my stomach, both from my hangover and his suggestion. "You want to go search the woods for a missing girl?"

He squinted. "Don't you?"

"I don't know, Deck."

"You can't tell me you don't think these two cases are related. Both disappeared from their homes in the middle of the night, in neighboring towns, four months apart."

No. I couldn't say that. The case with Laurel had all of us siblings on edge. It was the closest thing to a clue we'd had in months. Still the thought of combing the woods and coming across something relating to May instead of Laurel made me squeamish.

Maybe I really didn't want to know what happened to her.

But my brother's expression was wide, as he looked up at me with all the expectation in the world. *Be my big sister. Help me*, it said. *Let me do something to try to not feel useless about all of this.*

"Yeah," I said. "We can go."

* * *

The meadow refracted copper specks in the gleam of afternoon sun. The shimmer to it felt blinding, unearthly—especially when juxtaposed with what we were there to do. I hopped out of the driver's seat of Auggie's truck, Deck in tow, and the two of us were soon joining the search party for Laurel Dillon.

Volunteers had turned up from all over the county to search for any sign of the missing girl, same as they had for May in the days immediately following her disappearance. My hope of actually finding anything was slim to none.

We were handed flyers first—to recognize her in the event we found a body—as if any body we found would be anyone other than Laurel Dillon's. But I stared down at the photo for too long anyway. It was the same one they were flashing repeatedly across the news. *She's just a kid,* I thought, a rather homely looking kid, in the way that only a sixteen-year-old girl yet to grow into herself can be. I focused on that gap-toothed smile again.

My best friend—okay, only real friend, Zoey, beelined over and handed us neon orange vests. "I figured y'all might show up."

Zoey had gone to Hazel's middle school, so we didn't meet until our freshman year. Her single-parent, alcoholic father, trailer-park status had made her into a school pariah. We had bonded instantly.

"Yeah. Well. Thought we should." I began weaving through the grass with the others and gestured to Deck in warning. "You stay in my line of sight, you hear?"

"Whatever, Kathy," he muttered, then began strutting up ahead in a cluster of other reflective vests.

"You been out here all day?" I asked Zoey.

She nodded, the bangles on her arms clattering along with her. I liked the Nine Inch Nails T-shirt she was sporting under her vest. "Started up at the creek this morning behind her house."

Dewey Meadow sat on the opposite side of Hazel from Laurel's street. But it was the only open let-out from the woods that didn't border the main artery of road that wove out of town to Pacific. It also had a campground and multiple hunting cabins speckled throughout its back stretch of forest. This was where all the people of Hazel and Pacific came to commit their nefarious acts: underage drinking, adolescent sex, marital affairs, drug deals. It was also where the homeless addicts tended to camp. I didn't want to begin to guess all that these woods had seen.

Zoey and I worked through the clearing along with all the rest, scanning the tall grasses and bracken as we searched for any signs of something out of the ordinary. The leader of the search party had instructed us to look for anything: blood, footprints, a disturbance in the grass. We were lucky it hadn't rained since Laurel's disappearance, an older woman pointed out.

I scanned the field, but kept one eye on Deck up ahead. I didn't trust him not to go wandering off, but I was pleased to find him studiously looking the same as everyone else.

I spotted some familiar faces across the field, parents and people I went to school with. We were all fascinated by the disappearance of Laurel Dillon, almost one of our own. Except that was the strange thing: was she?

"Hey Zo, how come we don't know her? If she's from Hazel, why doesn't she go to Pacific High?" Between the two towns, the combined high school only had eight hundred students. We sort of all knew, or knew of, each other. I'd never seen Laurel Dillon's face until it was on my television screen.

"Homeschooled apparently," Zoey supplied. "Only child. Daughter of conservative protestants. A couple of people recognized her from the Hazel library, but outside of that, she didn't really socialize or have a lot of friends."

"Interesting."

I caught sight of two familiar faces walking through the tree line up ahead: Clarence and Lydia Davidson, Pacific's mayor and first lady and Colton's parents. A look of venom appeared in Lydia's eyes when she spotted me. I guessed she'd heard.

Zoey followed my line of sight. "Colton Davidson has been calling all around town this morning saying you're a bitch and a tease."

"Let him." I'd been called worse.

"You want to talk about what happened?"

"Not really. You clearly heard enough of it."

"July, the whole damn town heard. You punched him in the middle of the drive-in. Even I knew by this morning." She paused mid-step. "What were you thinking? I know he's been acting sweet on you lately, but seriously? Are you stupid? Why the hell would you go out with someone like him?"

Zoey had a brusque way about her sometimes that made me want to smack *her* in the face. Maybe we were too similar in that way. "I wasn't thinking, okay? Now will you lay off?"

Zoey shrugged and leaned in close. "Look, I'm not trying to be a bitch here. I get you're going through it, but you're acting like an idiot lately. Taking stupid risks, even for you." Her nostrils widened. "And seriously? It's three PM on a Sunday. I can smell your breath."

I shoved her off me and popped a mint in my mouth to cover the stench of the airplane vodka bottle I'd downed in Pickens' bathroom. In my defense, it hadn't even made me tipsy and I needed it to get me through my shift after last night's hangover.

"You need to pull it together," she said.

"Mind your own business. You're such a nag sometimes."

I walked away from her, pissed, but only because I knew she was right. I was losing it, and last night had been proof of that. I plowed ahead through the woods past two other groups of volunteers until I was far off from the crowd. I was about to reach for the other airplane bottle I had concealed in my front pocket when a voice stopped me.

"You make friends everywhere you go?"

I spun. Gabe was five feet from me. He'd clearly witnessed my rapid departure from Zoey.

"You butt into everything?" I snapped. I immediately regretted it when his eyebrows went up and he was about to turn away.

"Wait. Gabe. Sorry."

He flipped back. "Doesn't seem like you're having the best twenty-four hours."

"Try four months."

A fragile peace was established. With that, we began to move in tandem, weaving through the trees. That was something I always appreciated about Gabe—his utter willingness to go quiet. There was a comfort in it.

I, on the other hand, felt raw energy rattling up and down my spine simply by being in his presence. All I wanted to do was hear him talk. I had to admit I'd felt this way about him since I was a little kid.

"You sticking around for the Fourth?" I asked him.

"Promised Daniela's kids I would."

"That'll make them happy."

I followed his gaze to where the Davidsons were weaving through a cluster of volunteers up ahead. He frowned.

"If I'd known why you needed a ride last night . . ." He stared down at my bruised knuckles. It had probably been too dark for him to notice them the night before.

I felt my cheeks flame. "You what? Would have gone over and confronted the son of the man who keeps half your family employed?"

I didn't intend for it to be mean, but it was the truth. It was a large reason why I hadn't told Gabe what happened with Colton last night. If Gabe had confronted him, the first thing Clarence Davidson would have done this morning was make sure Maria Santana and her daughters lost their jobs at every house in town. I liked their family too much for that. Besides, I could fight my own battles.

Gabe was clearly bothered by this reality, too. His jaw clenched.

"I can take care of myself," I told him.

"I know that."

The air between us suddenly felt thick in that alcove of trees. I don't know if it was born of hostility or something else, but it was broken by a scream.

I knew in an instant who it belonged to. I'd heard that sound emitted a thousand times in my childhood—when he jumped off the dock at the end of spring, when our older brothers trapped him beneath them as a toddler to tickle him, when Harry spanked him for leaving the old chicken coop open one night for a fox to turn the wired container into a massacre site.

"Deck," I breathed, then was off.

Charging through the trees, running as if his life was literally at stake—which in my panic I thought it might reasonably be—I launched myself through the bracken, lunged over the thick streaks of stream, and called out his name, over and over and over again.

"July, he's okay. He's over here," someone called through the trees to my left. It was Zoey.

My heart thumped as I trudged over the next hill, where I saw Deck kneeling down over the riverbank. He was vomiting, Zoey rubbing his back, surrounded by two other concerned volunteers.

"What happened?" I cried, falling to my knees beside him.

My brother was dry heaving at this point, the contents of his chocolate milkshake having already met the water.

"He got scared," Zoey said.

"By what?" I asked.

Zoey nodded her head back over the ridge. "He and a few boys found one of the hunting cabins. It's bad."

"May," Deck cried. He was half delirious. "May."

"Hold him," I ordered and got back to my feet, suddenly feeling wobbly myself.

"July," Zoey called.

But I was already stumbling over the small ridge where I knew the hunting cabin would be. A group of middle-aged volunteers were herding a couple of teenagers back who must have found the cabin along with Deck. Another was calling the police on a walkie-talkie.

I moved toward the falling eight-by-eight-foot cabin, the rusted windows coated by what I suspected was dried blood. I braced myself, felt a stone in my throat, and clutched the airplane bottle in my jean pocket. I felt the cabin calling to me. There were answers inside I had to see. I stepped onto the small porch. A faint odor I couldn't place wafted toward me.

"Don't," Gabe said, coming out the front door. How had he gotten here so fast? He grabbed my arm in an attempt to yank me back.

"Let me go," I said. My voice was morbidly calm.

His expression was haunted. "No. What's in there, you don't need to see."

I stared into the whites of his eyes, at the determined immovability there. He had me in a near identical hold Colton had the night before, only one had been trying to restrain me, the other now to protect. I didn't need either.

I yanked my arm back and surged past him through the entrance. The smell hit me first, and now I recognized it—rotting meat. It was so intense that my fingers went to cover my nose instinctually and I had to resist the urge to gag. That was when I saw what had horrified Deck so thoroughly. The cabin was not abandoned like all of the others I had been in before in these woods. No, there was furniture in here—or rather tools. A workbench with saws and pliers, rusted blood adhered to all the handles and blades. The walls were plastered in photos. Of girls. Dozens upon dozens of women and girls, some from magazines—celebrities and over-sexed cartoon characters, porn stars; the other half photographs—most of women, young and old, that I recognized from both Hazel and Pacific. The latter were all candid shots, taken when the individuals were going about their daily routines outside; most didn't even notice the camera. I caught Laurel Dillon in the middle of the collage and prayed

I wouldn't find May as well. There were patterns, swirls of blood that ran curlicues up and down the makeshift wallpaper. It matched the blood on the floor. Collapsed duffel bags were thrown into the far corner. It was what hung from the center of the room that made me want to run.

Suspended from a rope upside down, coated in an armor of metallic flies, was a buck. Its lifeless black eyes stared at me like an omen, its nose hitting the ground and scraping against the entrails that had been gutted from its center. I wouldn't have known it was a deer, but it had been scalped. Its antlers sat upright on the floor before it, along with words traced in perfect red. *I am the king.*

Now I knew I would be sick. I was pulled from the cabin with force, and Gabe had me down the steps, fifty feet from the scene, with my back turned and my rear down on rock, before I could process what was happening. I couldn't breathe. I felt the world go fuzzy, spinning. My heart pounded in my eardrums, a deafening roar, tribal. My body rocked, myself, heaving.

"Put your head between your legs," Gabe commanded me. "Focus on your breathing."

I did as he said, feeling like I might actually die of shock, or whatever this was.

"Breathe. Just breathe, July. You're having an anxiety attack."

May, the only thought that kept repeating over and over through the grips of my panic, *what if that buck had been May?*

CHAPTER

9

Then

I T COULD HAVE been some kids screwing around. That was what the crowd, which had only swelled in the last thirty minutes, was saying. Some teenage hunters who had seen the report of Laurel Dillon on the news and thought it would be a funny prank to set the cabin up for a search party to stumble upon.

But most of the people who said that hadn't been allowed inside.

The local cops had arrived within the hour and roped the entire place off, pushing volunteers and newly arrived busybodies back as far as they could. A team was already combing through the evidence of the cabin. I overheard one of the two forensic guys relaying to the lead detective, Rafael—he had headed May's case too—that the buck was completely drained of blood. They suspected that was what had been used on the walls, not human blood. But the second forensic suit wasn't so sure. "I still want to run the tests."

Deck and I had been ushered over to a waiting ambulance where we were sat on the bumper and wrapped in foil blankets like we'd just survived a natural disaster. *You should be combing these whole damn woods for an actual body,*

I thought to the cops we watched. Because after what I'd just seen, whether that blood belonged to that buck or not, there was a body around here somewhere and no one was going to convince me that this was all some teenage trick.

What happened in that cabin was the work of a sick, depraved mind. That buck's throat hadn't been slit. I'd been along on enough hunting trips with Harry and my two oldest brothers to know what it looked like when you didn't put an animal out of its misery quickly. It had been gutted alive, left to bleed out. I was certain that whoever had left that message was behind what happened to Laurel Dillon. Probably May, too.

Deck and I sat in silence, waiting. Someone had taken my keys, saying I shouldn't drive and that Harry was on his way to get us. Zoey had been ushered off the scene along with all the other teenagers by concerned parents, leaving my brother and me once again with only one familiar face. Gabe stood about thirty feet away, being questioned by a detective on how we had stumbled upon the cabin. I watched his back, his hands sliding inside his pockets, only turning the other direction when I heard Auggie call my name.

He bounded out of the passenger side of Harry's Jeep five cars away, Harry trudging determinedly after, both sets of eyes on Deck and me.

Auggie halted in front of the ambulance bumper, not knowing who to go to first.

"You two all right?" he asked.

"No. That scared the living shit out of me," said Deck.

Auggie grabbed us both into massive hugs, holding me a second longer to examine my face. I'm sure I looked like shit. I felt like it.

"We're fine, Aug," I said.

He nodded and released me, just as Harry reached us. My father actually looked uncomfortable at the open act of affection between his two eldest children. We'd all stopped embracing him years ago.

He cleared his throat, stared at the cabin. "They found something?"

"Thanks for the fatherly concern," I said dryly.

Harry sighed. "You're clearly all right, Livewire. They told us that much on the phone. They said Deck stumbled upon something in that cabin, and you saw it, too. Must have had something to do with the case to have you both this riled up."

"Seriously?" Auggie spat.

But our father had actual excitement in his eyes. He looked high.

"They don't know if it's legit or not," I said, not even believing my own words. "Might be some kids who staged it. It's a dead deer with pictures of women all over the walls . . . some are women from town."

"I'm going to go see," our father said.

"I wouldn't do that if I were you," said Gabe, having returned to us now that he was finished with the detective. "It's . . . disturbing."

"Gabriel," said Harry. "Good to see you back. But believe me, young man, I've become more than accustomed to disturbing in the last few months."

My father wandered off toward the crime scene, was turned away by the first cop at the yellow tape line.

"They're never going to let him through," Gabe said.

"The key word being *let* him, Santana. I think you've forgotten what Harry Weaver's like," I said.

I jumped off the bumper and leaned against the side of the emergency vehicle. I just wanted to see my father's reaction. From there, I watched him weave through the crowd, circling the crime scene tape as if casually walking the perimeter, but I knew better.

"Three. Two. One," said Auggie.

In the last crowded spot, Harry sprung like a cat—limboing under the tape in one go and running for the cabin door. He got right up to the yellow CAUTION tape X over the front, gazed inside stone-faced, before two police officers hauled him back. He howled about his constitutional rights as an American and as a father, as the cops yelled at him all the way to a police car, where Harry was promptly hand-cuffed and pushed down to lean against a tire. All the local officers knew he was harmless, but restraining him would be the only way to keep him contained.

"Our women are being hunted!" he roared from his pathetic perch at the cops. "Do your jobs! I warned you this was a pattern!"

The cop standing next to him looked like he'd enjoy nothing more than to kick my father in the face.

"Laurel Dillon's picture's on that wall," muttered Deck to our group of four. "I saw it."

Auggie looked to me. "Is . . . ?"

He didn't need to finish that sentence. I shook my head. "No. Not that I saw."

My eldest brother appeared slightly green when he sat down on the bumper beside Deck. I handed him my blanket. He took it gratefully and cocooned himself in it.

"I should probably go," said Gabe. "Y'all all right?"

We nodded, and with a final look to me, Gabe turned and walked to his truck at the end of the field.

"What's with that guy?" Auggie grumbled.

"What's your problem? You didn't mind Gabe when we were kids," I said.

"I didn't. Except now he keeps showing up with my underage sister and it's weird."

"Chill, Harry."

He hated being called Harry about as much as I hated being called Kathy.

Detective Rafael had broken away from the crime scene, undone Harry's handcuffs, and was now escorting our father back over to us.

"Seriously, Harold," he said. "You can't help yourself, can you?"

"I'm the father of one of the missing girls. It's my right . . ."

But Rafael silenced him by holding up a hand. I wasn't a tremendous fan of the detective, seeing as he'd gotten nowhere in May's case, but I always appreciated how he handled our father.

"Kids," the detective asked, "Do y'all have another way home? Otherwise, I have a few more questions to ask your father, then y'all can be on your way."

"My children saw whatever this is, Detective. It concerns their sister. You can ask whatever it is you want to ask me right here, right now, with them as my witnesses," Harry said.

"Fine," the detective said. "You want to tell me where you were last night?"

"Last night?" Harry asked, scratching his head, like he really had to think about it. "I was at the station talking to you, detective."

Rafael produced a small notebook from his pocket, checked it. "You left the station around five PM. Where'd you go after that?"

"Home, of course."

"What time did you arrive back at your residence?"

"Shortly after," Harry said, this time sterner, annoyed.

His sass was grating on my nerves. I wanted to yell, *Just answer the questions.*

"Could anyone verify that?"

"My wife was home."

The detective paused. He didn't have to say it—Kathy wasn't considered a credible witness, and we all knew it. "Any of your children?"

"Of course," Harry said, looking to us for aid. "Someone's always home."

I expected all of us to clamp our mouths shut. I didn't get home until after ten and Harry's car still wasn't in the driveway.

"I saw him when he came in," said Auggie.

My head whipped to my brother. He'd been standing on the porch half the night. He knew damn well Harry hadn't been home by six. Why the hell was Auggie lying?

"What time?" Rafael asked.

"Don't know," said Auggie. "Around five forty five, six fifteen, maybe? I wasn't checking the clock."

Harry had the actual gall to look vindicated, and crossed his arms.

"And what time did you leave this morning?" Rafael asked.

"Thirty minutes ago, when your team called me to come pick these two up. Which can also be verified by Auggie, as he was with me."

Auggie nodded and I thought I might be sick. He didn't even twitch.

"You want to tell me why you're asking about my where-abouts, detective?" Harry asked. "Or are you just lining up your same list of dead ends again?"

The detective frowned. "It's looking like this incident," Rafael gestured back to the cabin with his pen, "occurred sometime last night. We've got a few eyewitness reports from campers staying on the campground that they saw a tall Cau-casian man in black moving around the woods somewhere around one AM. I have the feeling that when the blood comes back, we're going to realize it was painted around that same time."

"That deer doesn't look fresh," said Deck. He had a point: the flies.

"The deer appears to have been hung there last night, but it's been allowed to decay for some time. Someone wanted us to find this place. It's a clear message. We think the individual is someone trying to brag about what he's done, or at the very least someone attempting to take credit for it."

"For what he's done to Laurel Dillon and our sister," I said, because he might as well have come out and said it.

Rafael closed his notepad. "Like I said, we'll have to wait on the blood. In the meantime . . ." He scanned us all over. "Do me a favor, and y'all stick to town the next few days, all right?"

"Are we all suspects now?" I asked. "What? Murdering our own sister wasn't enough? We had to go off and kill another random girl and spray deer guts all over a hunting cabin too?"

"July," Auggie said. "That isn't helping."

"Neither is he," I said. "Four months. We don't know any more about what happened to May than the morning after she disappeared. Now because of that, some other girl is missing, probably dead, and you're wasting time pointing fingers at all of us, so you can pretend you're actually doing your job."

Deck whistled.

Rafael's lips tightened as my father beamed. "It's a rather large coincidence, Miss July, that you and your brother were the ones to stumble upon this cabin. Of all people."

"Yeah. Us and ten other volunteers!" yelled Deck. "We were just trying to find our sister."

"I suggest you cease throwing around false accusations about my children," said Harry, "unless you have proof to back them up."

Rafael held up his hand. "It's not my goal to accuse anyone of anything. I'm simply trying to find out what happened to these missing girls. I want to find your daughter, too." He took a step back, agitated. "Why don't we all take a beat here? I'll call you, Harold. In the meantime, your kids have already given their statements. Y'all can head on home."

"I'm going to want to see copies of those crime photos," Harry said to the detective's retreating back, then he put his hand on Deck's shoulder. "Let's go."

Deck ripped out of his grasp and dropped the blanket down in a heap, to run for our father's Jeep. It wasn't joyous like the other night. It was tormented. I knew that look on my little brother's face. He'd been fighting back tears for the last hour.

We followed behind, and Harry stiffened once Deck was closed within the car. He stopped midfield to face Auggie and me, pissed. "What the hell were you thinking, Livewire?"

"Excuse me?"

"You two never should have been here. That," he jabbed a callused finger toward the cabin, his voice the tone I had feared as a child, "that's what I've been trying to keep y'all from. That's not something I ever wanted any of you to see—and you brought your little brother here, and threw him right in front of it."

"Are you seriously lecturing me on parental choices right now?"

Auggie grabbed me and yanked me back, knowing me well enough to know I was about to get in our father's face and gain the crowd's attention. Like father, like daughter.

"Lower your voice," Harry commanded.

I puffed up my chest. I didn't care that he was my father and still intimidating to me. I matched his menacing tone, adding an extra layer of mockery to it. "Why? You scared I'm gonna make a scene, and embarrass this family more in the eyes of this town?" I raised my voice so half the field could hear. "Take a look around you, Harry. We're already freakshows. Hell, you're the prime suspect in your own daughter's murder. Do you know what they say around town about what they think you did to her?"

Harry's eyes bulged, then flattened into two hard stones. His body sagged visibly. Had he been anyone else, I would have felt like a complete monster, but this was Harry. He had hurt me, abandoned me, left me to raise myself and everyone else in this family time and time again. Harry's little Livewire. His spitting image in girl form. I got his temper. I hoped to hell nothing else.

"We need to go home," Auggie said, trying to defuse the hate this open field wasn't big enough to contain. "This day's getting to all of us. We don't mean it."

"Oh, I mean it," I said. "Every goddamn word."

I shoved past them both, making for Auggie's truck.

I slammed the passenger side door closed, too emotionally fried to drive, and banged my hand against the glove compartment, cursing. *Fuck. Fuck. Fuck.*

Auggie didn't say anything when he slid in beside me, only put the key in the ignition and waited.

"Why would you do that?" I asked, staring straight ahead. I took several conscious breaths to calm myself down so I wouldn't take all my anger out on him.

"Do what?"

"Why would you tell Rafael that Harry was home last night, when he wasn't?"

"Harry was home. It was just later than he said it was."

"His car didn't pull into the drive until after midnight. I saw the headlights from my window."

Auggie sighed, ran a hand through his hair. "You really want our father arrested for murder?"

I scoffed. "If he did it."

"Come on. You really believe Harry of all people would be capable of doing something to hurt May? Or that other girl?"

"No, but . . ."

Auggie cut me off. "No buts. You said it back there yourself. The more time the police spend looking into Harry as a suspect, or any of us, the less time they're out there actually looking for whoever did this, and finding out what happened to May. You want that?"

I glared at him. "You know I don't."

"Then stop making everything harder on all of us. You're too freaking good at it sometimes."

I sank back in my seat. I felt wounded, like he'd gotten me beneath a rib. My greatest ally. If Auggie was against me, then I really must have been messing up. We'd never fought as much as we had in the last few days.

"Okay," I said, promising with that one word to do better. "I'll cool it."

"Thank you." He started the engine and pulled out of the campsite. I could barely make out the roof of the hunting cabin through the trees, the yellow tape as we retreated. That room flashed back to me. The words written in blood.

I am the king.

There was something I hadn't brought up to Rafael or the other members of my family—something I'd seen in the collage of women and blood. It was a long-lensed shot of a girl stepping out of Pickens, her face full of laugh lines, wearing a thick coat in what looked like the dead of winter, peering back through the open door to wave goodbye to some unseen figure.

Deck, Gabe, my father, the cops—they either had all been too overwhelmed by everything they'd seen to notice the specific photo, or hoped I hadn't. But I'd spotted it almost the moment I walked through that half-collapsed doorway, curving in a thin peel around a high corner of the right wall, a streak of blood right through the girl's face.

My face.

PART II

10

Now

I WISH I COULD say that Auggie's plan for all of us to settle back into the house on Pacific Lake has gone smoothly, as if the past and ensuing gap of years immediately bridged, but that hasn't been the case. As promised, within two days, Mark returned to New York, voicing his need to get back to Lindsay and his stockbroker job—after promising Auggie that he would be back in a few weeks for the Fourth.

As for the rest of us, we've undertaken the meticulous chore of actively avoiding one another. April is never home, other than to preen the house's jungle, and then she acts as a sprite, slipping in and out of rooms, the two of us hardly exchanging a word. Kathy spends most of her days in the greenhouse reading romance novels or on the couch in the foyer watching TV. There have been no repeats of her bizarre warning since my first night back, but that's likely only because I've tried to avoid being alone with her. Auggie, the eternal hypocrite, is knee deep in final wedding plans with Bridget, and working every hour, all hours, overseeing his construction sites.

My current project, Deck, sleeps a lot, claiming to still be in withdrawal. He forgets that I know withdrawal, and his worst symptoms cleared up around two weeks ago when we checked him out of the hospital. As for his antipsychotics, they should be well on their way to full effect, although it could take him another few weeks to fully stabilize. I spend my days alternating between carting him to NA meetings and mental illness support groups, and working on songs for Kade's next album in my room.

Somehow, every night, when insomnia grips my body, I end up on the end of our dock. I don't know what I am waiting for—there's never that familiar speck of dust on the horizon, no Harry gliding toward me from the other side of the lake. Still, I wait. I watch the dark water. It's become an obsession.

The longer I remain in Pacific, the more I feel myself being surrounded by ghosts. So I guess I shouldn't be surprised when I run right into the chest of one in the freezer section of Kroger one June afternoon.

I'm staring down at my grocery list, having just retrieved a pack of frozen peas from one of the freezer cases, when it happens. We strike so hard the contents in both our hands hit the linoleum floor.

"Sorry," I say, diving to pick up the hamburger rolls and eggs I've knocked from this poor guy's hands.

"Not a problem at all." He squats down in his dress shirt and slacks to help me, then looks at my face. "Well, hello, July Weaver."

I'm a firecracker, up and shoving the rolls into his hands. I'm holding the half-cracked carton of eggs. There's yolk running down my fingers as I try to hide my alarm. "Colton."

I instinctively dart my head around, scanning the aisle of glass doors, but it's only the two of us beneath the harsh fluorescent lights at this end of the store. Damn. I wanted to avoid this.

Colton grins, smug. I can't stand the sight of him any more than I could nine years ago, and that's saying something. But I'm also overwhelmed by shame over what happened the final night we met that last summer.

"I heard you were back in town," he says, perfectly friendly. It's odd to see him grown up in a suit. "Can't say I wasn't hoping I'd run into you eventually."

"Yeah, well." I step back from him. "I'd say it was good to see you, Davidson, but . . ."

"What? Two old friends can't exchange more than a hello?"

I walk to the end of the aisle and drop the cracked eggs into the upper carriage of my cart to ditch them at the register. I start to push despite my slimy fingers. "Is that what we were?"

"Man, you're as hilarious as ever."

Colton keeps pace with me as I wheel my cart toward the front of the store past the bread and flower sections. His presence draws curious glances from the other customers. Everyone in this town knows who Colton Davidson is.

We pass the meat section, but I decide to scrap it. The Weavers can be vegetarians for the night. I'm beelining for the register, feeling the need to get out of here fast.

Colton's grin never wavers. "I'll have to tell Nicole I ran into you. She won't believe it."

Nicole, as in the former Nicole Sheridan—Mark's high school girlfriend, and Colton's never-a-nail-out-of-place, playing tennis at the country club while Colton runs his daddy's real estate empire, mother of two perfect kids—wife. At least that's what Auggie's told me.

"That's nice." I say. "Give the ole bitch and her harpy squad my regards."

He only laughs.

I get to the register, hoping that's it, but he's my shadow. I pointedly ignore him, as I unload my groceries onto the belt as the pimpled teenage cashier rings me up, and apologize for the broken eggs.

"You can put all her things on me, Darlene," Colton says holding out his card.

I have the equivalent of $100 in groceries and all he has is a package of hamburger rolls. I rip my card out and shove it into the girl's hand.

"I don't need your money," I bark back at him.

"Okay, then," Colton says, more amused.

He must practically throw money at the cashier for the rolls, because he's back at my side outside the parking lot in thirty seconds. I've had it. I slam the cart to a stop and cut him off.

"Just come on out with it, Colton," I spit. "Your tactics haven't changed all that much in a decade. What do you want?"

He edges a step closer, breaking into my personal space. "I don't want to be enemies with you here, July. We come from the same town. If you're coming back like I hear you are, I think it's best we get along, don't you?"

Now why would I want to do that?

"I've got nothing against you. We're good."

He laughs, rakes a hand over his head. "Yeah. You don't have much for me, either."

"So what? I don't know why you'd want to be on friendly terms with me anyhow."

He smiles, sweet but tight. Apparently he's still used to people complying without hesitation. "I don't know if you've heard, but I'm running in this upcoming election."

Of course I have. There are Davidson posters on every lawn. You'd think the man is running for Congress, not small-town mayor. Like father, like son. The election is a few months away. "I had heard someone mention it."

"Well." He darts a glance around the parking lot, as if there are prying ears everywhere looking to Watergate him. "I have a reputation. I'm a family man now, and there are certain things I'd rather not come out that would do damage to that family."

I cross my arms, amused, finally understanding what he's getting at. "You're worried that I'll open my mouth about the last night we saw each other." *Oh, this is too good.* "What? Will it ruin your campaign, if Pacific's good people find out you were the last one to see the Weaver girl before she was attacked in the woods?"

I don't bother going into what happened during that final interaction. He knows it's damning. That's why he's bothering to have this conversation. July Weaver returning to town at this exact moment, deciding to finally talk? That would be the election right there. The thought gives me joy.

Colton squints with a trace of annoyance. "I heard you're a musician up in Nashville. You've done well for yourself, *Jules Thomas*. It's nice to see that from one of our own. You know, my college roommate's actually a producer at Channel 5 in Nashville. Serial killer's daughter changes her name to become successful songwriter? Now, if that's not a story, I don't know what is."

My heart stills. How does Colton know about my career? I've taken great pains over the years to conceal any connection between Jules Thomas and July Weaver. And Auggie knows better than to tell anyone local about my life in Nashville.

"You want my silence for yours," I say. "About that night."

"And everything else in the cops' report on me back then—what we both know you are well aware of."

Clearly, I'm not, because I don't know what the hell he's talking about. I never saw Rafael's investigative report on Colton. With all his influence, Clarence Davidson had made his son's file—and any apparent involvement in the case—disappear around the time of Harry's arraignment. Had Colton been more involved in the events surrounding the murders than just that night with me?

I force a poker face. "You think you can blackmail me?"

Colton smiles. "My career is important to me, July. Just how important is yours to you?"

I clench my jaw. He has me there, and he knows it—I'm the one with more to lose. But I play it off. "Don't worry, Davidson. Haven't you heard why I'm back? I've got my hands full with crazy Weavers. I have no time or interest in messing with your high society bullshit. Are we done then?"

"Great seeing you."

And he's off toward his Range Rover two rows over. I am left standing in the middle of the lot, fuming.

I load my groceries into the back of my car and fantasize about running Colton over, until I'm pulling halfway out of the shopping center. It's a good thing I have to stop to glance over my shoulder before turning onto the main road, or I might have run my baby sister clean over. April jumps out of the way of the car, wide armed, staring at me with a *what the hell* face.

"Can I help you?" I ask, rolling down my window. I'm boiling, and not in the mood to deal with her adolescent attitude.

"I need a ride."

I stare around to the parked pickup she's come from a row away. The bed's full of laughing teenagers.

"All right," I say. It's the most words we've said to one another since I got home. "Get in."

She climbs into the passenger seat and I'm about to resume turning right when she jabs her finger left. "No. Go that way."

"Home's the other way."

"I never said I needed a ride home."

I sigh and turn left. This kid is lucky I abandoned her nine years ago or I wouldn't be going out of my way to do this. "And where exactly do you need a ride to?"

The paved road's smoking, it's so hot out, the two faded golden stripes appearing kissed by the sun.

"This local artist's house. We've got a fundraiser at the end of July for the upcoming seniors. Local shops donate stuff to be auctioned off to support their class trip. I'm in charge of picking out one of his pieces at his shop."

"And where exactly is his shop?"

"North end of the lake."

We ride in silence, and I have to admit that my mind isn't on my little sister at all, though I suppose I should be making the most of this time with her. I'm incapable of it right now. My thoughts are thoroughly fixated on Colton and his threat. About what he meant by "everything else" in his investigation file. And what if he does say to hell with it, and goes to the press anyway about my dual identities? He hates me as much as I hate him.

I force myself to focus on April's instructions as she guides me through several turns that push us toward the outskirts of town. At some point she says to bear straight until she tells me to stop and flips on the radio. "Sugar, We're Goin Down" by Fall Out Boy is halfway through.

"I was expecting country," she says. "Isn't that your thing?"

"I write for a lot of genres," I say. "Country is just my biggest hits." I look at her, suddenly curious how closely my sister has followed my career. "Do you know any of my songs?"

"Not really," she says. "I hate country."

She seems content to let the subject die there, but now that she's talking, I don't want her to stop. Maybe this is my way in. "I like alternative best," I say. "Indie. Rock. Bands like this. The ones that make you feel something. I wish I could write more for this genre."

"Then why don't you?" There's accusation in her tone.

"Because Nashville's more country. The first stuff I put out there was a bunch of love songs that got snatched up by a couple of girl country bands. It sort of unintentionally became my brand."

She puts her feet up on the dash. It's a move so like the teenage version of me, I want to shove them down.

"So, why botany?" I ask. "The April I knew never looked twice at a plant unless it was to stick a flower in her hair."

"The April you knew died a long time ago," she says.

I mentally roll my eyes. "Okay. I get you're a teenager and all, but that's a little dramatic."

"What? My twin vanishes and the rest of you get to be messed up but I'm not allowed to be because I was young? I remember plenty from that summer, too."

"I never said you weren't or didn't." I hold up my hands from the steering wheel in placation. "May was your twin. If anyone got to be devastated by what happened to her, it was you."

The lake begins to twist into view along the left side of the road, a line of pines hugging the shore.

April sinks into her seat. "Auggie doesn't seem to think so."

This is what I want, confiding mode. "What do you mean?"

"He's thinks I'm not supposed to be affected by it, because I don't remember everything. I ran from the room when Kathy finally lost it, and I don't remember Harry's arrest, so I'm supposed to be perfectly adjusted. No Harry around. None of you. Kathy 'normal'."

"But you're not."

"No. I'm not." She points to the next drive near the end of the road. "Turn here."

I do, and we're instantly stitched in by woods on either side, the brush so dense overhead that we're shrouded in shade. I can see the modest cabin budding along the lake's edge up ahead, a matching barn twice the size descending off its shoulder. It all appears recently built, the telltale signs of weathering and mold having yet to fully encompass the slats of wood on either structure.

"You sure this is the right place?" I ask. "It looks like a house."

"It is. He lives in the cabin. The barn's his studio."

I put the car into park and April is out before me, heading for the open barn door like she's been here countless times before. I follow her and stop in the doorway.

The outside of the barn isn't a fair indicator for the precision and the elegance that is the workshop inside. The walls are an almost-yellow stained wood, the knots darkened at the spots of forgotten branch rings. There are tables stretched out throughout the room, woodworking tools, saws, paintbrushes, stain and glycerin containers. Sawdust and wood stain waft to me all in one instant. I can't help but have a momentary flashback to the hunting cabin.

But then I take in the furniture staggered throughout the space. The artist has painstakingly crafted and stained dozens of pieces: tables and chairs, dressers and antique chests, armoires and mirror frames. I understand why April referred to them as art, because that is what they are—each individually warped in patterns and colored resin that cut through at angles like lightning sizzling midair or rivers piercing through mountaintops, sharp and vibrant with powerful swirls and curlicues and thick lines all chiseled out of the natural wood. They're breathtaking, and I've seen their kind before. I don't know how I didn't immediately know who this workshop belonged to the moment I smelled sawdust.

His back is to us, his dark hair as short as I remember, but his frame is thicker, the cords that run up his forearms new. April calls his name. When he turns, he's sporting a goatee, a pencil behind his ear, and a face he's grown into now that he's in his mid-thirties.

He's as shocked to see me as I am him. It's like a current ricocheting between us—like no time has passed at all, like all the time has passed. I can't breathe. I want to run. I want to get as far away from this man who broke my heart nine years ago as I possibly can. But it's too late now. I'm meeting his eyes.

"July," he breathes.

"Hi, Gabe."

CHAPTER

11

> You said I was too young babe
> That you'd split my heart in two
> I didn't believe you then babe
> But that's the crime of youth
> —"The Crime of Youth," written by Jules Thomas

I F A SINGULAR look could gut me, this would be it. Gabe's eyes are a pool of memories and regret, his body rigid as he clenches his knuckles on the worktable.

"Surprise," says April from behind him. "I thought you two might want to catch up."

As she walks the barn studio to observe the furniture pieces, I want to believe that this was done in innocence, that there is no possibility my sister could have known the history between Gabe and me. But then I catch the smirk on her face and I know the truth: she did this on purpose. To hurt me.

Gabe doesn't catch it. "I . . . I didn't know you were back."

He runs a hand over the back of his neck, and the fact that he stammers pulls at me just a bit. That feeling is quickly replaced by the stone wall that comes down over my heart.

"I'm not," I snap, then whip to my maniacal sister, whom I'm pretty sure has inherited the sociopath gene. "Pick out your damn furniture piece and meet me in the car."

I am out of there like my ass is on fire, determined with every fiber of my being to get as far away from Gabe Santana as I possibly can. I'll pitch myself into the lake if I have to.

I'm to the car, my hand on the driver's side door handle, when he calls after me.

"July, wait."

My name on his breath is enough to still me, to shoot a look back to where he shuts the barn door, walling my sister from our conversation.

"Wait for what?" I ask. "You want to make the 'let's be friends because it been so long speech'? Save it."

"I didn't think you'd come back," he says. "I heard about what happened to Deck, but I didn't think . . ."

I rip my door open. "Yeah, well, me neither."

"I want to talk to you, while you're home."

"You're a decade late with your closure crap." I hop into the car and slam the door, signaling an end to the conversation.

To Gabe's credit, he stares me down for only about five seconds before returning inside. I wait, and fidget with the radio, my fingers clenching the steering wheel as I curse Auggie for the hundredth time for making me return to this town. April pops out of the barn ten minutes later and slides into the car without looking at me.

I have the vehicle in reverse through the mud, then flying down the driveway before she so much as has her seatbelt on. We're on the main road in a ripping flash, me cutting off a honking tractor on the turn out.

"Jesus," April shrieks, "Are you trying to kill us?"

I'm going twenty miles over the speed limit. "Do you think it's funny to fuck with my life?"

I know the woods are barreling past us at a dangerous pace, but I can't seem to lighten my foot on the accelerator. I'm enraged; all logic has departed me.

"Slow down," April says calmly.

It's so like how Auggie would approach me in this situation, I want to smack her.

"Answer me."

She's not even scared. She's only staring at me, her face unreadable, hard. This reminds me of Mark. "I don't know what you're talking about."

"Don't play dumb," I snap. "You were young, but you were the smartest goddamn eight-year-old I ever met. And you found out about everything that happened that final summer during Harry's trial. You knew about Gabe and me. Do you really hate me that much, that you would let me walk in there like that?"

April feigns a cruel pout. "Poor July. She's the only one in the Weaver family that had it bad. She got dumped. She was the one who found the hunting cabin. She was the only one who ever had to put up with Kathy and Harry and she was the one to get attacked in the woods, so we all need to feel sorry for her. Jesus Christ. You make everything about you, don't you? Even May dying."

Now I really want to strike her. "Don't you ever say that to me again. We all lost May. We all loved May."

"I didn't love her," April snaps. "I didn't love her at all. May was a bitch."

I slam my foot on the brakes and the car lets out a wild hiss as I shove it off the road's shoulder. We spin half a clock as April shrieks. I pop the gearshift into park and stare at her.

"Get the hell out."

She's horrified. "Are you crazy?"

"Get out," I say it louder this time.

"We're five miles from home. It's going to be dark soon."

"Then I suggest you and your ungrateful ass get walking."

"You're not serious?" She darts her gaze to the open road. "I'm a seventeen-year-old girl alone. This isn't safe. My sister was murdered, for crying out loud."

I lean closer. "Then it's a good thing your other narcissist sister got the town's resident serial killer locked up then, isn't it? Now get the hell out of my car. Before. I. Throw. You. Out."

April undoes her seatbelt and climbs out. There's disbelief and worry on her face as I accelerate the car back onto the road. But I don't care. By the time I look back again, she's already a dot on the horizon.

Apoplectic doesn't come close to describing how enraged I still am by the time I'm slamming doors in the manor's foyer and calling for Deck at the top of my lungs. He appears frantic on the stairs' landing, with towels twisted around his hair and waist, and his emaciated body glistening from the shower. In any other moment I'd find the look comedic.

"What? What's wrong?" he asks.

"Get dressed. We're going to a meeting," I bark.

"Now?"

"Yes, now. If you're not in my car in five minutes, I'll forcibly recommit you myself."

He curses under his breath, as I head down the hall to the kitchen, knocking into Kathy along the way. She staggers back, like a wounded animal.

"Sorry," I mutter.

I shove past her, because if I open my mouth again, I might say something I regret.

*   *   *

I'm still full batshit by the time Deck and I pull into the rundown strip mall that houses Huntington's community center twenty minutes later. The lot's abandoned, being that it's seven PM and the only other occupants of this sad excuse of a cracked cement building are a discount boutique and a dentist's office.

I cut the engine, silencing the rock music I've been blasting to prevent Deck from talking the entire drive. I'm about to open my door, but Deck grabs my arm.

"I feel that this would be an opportune time to tell you that you got the wrong NA/AA meeting site," he says.

"What?"

He nods through the dashboard at the community center. It's only now that I realize there are no lights on. Then I remember: it's Wednesday. The closest seven PM meeting is at the Hazel Baptist Church tonight. The meeting here is tomorrow. I drop my head against the steering wheel and blare the horn. "You didn't think to mention that until now?"

Deck whistles. "Hard to get a word in between the shrieking rock bands and your fuck-the-world attitude."

I glare at him, but Deck is about the only person in the world this has little effect on.

"Hold that thought, ice queen." He points behind us to the main road. "There's a Burger King a quarter mile up."

I sigh and drive out of the lot. Fifteen minutes later, our seats are pushed back with our feet on the dash, in another quiet parking lot, the two of us eating burgers and fries as we stare up at a flickering traffic light at the end of the street. There's a hard slice of black through each of the green and yellow panels. Red is the only color not malfunctioning. Not that that matters; there are hardly any cars on the road and only a handful pulling in and out of this lot for the drive-through. Got to love the South. We have a greasy food chain on every corner.

Deck bunches up his burger wrapper and tosses it into the backseat, then washes it down with a guzzle of milkshake. He's always been a surprisingly shitty eater for what a rail he is. Probably because he only eats one meal a day.

"All right," he begins. "Now that we're thoroughly sated, you want to tell me what got the ole Livewire so triggered up tonight? I'll start us off properly first. Hi, I'm December "Deck" Weaver and I'm a goddamn addict."

I pop a fry into my mouth. "What're you doing?"

Deck holds out his hands. "You wanted a meeting. Let's have our own. Right here in this car. Just you and me."

"That's not how it works."

"Says who? What? You need me to throw in a serenity prayer to make it feel more authentic?"

I roll my eyes and drop my fries into the center console. I need to get this off my chest to someone. "April took me to see Gabe Santana today."

Deck nods. Of all of my siblings, he knows the most about that chapter of my life, and that is only the barest tidbits he's pulled out of me over the years—usually when I was drunk. "Ah, there it is. The heartbreaker. So he's back in town, too?"

"Apparently."

Deck frowns. "Why would April take you to see him? Doesn't she know the history?"

"She needed to go over to his workshop to pick out a piece of his furniture for her school fundraiser. But she knew. It was an ambush."

Deck took another slurp of his shake. "Damn, maybe the kid's a Weaver after all."

"You should have seen her face afterwards. It was something right out of Mark's teenage playbook. She hates me."

My brother shakes his head. "Nah. She doesn't hate you. She hates Harry and Kathy for being shitty parents, like all the rest of us. It's just a hell of a lot easier to take it out on you, because you're the one that left."

"I made her walk the last few miles home."

For either of our other brothers, this would have earned me a reprimand. But Deck takes the news by throwing his head back and laughing. "Sounds like the brat deserved it."

Shame fills me. "It was immature of me. But you should have heard what she said about May."

"What?"

I force myself to repeat it, even though it makes my skin crawl. "She called May a bitch."

Deck gulps his shake. But there's a guilty look to his expression.

"What?" I demand.

He's sheepish. "I mean . . . I know it's shitty to speak bad about the dead, but April isn't exactly wrong."

He holds up his hand to stop me, clearly seeing the outrage about to flood out. "Now, before you go crucifying me," he says. "Just think about it for a second. There's a bit of a generational gap between Auggie, you, and Mark from the twins and me. I might only be two years younger than the rest of you, but I always got roped in with the twins. I saw more shit that went down between the two of them growing up than the rest of y'all did."

"Like what?"

"Like that May was a bully. She tormented April most days. Me too, half the time."

"What are you talking about?" I can't believe it. I won't.

Deck sighs. "You always wore rose-colored glasses with the twins or were off doing your own thing. I'd walk in on May ripping April's toys out of her hands all the time. She smacked her around. She'd misbehave and do shit around the house, then blame it on either me or April. And everyone always believed her, because she was the quietest one. When the rest of you and the parentals were in the room, she acted like this doting angel . . . but behind closed doors, she was a tattletale. April and I couldn't stand her."

A revelation. This entire time I have practically been sanctifying my dead sister. But does this give new context to her murder? A darker side that I refused to see?

"You think that's why Harry killed her? Because she did or saw something, and was gonna tell someone?"

Deck shrugs. "Maybe. We'll never know. Unless you want to go question the liar in prison, which I don't recommend."

To this day, Harry still maintains he's innocent to any media outlet that will give him the time of day. None of the Weaver siblings have been to see him since he was arrested.

He's on death row now, but with the judicial process, he's likely still years away from execution.

I study my youngest brother. "Do you resent me for not letting you go see him back then?"

Deck had wanted to visit, once, about a year after Harry was locked up, but I stopped him. It was right after his first rehab stint and I was afraid that family reunion would send my brother back over the edge. Deck never brought it up again.

"I get why you didn't," he says. "And it's not like I've tried to go on my own, since."

"But?"

Deck meets my eyes. "It's just sometimes . . . do you ever wonder if we should have asked more questions back then? Let him explain his perspective on everything that happened that summer? There are just things that have never made much sense."

"You *do* think he's innocent," I realize. "What you told Auggie when you were high—about thinking Adrian Bennet was killed by the Pacific Lake Killer, that Harry was framed." The truth is an anvil on my head. "Why would you lie to all of us when we asked you in the diner?"

Deck purses his lips. "I never said I thought he was innocent. I only said there are things that don't make sense. There's a difference."

"But you question it?"

He throws his hands up. "I don't know. That was obviously my imbalanced brain trying to connect dots that aren't there with the Adrian Bennet thing. But I'll admit that I've never been entirely convinced that Harry was the Pacific Lake Killer. And forgive me if I didn't own up to that in front of our brothers. I was a bit concerned I'd sound epically paranoid, and they'd throw me right back into the hospital."

"And you think I won't?"

Deck shakes his head. "No. You won't. Because despite what Auggie might believe, I know you better than any of our siblings now. I was the one with you in those first few years in Nashville, when you were drunk off your ass, trying to sort through all of this. Something about how that last summer ended never sat right with you either. I think you've always doubted it was Harry."

"You're wrong," I say, sounding more rattled than I should. "I know it was him."

"Sure," says Deck picking up my discarded fries. "Just like you knew the whole story with May, right?"

*   *   *

That night, I dream of May, and I try to dream her mean—the girl my younger siblings claim to have known, but the images won't fit. All I see are flashes: a reserved, pudgier twin in the corner, a girl so introverted she perpetually seems like she wants to fold in on herself. April dancing to their boom box, singing along to a CD, trying to coax May out of herself. But the child won't budge. A corner. A book. A walk about the grounds by herself—that is who May is. We find her asleep in a corner of the greenhouse, or cross-legged beneath Father Time, staring up at the skylight, or on the end of the dock with her feet dangling over the edge as she has conversations with the sunfish underneath. May is odd; I've always known this.

But mean? I can't catch hold of that glimmer of her. Not until my restless sleep leads me to another dream. This one forms more concretely than the others, so vivid I can taste it on my tongue. May.

She is screaming. It is only a few months before her disappearance, right after Christmas. I hear her from my room, but don't bother going to investigate. There is only the typical level of Weaver trauma in these days. Two oddball parents, one of which is on and off her meds. But without a missing sister, my overprotective sibling instincts have yet to fully smash into place. Auggie will handle the matter, if Kathy doesn't, I think. I'm messing with my guitar, trying to find the right chords.

But then May crashes into my room. So uncharacteristic of her, and she's sobbing. Sobbing as she clutches her cheek. It only takes a second to realize she has a scratch there, one that runs from the tip of her nose almost to her ear. A line of blood peppering it.

I jump up, running to examine her face. "What happened?"

May is so inconsolable, she is heaving. She can hardly get a word out. "April." Heave. "April." Heave. "Scratched me."

"Why?"

"She . . . she took my coloring book, and I tried to . . . to . . ."

"Calm down, sweetie."

"She scratched me."

Kathy appears at the door. "What was that screaming?" Then she sees May's face, and cries out, coming to her knees before her. "What happened to your face?"

"April scratched her," I say.

"Oh, you poor baby," Kathy says, beginning to fuss over her youngest child.

"You should put hydrogen peroxide on that," I tell my mother. I don't trust her to remember to do it. "I'll go talk to April."

I leave Kathy with a shaking, red-faced May, and head for the twins' room. I'm not mad at April—I know better than to take sides in their fights—but I certainly am not going to take it easy on her either. That is why I left Kathy with May. She never has been capable of handling sibling conflict resolution. She'll lose interest in a few minutes and be on to the next thing.

I find April curled up against a wall on the twins' bedroom floor. She, too, is sobbing. I sit down beside her. No visible marks on her, but she's just as flushed as her twin.

"You want to tell me what happened?" I ask. "Why you scratched May's face?"

April wipes her eyes. "I didn't mean to!"

"What happened?"

April shakes her head too quickly.

"April, May said you took her coloring book, and when she tried to take it back, you scratched her. Is that true?"

"No!" April barks. "May lies. May lies all the time."

I sigh, chalking it up to equal parts twins' fault. But then I notice April tugging down her sleeves to her wrists.

"April, show me your arms."

My little sister hesitates. "She'll be mad if I show you."

"Who'll be mad?"

"May."

I am running out of patience for this. "April, show me your arms, now."

April obeys, hiking up her sleeves. I inhale sharply. There are five crescent piercings on each arm. Ten deep half-moons of blood where May's nails have squeezed down, broken skin.

But this isn't a dream. It's a memory.

12

Then

A NY FLIMSY PLANS for the Fourth of July evaporated in the wake of Harry returning home and the discovery of the cabin. If our family's desire to celebrate before had been minimal, it became entirely nonexistent once Detective Rafael appeared at our door the morning of. His purpose: to requestion our family on our whereabouts the night Laurel Dillon went missing.

The truth came out to the rest of the Weavers that I was one of the women to have my face spotlighted on the sicko's cabin walls. When Rafael sat my father, brothers, and me down in the living room to relay that I was in one of the photos, I couldn't help but dart my gaze around to gauge their reactions. Deck's eyes looked like they wanted to pop out of his skull, while Mark took the news without blinking. Auggie predictably clutched my shoulder in protective alarm. But it was Harry's reaction that I was least expecting. No shouting or pontificating. My father simply removed himself from the room.

Rafael explained that the cops were going door to door questioning every woman in the county they recognized in the blood-soaked images: Have you ever felt like you're being followed? Has anyone strange approached you? Any weird encounters at all? Ex-boyfriends? Creepy neighbors? They wanted to know—why me and the others pictured, not April or Zoey or Kathy or Nicole Sheridan or Bridget Cane or any of the other hundreds of women in Pacific and the neighboring towns, were the ones targeted. My answer was no to everything. I'd never felt followed, only stared at. But that was by everyone in town. My family was weird to begin with, and my kid sister just disappeared.

At the end of the interview, Auggie walked the detective out, and Deck left soon after with an "I can't with this shit." I remained on the couch and tried not to let it shake me. There were a lot of local women on the walls of that cabin, but I knew I had to stay on the alert. Whoever the person was who had taken those photos, they'd had their eye on me since winter. Same as they probably had May.

I turned to Mark. He was staring at the photo of Laurel Dillon left behind on the coffee table. Rafael brought it to see if any of us recognized her. The four of us had all given a resounding no. But based on the haunted expression on Mark's face, I wasn't so sure if that was the truth.

"Did you know her?" I asked.

Mark shrugged. "Looks like every other dumb bitch in this town."

His words unnerved me, but his voice was choked as he headed for the door. He slammed it, leaving me more alone than ever.

*   *   *

"July," said Kathy as I stepped into the kitchen later that afternoon. She was standing at the sink, scrubbing dishes while April stood on the stool beside her, drying. My mother offered me a weary smile. "Daniela brought us trays for dinner. She said to say hello."

I was on my guard as usual whenever Kathy seemed coherent. Harry had done his best to stabilize her on her meds over the last few weeks since he'd come home. The result was my mother happier, more herself. Out of habit, I couldn't help but pop my head over the sink to make sure there were no knives in their soaking pile that she could accidentally cut her hand on.

"There are hot dogs and potato salad," April said.

She beamed up at our mother. I was momentarily jealous of the innocence of childhood—so willing to forgive.

Kathy cupped the little girl's shoulder. "We will eat them, then go out on the water, like your father promised. Won't it be fun to watch the fireworks over the lake?"

That's what we did every year, but Kathy made it sound like it was a first-time thing. Maybe in her warped mind it was.

April nodded fiercely and Kathy turned to me. "July? What about you? Your brothers don't seem interested."

"I'm gonna pass, too." I kissed my sister on the top of her head. "But I'll see you when you get back."

Harry walked in then, carrying a rifle. He must have pulled it from his gun safe in the basement. The sight of it in the house, this close to both Kathy and April, unsettled me.

"What the hell are you doing with that?" I asked.

"Protecting my family," he said, pushing through the door to the foyer.

I chased him down the hall, stopping him in front of Father Time. "Are you insane?" I hissed. "With Kathy the way she is?"

"It's not loaded," he said. "But it's no good to us locked in that basement. I'm putting it in your closet. If one of us needs it, it'll be close by. Besides, it's the last place your mother would think to look." Harry dropped three shell casings into my palm and closed my fist around them. "I need you to protect yourself, Livewire. Keep those somewhere safe where only you can find them. You're a good shot."

"You think he's gonna come after me, too," I realized. "Of all those women on the walls, you think I'm high on the list."

Harry's lips tightened. "Be diligent. The only person you should trust now is yourself. And don't go anywhere alone."

He hurried up the stairs.

"I still think the gun's a stupid idea," I called after him.

* * *

I hardly saw my family the rest of the day. Mark went off to get drunk with Nicole and the rest of his letterman/pom pom crew; Deck planted himself in his room on the PlayStation—an immovable object; Auggie reluctantly went out with Dan after I forced him to; and my parents took April out on the lake for the fireworks show. I could have gone with them, but something about being trapped in a boat with my parents felt like a special kind of torture. I could have called Zoey, but I was still a little pissed at her, so I contented myself with cleaning up dinner after everyone left.

It was only seven-thirty when I finished the dishes. I was too wired to sit and practice my guitar, too awake to go to bed. It occurred to me that I could bring back Daniela's trays. Even driving three miles down the road and back would be better than sitting around this house alone. And if I was honest with myself, I was sort of hoping that Daniela would welcome me into her own family celebration for an hour or two, so I could forget my own.

I packed everything into Harry's Jeep and took off. My father would be annoyed later that I ignored his warning to not go anywhere alone, but as I saw it, I was just as likely to get murdered sitting at home with a headphone-clad Deck a room away than I was driving by myself.

Daniela's house was also on the lake, in a more populated neighborhood. It was a single-family ranch house on a quarter-acre lot with a porch that overlooked the water. The only difference between it and the matching five houses around it was the silver Airstream parked in the backyard. Daniela used it as a guest house. I'd spent more than one night passed out drunk in that bed when it was too far to walk home after a party.

I hopped out of the Jeep, carried the metal trays up to the porch, and banged on the front door. There was no answer, even after the third knock. I looked at my watch. Fireworks were in half an hour. Daniela and her husband had to have already taken her kids out on the water. Damn.

I sighed and dropped the trays down on the porch's picnic table, then headed back for the car. A night home alone it was.

"What're you doing here?" came a voice behind me.

I jumped about five feet.

"Sorry," Gabe said. He was carrying a pile of firewood in his arms, having come from the side of the house. "I didn't mean to sneak up on you."

I shook my head. "It's okay. I'm just on edge."

"I can imagine." He nodded up to the porch. "You looking for Daniela? She's already out on the lake."

"Yeah. I figured that. I was just dropping off the trays she brought over earlier." I nodded to the wood in his hands. "You prepping for winter already?"

"I was gonna get the firepit going in her backyard."

"You don't want to be down watching the fireworks with the kids?" I asked.

Gabe shook his head. "I'm not a fan of popping noises, after being in the service. Why aren't you out there with your friends?"

I laughed. "I don't exactly have a lot of those these days."

Gabe looked like he didn't know how to respond to that. He hesitated, "You want a soda?"

It was a pity invite, but I shrugged. I had nothing better to do. "Only if you let me help you build that fire."

He led me around back to the patch of lawn between the house and Airstream. There was a firepit set up with lawn chairs all around it. The other two sides were bracketed in by woods. You couldn't even see the lake from here.

"Cooler's on the back deck," he said, dropping the firewood down next to the pit. "Grab me a beer, will you?"

I stepped onto the deck and opened the cooler. It was full of Sam Adams, Coke, and Sprite. I brought out two beers, and popped the tops on the deck railing before walking back over to Gabe. He had the fire going at that point, was shifting wood around to light off the starter log. I handed him his beer and sank down into one of the lawn chairs with my own.

"Aren't you a little young for that?" he nodded with his drink to mine.

"Aren't you a little young to be acting like my father?"

He shook his head, but pulled the nearest lawn chair away from mine before sitting down. Putting distance between us.

"Will you chill?" I asked. "We're old family friends."

"I'm trying not to come off like a creep here."

But that's the last thing I'd ever think Gabe Santana was. He was such a decent person. I'd watched him interact with people around town my entire life. The last thing he'd ever do was hit on a minor. I wished he would.

"I could never think that."

We drank our beer and I picked at the label to mine. Fireflies lit the grass as the sky descended into blackness, a curtain of stars pulling up above. I thought of May, wondering if wherever she was, dead or alive, she could see the same set of stars I could. The piecemealed moon.

"I heard Rafael was making the rounds to all the women pictured in the cabin," Gabe said. "Did he come see you?"

"This morning. Apparently the man doesn't believe in holidays. You saw it when you went in too, then?"

Gabe nodded. "I was hoping you wouldn't."

I shrugged. "Might be random."

Gabe's eyebrows went up. "Might not be. You should be careful . . ."

I held up my hand to cut him off. "Let's not, yeah? I thought you and I already established that I can handle myself."

Gabe answered by taking another gulp of his beer, subject dropped.

I peeked back over at the rusted Airstream. "That where you're staying?"

"Yup."

"That's got to be a little different from the army."

"It is. Softer bed."

We laughed.

"Where were you this whole time?" I asked.

"Mostly stayed in the South."

That seemed deliberately vague.

"Are you glad you went in?"

"Made me who I am."

"You didn't answer my question."

Gabe leaned forward and stroked the fire. "I didn't have a lot of options when I finished high school. We didn't have money for college. It was enlist or go work for Ma's cleaning company or Daniela's diner." He met my eyes over the flames. "I wanted out of this town."

An unspoken understanding passed between us. "And are you happier now that you left?"

I needed to know, needed to believe that it was better out there somewhere.

"Sometimes. But family . . . they have a way of bringing you back."

"I don't know the feeling. I can't wait to get away from my family."

"Your parents, sure. But do you really feel that way about all of them? Your siblings?"

I nursed my beer, thinking about it. "No. Not Auggie. Or the younger ones. Mark and I are like cats and dogs, though."

"They're your people," Gabe said. "You can't ever truly shake them. Even if you do for a little while."

There was sincerity to his words. I could see it on his face lit orange by the fire. I was so attracted to him, it hurt. I noticed that he'd unconsciously leaned in my direction, too.

"What happened with the girl from the drive-in?" I whispered.

That seemed to wake Gabe up, because he sat back in his chair again. "Drink your beer."

"July," called a voice behind me.

Daniela was standing on the back porch, a simultaneous look of confusion at the two of us sitting together at the bonfire, and something else. Fear.

"What is it?" Gabe asked. He had already sprung up. "What's wrong?"

"A body," Daniela said, her eyes trained on me. "All the boat traffic on the lake. It dredged up a body."

I was on my feet, too, in a flash. "Who?"

"I don't know." The woman shook her head. "The screaming started when the fireworks started going off. It was floating in the water."

"Where?"

"Sullivan's Point." Daniela's eyes welled. "Sweetheart, you should head on home. Your parents will be getting back soon."

I was already past her and Gabe, my beer forgotten in the grass, as I scrambled to reach the Jeep.

"July, wait," Gabe called after me.

But I was already scurrying into the driver's seat, my hands moving ahead of my mind. I had to get there. I had to get to Sullivan's Point right now.

Gabe climbed into the passenger's seat before I could blink.

"What are you doing?" I demanded.

"Going with you," Gabe said. "I know you're not going home."

I backed out of Daniela's driveway without bothering to look either way. There was never oncoming traffic on this road.

"You should let me drive," Gabe said. "You're too emotional."

"Too bad," I barked, ramming Harry's gear stick into drive.

I tore the two miles down the road. It was faster to take Mulberry Drive around the rim of the lake to get to Sullivan's Point than to head back into town, then dart over. I barely registered the dark lake on my left, except that the fireworks were over, the night a thick ash to block out the stars. They must have ended the show early, when the screaming started.

Sullivan's Point was a mess of people and cars. Yellow police tape roped off the beach, but there wasn't enough manpower on such short notice, so people flooded the shoreline. Gabe and I got out, and joined the others.

A group of men, some cops, some locals, were wading to their hips to meet an approaching boat. Mitch Harkins, the Pacific Lake Middle School football coach, drove his troller as shallow as he could before being forced to stop. The other men met him, a handful climbing into the boat. They picked up a large, wrapped mass, in what looked like duct-taped black garbage bags, and handed it over to the other waiting men in the water.

"You shouldn't be here for this," Gabe said to me.

I ignored him, shoving forward to get a better view, waiting as the men waded to shore with the dark form. They laid it on the beach. I was right about the garbage bags. A thick line of duct tape was around the neck, the torso, the legs. I knew immediately on closer inspection that it couldn't be May. The body was too long, probably as tall as me. It had to be Laurel Dillon.

Cops began to push the crowd back and yell to leave the body where it was; this was an active crime scene now. But one of the men who'd hauled it to shore didn't bother to wait. I recognized him from the news as Laurel Dillon's father. He took a penknife from his pocket and leaned over the top of the body.

"You cannot tamper with that!" one of the cops yelled, hurrying toward him.

"It's my daughter," the man spat, and ripped his knife through the material, pulling the garbage bag away from the face.

I heard multiple breaths catch, and my fingers laced through Gabe's. The body was certainly female. Bloated and gray. It wasn't May. But it also wasn't Laurel Dillon. No, this was someone else I knew, someone who had been one of the biggest gossips since the moment May disappeared. Some-one no one even knew was missing until now. A third dead woman.

Kelly Anders.

13

Now

I WOULD BE INTENT to let the day and the week of the Fourth of July go by completely unremarked upon, but Auggie is having none of it. Mark is flying in for the holiday begrudgingly, leaving Lindsay back in the Hamptons, and according to Auggie, we are all to assume the roles of one big happy family for Bridget's sake.

I can't help but still feel odd about their upcoming nuptials. For one thing, I haven't so much as laid eyes on Bridget since returning to Pacific a month ago, other than one awkward time I bumped into her coming out of the post office.

Auggie has done his best to shelter her from our reunited family, going over to her place several nights a week instead of having her to ours. He doesn't offer an explanation for this, but I get why: not only would Bridget have to contend with his schizophrenic mama, but also his schizophrenic drug addict brother and his cynical recovering alcoholic sister. We're a lot. But the inevitable has come and Bridget's first re-exposure to the full Weaver clan is finally here.

This distance up until now has also mercifully meant that I've been spared from having to help with wedding preparations. The first and last time Auggie summons me is for his final tux fitting. I don't know the first thing about formal wear, but Auggie begs me to come along anyway. Apparently, Mr. Lumberjack is even more lost than I am.

So I sit bored in a lounge chair that afternoon, while my oldest brother changes in the dressing room. I have a magazine in my hands but I'm not reading it. My mind is focused on May. I haven't gotten Auggie alone for more than a few minutes since April and Deck's bombshell, and I'd be lying if I didn't admit I came along today so that I could talk to him about it.

"What do you think?"

My brother emerges from the dressing room a different man. Gone is the plaid-and-jeans construction project manager, replaced by a full navy suit and crimson tie—wearing stranger. Auggie's handsome as hell, and it hits me for the first time that he's starting this next chapter in his life. I'm happy for him; he deserves it more than any of us.

"You're a regular James Bond," I say.

He grins and steps in front of the three-way mirror, pulling at his cuffs. "I don't really know how to do these."

I go to him and button the cufflinks. Our reflections stare back at us in the mirror. "I can't believe you're getting married."

Auggie inhales. "Me, neither."

"Try to say that with a little more enthusiasm, why don't you?" I hit him in the ribs, then face the real him. "I'm proud of you. You know that, right? I'm sorry I acted so surprised when you first told me."

Auggie shrugs, pulling at his tie uncomfortably. He's not a fish out of water; he's a fish in space. "You were right to be taken off guard. I wasn't even with her when I came to see you last time in Nashville."

"But you're happy?" This is what is most important to me. Far more insane things have happened in this family than short-term engagements.

Auggie nods. A truth lies behind his expression, perhaps one only I can fully understand. "I want to be."

"What happens after the wedding?" The question only skates across my mind now. How life in the Weaver household might change with the addition of an outsider.

"What do you mean?"

"Well, April will stay with you another year until she finishes high school. Deck and I'll go back to Nashville at the end of summer. But what about Kathy? Is Bridget going to move into the house?" I want to find the right time to talk to Auggie about Kathy's medication, but this doesn't seem like it. He's stressed enough.

Auggie shrugs. "Bridget's fine with it. She knows Kathy, and gets why I have to take care of her."

"Got to admire the woman. This is a lot of family baggage she's taking on."

"Yeah, well, it's not like she has much of a choice," my brother says, unbuttoning the jacket.

I frown at him. "Meaning?"

Auggie turns back to me, guilty. "She's pregnant."

"Oh." I have to lean against one of the mirrors, I'm so taken aback. "So this actually is a shotgun wedding."

My brother's face is a display of mixed emotions. "I didn't want you to think that was the only reason why I'm marrying her."

"Is it the only reason why you're marrying her?" It's a valid question. It also explains a lot.

Auggie rubs his beard, then steps off the mirrored pedestal. "I want a family. A normal family."

"I get that." He has no idea how much I get that. Although kids have never been part of my plan, Auggie was born to be a father.

"So, you're not judging me?"

"Auggie, you're my brother." I smile. "Of course I'm judging you."

He laughs at that, which was my intention.

"You're going to make a great dad."

He pulls his jacket off and folds it over his arm. I don't know how he's going to get through an entire ceremony wearing it. "Thanks. I'm honestly terrified."

"Don't be. You've done a great job with April." I pause. "Other than the fact that she's a bit of a satanic brat."

I mean it jokingly, but he catches the truth in my tone. He lifts an eyebrow. "Says the sister who left her on the side of the road."

"You heard about that?" *Great.* I'm freaking sister of the year.

"Of course I did. April tells me everything. Not one of your finer moments."

I push down the shame Auggie is so damn good at inflicting. "Yeah, well. I knew that already." I decide to take this as my opening. "Did she tell you why I kicked her out of the car?"

Auggie's expression darkens as he undoes his tie. "She admitted that she ambushed you at Santana's shop. I told her she was lucky you already made her walk home, or I would have grounded her for weeks."

He sounds like a father already, and is still infinitely overprotective of me. There are few people who hate Gabe Santana more than my eldest brother. Auggie lived through the tail end of that night with me. In many ways, he blames Gabe for me being attacked at all.

"I didn't think he'd still be here," I say. "Why didn't you tell me he came back?"

Auggie looks at me pointedly. "How would knowing that have helped you? You were doing great in Nashville. You didn't need to know that piece of shit had moved home."

"Yeah, well it would have been nice to have had a warning. So I wouldn't have been surprised when I literally showed up at his house."

"Sorry."

I shrug, it already forgiven. "And that's not the only reason I kicked that delinquent's ass out of my car. She called May a bitch."

Auggie stiffens at that. "That was left out of April's explanation."

"Convenient."

"Why would she say that?"

"Why don't you tell me, big brother? You know April better than me. She claims that the rest of us didn't know the real May, that she was mean and manipulative. I didn't believe it, but then Deck confirmed as much. He says that May acted differently around us older kids than him and April." I collapse down on the sofa. "Since then, I've started to think about it, and remember some stuff from when her and April were little. Maybe they're right."

There's disbelief on Auggie's face. "No chance. April was always the instigator. May was a sweetheart."

"Are you sure about that? Really sure? Or was she just the quieter one?"

Auggie maneuvers back toward his dressing room, his hand going for the curtain. "What does it even matter now?"

That is the question, really. Why am I so fixated on this? "I don't know. It just does. What if it had to do with why Harry chose to kill her specifically?"

My brother kicks off his loafers, probably too roughly for what they cost. "Why did Harry pick any of them? Why Laurel Dillon? Why Kelly Anders? Why you? There's no point in trying to find explanations in the mind of a madman, especially not one who chose his own daughters as two of his victims."

I'm not trying to upset him, but . . . "I know. I just . . . Then there's the whole Colton Davidson thing."

Auggie's eyebrows go up. "What Colton Davidson thing?"

I rub my forehead. "I ran into him in Kroger. He's worried I'm going to start talking about what was in his file from the investigation. Like there was more there than just his interaction with me the night of my attack."

Auggie pulls the curtain all the way over, but his head sticks out the slit. "Well, yeah. There was. He was hooking up with Kelly Anders all that summer." He frowns. "I thought you knew that."

I most certainly didn't. No one thought to mention that to me? "Are you saying that Colton Davidson had something going with two of Harry's victims? Anders and me?"

Auggie shoves the curtain fully open again, still in his dress shirt and slacks. "Stop."

"Stop what?"

"Whatever it is you're overthinking in that brain of yours. Davidson was a man whore, but he was cleared of any further involvement. Harry killed those women. Harry killed May."

"I know that," I snap.

"Then let this go," he says annoyed. "All you're going to do is drive yourself crazy trying to find meanings back then where there were none. Okay? We were raised by a sociopath. End of story." He goes back behind the curtain. "And for the love of God, can you stop listening to the seventeen-year-old and the guy who just got out of the hospital when you're formulating your wild theories?"

The authority is his tone is enough to make me clamp my mouth shut. He's right. I'm overanalyzing everything. It has to be this place getting to me. What I need to do instead is focus on Deck's recovery and Kade's album. Then at the end of this summer, I can leave Pacific. No more thinking about May or Harry. No looking back.

"You're right," I say.

He pops his head back out, clearly relieved. "Good. There's one more thing we need to talk about then before you get over being pissed. I'm making you my best man."

I open my mouth to object, but the curtain slams closed before I can.

*   *   *

Mark arrives with a grumble the morning of the Fourth, decked out in flamboyant swim trunks and douchey sunglasses. I have to bite my tongue to keep from making fun of him. Deck fortunately takes over that role for me as the two of them spend most of the day out on the dock—Deck spiraling into the lake, launching cannonball after cannonball, while Mark looks on unimpressed. The real action begins when Deck trips him and Mark faceplants into the lake. He's furious the first second, then racing Deck to the swim float the next. April is out on a boat somewhere with friends, and I'll admit that I'm not sorry she's gone. We haven't reconciled since that day at Gabe's, and I think it's a relief to both of us to avoid each other for the holiday.

My role for the day gets assigned by Auggie. It's half because he knows I can't stand the thought of jumping in that lake and half what I expect to be a getting-to-know-Bridget effort. While Auggie turns over burgers and dogs on the grill, Bridget, Kathy, and I sit on the porch husking corn. Bridget passes the time by regaling us with the story of how the two of them began dating six months ago after years of being neighbors. I'm only half paying attention.

My brother's fiancée is average looking, encroaching on pretty, her face long and hair dyed brunette. Her appearance isn't much changed since I last saw her in passing that final summer, aside from a few added laugh lines. She's nice, I determine, tripping over herself at every turn to make me like her. I can tell she'll be a sweet mom, and by the way she looks at Auggie, she worships the ground he walks on. It's all I've ever wanted for him. Only problem is, I can see it in his eyes when he looks at her—he likes her well enough, but it isn't love. I hope that comes for him in time.

It also proves a relief to have Bridget here when we all finally sit down for dinner. Had it been only us Weavers, on this of all days, the meal would likely have been painfully tolerated in silence. But with the absence of April and the addition of a new partner, our family takes on a new tenor. Auggie sits at the head of the table stroking Bridget's hand, as Deck entertains us with stories from Nashville, periodically pulling the same from Mark and his life in New York. I'm actually laughing, adding bits and pieces to what Deck leaves out, and even Kathy seems a little more enthralled than usual from her end of the table. She smiles and laughs at Deck's ramblings, although she doesn't say much.

Bridget is polite and attentive and keeps asking questions until she's hearing the entire history of the Weaver clan. We tell her of the childhood before May died, leaving out Kathy's episodes and any mention of Harry at all. Instead, my brothers rotate telling stories of the chaotic adventures of the six Weaver children—stealing Harry's boat to roam out on the lake; the time Deck set up a throne room in the greenhouse and convinced the twins to wait on him for an entire weekend; the nights standing up in the bed of Auggie's truck, wind in our hair, as we tore through the breeze. It wasn't all bad, I have to remind myself. This, right here, my siblings, were the good parts of growing up, united in dysfunction, as we half raised each other along with ourselves. I don't realize how much I've missed them, all of us together, until this very moment.

When the hour ebbs and sunset pulls a blanket over the sun, the sounds of boat motors on the lake spike. It's a hot night, sticky and thick as only Georgia humidity can be, but the sky is clear. It will be a perfect night for the fireworks over the lake, but I certainly won't be watching. I put the fear of God in Deck when he says he's going out to meet some old high school friends on a boat, threatening him with fratricide if he so much as touches a beer, joint, needle, powder, or pill.

Kathy heads off to the foyer to watch TV on the projector, and Auggie agrees to take Bridget out on the lake, just the two of them. Of the siblings, it is ironically only Mark and I who are in agreement to stay off the water tonight.

The two of us clean up the porch and kitchen with hardly a passing word to one another. I try to think of the last time I was alone with him and realize it was that day outside the police station. We're both uncomfortable and it's a relief when he goes to take Lindsay's call outside. Time doesn't mend all wounds.

I finish the dishes and decide to turn in early. There's a duet I'm halfway through that I think might fit Kade's brand and I want to finish it before the lyrics leave my head. I pour myself a glass of water and head through the house.

The jungle hallway is dark. I'd flip on a light but I wouldn't begin to know what vine the switch is hiding under. But there is the blue light from Kathy's projector in the foyer that guides me forward. I head for it, breathing in the smell of moss and dirt.

Auggie set up a projector screen behind Father Time years ago for Kathy to sit and watch TV. Something about this room has always calmed her for whatever reason—maybe it's the tree or its bracketing square patch of stars.

Her pale face is lit from the screen and I can't help but walk over and see what she's watching before I head upstairs. Usually it's the news, but Auggie also has a VCR player hooked up, so our mother can watch her old movie musicals.

"What are you watching?"

"Home movies," Kathy says without turning her face from the screen.

I look up, and sure enough, there is grainy footage of Pacific Lake. Auggie and Mark, beaming on the shoreline, both under six years old. A two-year-old Deck waddles into frame and collides with Auggie's chest, as the camera shakes with Kathy's laughter.

"What are y'all doing?" she asks with motherly devotion.

"Building sandcastle," Mark says with the same bitter expression he carries in adulthood. He clumps muddy sand into a mound before them. Deck proceeds to ram his fist into it and Mark screams.

"Deck," Harry's voice echoes strict from out of frame.

Kathy pans the camera and there is Harry further down the shoreline, his back to the camera, but his head cocked around to his sons. Something comes skidding down the dock toward him. It's four-year-old me.

I'm screaming, "Daddy! Daddy! Daddy!"

My father pitches back and I can hear the smile in his voice when he says, "Come here, Livewire."

I run into his arms and he hoists me up. The frame stops on the back of both our heads staring out over the water.

"Sit down," present Kathy says to me, nodding to the chair beside hers. "There are more. They're fun."

I don't know what comes over me, but I do. Maybe it's time I let my mother back in, even if it's just a little. Nothing that happened back then was her fault, not really. I understand that better now than when I was seventeen.

So I sit and I watch the Weaver family reel of home movies with her for I don't know how long. I can't look away from the fishing trips, the boat rides, the trail climbs as the four oldest Weaver children grow in age. Eventually the two bundles of May and April appear, though the footage doesn't go past about when they're two years old—that was when Kathy's disease began to truly take hold.

The truth is I'm watching for one person and one person only—my father. I don't know why I think I will find meanings for why Harry did what he did in these videos, but I look all the same. Is he staring at May and me in a particular way different from the others? Are there any signs of the double life he would someday lead? A sinister expression? I don't find answers to any of these questions. The Harry Weaver of these videos is the same big-ideaed, crazy-scheming, loud and opinionated father I remember. There's no hint of anything else. No closure.

I stand up. I can't bear to watch his face any longer.

"Wait," Kathy says to me, just as I turn my back. "You need to see this one."

I look back to the screen, highly doubting that. There's no one in the frame, only a backyard in late fall, orange leaves carpeting the dirt and the side of a periwinkle-colored house with a broken gutter extending off its roof.

"What're you doing?" asks a familiar voice.

The camera pivots to Mark. Only, he's older here. Sixteen or seventeen. In his football jersey with shaggy hair. Holy shit.

"Nothing," says the girl holding the camera.

"Cut it out," says Mark.

"Or what?" The frame moves out of the way as he reaches for it.

But Mark must catch her, because suddenly the camera is turned sideways and only an angle of his face is visible. He must be holding it now.

"I told you not to film me," he growls.

"What? Scared that someone will see us?" the girl mocks, but there is a note of sincerity to her voice, hurt. "Relax. This's just for us. Now are you gonna kiss me or not? I know you wanna."

The girl's back is to the frame, but I can see her light brown hair. The long shapeless dress she's wearing. She sounds like she's our age.

"No, I don't."

The girl sidles up closer to Mark, her face an inch from his. "Liar."

Then Mark does kiss her, his hand cupping her throat in a possessive, almost choking, gesture. But then he pulls away as if struck. He looks into the lens. "Shit. It's still on."

"Don't delete it," the girl says and then she is reaching for the camera, her fingers outstretched. I finally see her face.

Laurel Dillon.

The film stops there.

"Guess she won that argument," whispers Kathy.

"You wanted me to see this," I say, more confused by my mother than ever.

Because I don't know what the hell I just watched. No, I do. That's what makes this so much worse. And yet again, my subdued mother proves there's more going on beneath the surface than she's allowing the others to see. A deliberate trail she's leading me down.

"Where the fuck did you find that?" says a voice behind us.

Mark. He's staring up at the screen, at Laurel's frozen face, in utter disgust.

"It was on the same tape as a bunch of other home movies," I say. "You want to explain that?"

Mark charges up to the VCR player, pounding the eject button and the tape pops out. Kathy must realize his intentions, because she's up in a flash, moving for him—quicker than I've seen her since arriving home.

"No! There're other movies on that! Don't!"

She throws herself at the tape, but Mark shoves her to the floor.

"Hey!" I yell, going for her.

Mark storms down the hall.

"Are you all right?" I ask my mother.

I help her stand up. A withered magnolia. "You needed to see," she whispers. "Your father's innocent. If you're not going to leave, July, you need to see it."

What I do is leave Kathy standing there and run after Mark. He's gone into the kitchen and by the time I find him, he's already ripped the film from the tape and shoved it down the garbage disposal. I hear the end of the film grinding into blade.

"Why would you do that?" I yell.

But Mark shuts off the disposal, tosses the empty tape in the trash, and hurries out the front door to the porch without responding.

I'm not letting him off that easy. I follow.

"Mark. What the fuck? Explain that."

When I step outside, he has his back to me and is leaning against a foundation pole as he stares out at the lake full of people. There are ricochets of sparks overhead: red and green embers over the trees in the distance, but my attention is on my middle brother. On unearthing this secret he has kept inside for so very long.

"I don't have to explain shit to you," my brother growls. "Get lost."

But I can't. Something in my brain flipped when I saw Laurel Dillon's face on that projector screen. I'm thinking about how Mark melted down when we found out May and the others were all dead, how he repeatedly brushed aside any mention of Laurel that last summer.

"You had a relationship with her." I think I guessed this even back then, but I believe it more than ever now.

The pure hate he offers me when he opens his eyes is enough to undo me. After all this time, I finally understand him better. Back then, Mark had been mourning not one, but two people he loved.

"How long did it go on for?" I ask. "I assume it was behind Nicole's back."

"It wasn't like that." He steadies his breath. "I barely touched her. She was my math tutor junior year. I used to go to her house. I didn't . . . I didn't want anyone to think . . ."

I thought about who I'd learned Laurel Dillon was over the course of the investigation into her disappearance. Shy. An outcast. A conservative Christian dressed in long dresses and frumpy sweaters. "You were embarrassed by her. You were scared what people would think, so you kept your relationship a secret. How very on brand for you."

"Fuck off. It wasn't like I was the only guy she was seeing. There was some older guy she was whoring herself out to that spring. Probably Harry."

I'm angry for Laurel, but I'm also sorry for Mark. The heated words he's speaking don't match the torment in his eyes. A man broken. That is who I see standing before me.

"Why didn't you tell the cops that you knew her, or about the older guy?"

"Why do you think?" Mark comes to loom over me. "And don't you dare tell anyone about this or I'll kill you. Do you understand me? I will finish what Harry started."

I'm shaking at the venom emanating off him. I've never been scared of Mark before. But in this moment, by the unhinged look on his face, I have every faith in the world that my brother means it. Like father, like son? Or maybe just son all along? I shake my head. Am I actually considering Mark as a suspect now, too? Even worse, am I starting to legitimately entertain Deck's theory that Harry might be innocent?

I don't try to follow Mark as he steps off the porch, descends the hill's stairs, and walks out to the end of the dock. Instead, I study his silhouette from here: the lake rippling as boats drift across the current before him, a curtain of golden light exploding over his head with the end of the fireworks show.

My mind is racing. Mark was the closest of us siblings to May. He had a secret relationship with Laurel Dillon. Kelly Anders was his girlfriend's best friend. He hated me. Mark is connected to all four victims in some way. So is it crazy to ask what if?

CHAPTER

14

Now

A STONE OF DREAD sits in my stomach in the weeks following. I never should have come back to Pacific. There are too many secrets whirling around me, too many confessions from my surviving siblings and the people around us that are setting my very knowing off kilter. I don't want to deal with any of it. I half consider throwing my bags in my car and making for Nashville in the middle of the night, damn it all to hell.

The only thing holding me here is Deck. I stare at his face over our morning coffee, him laughing and teasing April and Auggie, so much more himself than I've seen him in years. If I leave him behind, it will break him. The pressure of being the one thing standing between someone and their sobriety is a lot to shoulder.

Auggie seems to sense this shift in me, despite the fact that I don't tell him about the Mark/Dillon video, because he's suddenly more attentive. Asking me to come along on simple errands about town—the grocery store, takeout, a random wedding pickup. I feel his eyes on me like an overcautious shepherd. He's waiting for me to bolt.

Maybe I'm waiting for the same thing, when April's big senior fundraiser arrives. Every upcoming senior is expected to have a family member working the event. I don't know how that job got relegated to me over one of our three perfectly capable brothers, but I want to cry sexism. The dread at having to socialize with this entire town is only amplified when I pull up to the massive iron gate outside the allotted venue. Auggie warned me beforehand, but I'm still not quite prepared. This is Colton Davidson's house.

The would-be mayor apparently has a younger cousin in April's grade and has nobly offered his home to host the event. Convenient, considering over half of Pacific and Hazel are going to be in attendance. I expect a campaign speech at any moment.

"Oh my God, July," Nicole Sheridan—scratch that—Nicole Davidson greets me at the door, her smile fake and bright. At least her husband is nowhere in sight. "How are you? It's *so* nice to see you."

Mark's high school girlfriend is hardly recognizable through all the Botox, hair dye, and spray tan she's subjected her body to over the last nine years. Granted, I might be a little jaded. I should probably make an effort, since her best friend was one of Harry's victims, but we'd never liked each other. Not to mention, she dumped Mark the day after Harry was arrested.

"I'm freaking great," I say, meeting her mock cheeriness. "How're you?"

My tone goes over her head. "Just great. It's so good of you to come out and support April. It must be so nice to have you at one of these things after you've been absent for so long."

I bite my tongue. Maybe not totally over her head after all. "Where do you want me?"

Nicole leads me to the row of tables where baskets and donated goods from vendors across the county are being displayed. Busybody Pacific moms flutter about, arranging items and laying down bidding clipboards while spreading town gossip. I'm mercifully handed a roll of raffle tickets and left to my own devices. I begin setting up baskets in their proper numeral places, keeping my head down. I'm messing with a ribbon on one of Hazel's local boutique's offerings, when a voice comes beside me.

"What a surprise, your bow-tying skills are shit."

I smile before I straighten up. I'd know that voice anywhere.

"Zoey."

My old friend is smirking like a fiend, in tight jeans and a hell of a lot of dangly jewelry. Her profession could be either hippie or rock band groupie, and it's exactly how I pictured she'd look after all these years.

"Long time, no talk, Weaver."

I'm relieved there's no animosity in her tone. We lost touch like all the rest when I left town. I didn't have it in me to be a friend back then, and at the time, Zoey was a reminder of that day at the cabin.

I offer her a once-over. "Of all the people I expected to stay in this town, you weren't one of them."

"Yeah, well, technically I'm in Montgomery now."

"Wow, you made it over two whole town lines."

She narrows her eyes. "Least I kept my own damn name."

Apparently she knows about my dual identities, too. Jesus, does everyone in this town? "Touché."

We both grin. Warmer people might have hugged.

"So, what are you doing here?" I ask. "Because you sure aren't old enough to have a teenage kid."

Zoey laughs. "I'm one of the donors. I own a magic/tarot card shop over in Montgomery. I've got a basket for a psychic reading session around here somewhere."

"You're not serious?" Because that both weirdly fits and seems nothing like the Zoey I remember.

Zoey grins mischievously. "Five bucks a palm reading. I'll even communicate with your dead for a solid hundred and fifty bucks an hour if you want."

"No, thanks. I rather like my dead where they are."

Zoey was raised by two scam artists. She's clearly taken up the helm.

"Hey, ladies," says another volunteer coming up to us, probably someone's mom. "Nicole says there's a gentleman out back who needs help unloading a donation. Could y'all help us out?"

Zoey and I follow the woman through the foyer to the kitchen, then out what is undoubtedly the servants' entrance. The yard is vast and wide, with at least five acres of flat mowed land. Cars and catering vehicles line the massive driveway, but there is one in particular I notice that is backing up toward us on the stairs—a familiar navy Dodge pickup. I groan.

"Problem?" Zoey asks.

Gabe hops out of the driver's seat, and rounds the truck to pull the bed latch down. I catch sight of a gorgeous resin-soaked kitchen table with a strike of white through the center tied up in moving blankets and bungee cords.

Zoey is of course unaffected at my side. My history with Gabe isn't common knowledge, not even to my former best friend. I kept a lot of secrets that summer, him being the biggest one.

"Nope," I say and descend the stairs with the other volunteers.

Gabe undoes the bungee cords without looking at the four of us and drags the table back, careful to keep the moving blanket between the wood and the bed's ridges.

"Where's it going?" he asks us.

"We have a line of larger items set up on the floor in the main foyer. We'll carry it there," says the volunteer who recruited us.

It's only after the others grab the front corners and I take the final end from his hands that Gabe realizes it's me. He's six inches from me and his face goes stony.

"We need you to grab the other end," the woman calls to Gabe, and the moment's broken. He's hurrying to get the final corner.

It takes all six of us to carry the damn table in through the house and I'm silently cursing April the entire way.

As if summoned by the thought, my little sister is standing in the foyer with a clipboard and a pen in her hair. She lights up when she sees the table. "That's going over here."

She gestures to a space in a line of auction items: chairs, a dresser, a shoddy painting of a boy in a sailor hat on a boat. Our party places the table down and are then forced to pivot it to April's specifications.

"It looks so good," April says running her hand over the wood.

The other volunteers and Zoey are already moving on to the next project, leaving the two of us with Gabe.

"You had to pick the biggest piece of furniture in the shop, didn't you?" I say to my sister.

April ignores me and turns too big of a smile on Gabe. "Thanks for this. I'm going to put your business cards on the corner of it so people can take them."

"No problem," Gabe says, though his eyes are half on me. "I'm going to head out, then."

But my little sister frowns. "You can't leave. All of the donors are supposed to stick around and talk to the guests in case they have questions."

Gabe stares around at the dressed-up booster moms, the massive mansion we are currently standing in, then me. He's in jeans and a T-shirt. "It's not really my scene, April."

"Please, Gabe," April pouts. "We'll get a higher bid on the table if you're around to answer questions about how you made it."

Gabe exhales and looks to me. "Only if you don't care that I'm here."

"Why would I?" I say, then turn on my heels and am gone.

I have no intention of saying another damn word to Gabe for the rest of the night.

The place is beginning to fill with guests, the last of the tricky tray baskets and auction pieces set up. I feel as if I am standing in a swarm of bees. There's so much buzzing and everyone's face is indistinguishable from the rest. Auggie and Bridget have arrived and are talking with April in the foyer; Zoey has taken up residence in front of what I presume to be her basket, smiling and feigning interest in the palms of passersby; Nicole and other snotty women I recognize from high school are touring people about the room; Deck's burst through the door and saluted me before making for the buffet line with a couple of guys from his old gamer crew.

I still can't believe how accepting this town is of April and Auggie's remained presence within it—April specifically. There are certainly glares and whispers, but April seems entirely oblivious to them. She's popular in school, from everything Auggie's told me. Pitied for May's murder rather than ostracized for being the murderer's daughter. I envy her ease as she flits about the room.

I've contented myself to hide from raffle ticket duty on the landing of the second floor and people-watch. I don't feel much like talking right now. Mark is getting in for the weekend tomorrow morning and I don't know how I'm going to face him after the Fourth. Besides, I always find it better to remove myself from a scene where there are trays of Champagne every few feet. I realize I should probably be checking on Deck for the same reason, but my line of sight is cut off by the figure that comes up beside me.

"Well, hello, July Weaver."

"That greeting isn't any more cute than it was in high school."

Colton leans over the railing to watch the guests below. "Is there a reason you're standing on the second level of my house all by yourself?"

"Easy," I say, my eyes going to where Nicole is handing out flutes of Champagne to people. "I'm hiding from your bitch of a wife."

"Watch it," he warns, but there is no bite to his tone, only amusement. "You of all people should be more sympathetic to her. Kelly was her friend, after all."

I roll my eyes. Does she know that her husband was screwing that supposed friend the summer she was murdered? "You and I both know that Nicole was more concerned about the attention she got for being the dead girl's friend than the actual dead girl."

"Spoken like the daughter of a killer."

I want to punch him, July from back then would, but I clench my fists at my sides instead. God, growing up is difficult.

Colton's eyes are lit overlooking his crowd. "Now, you wouldn't want to make a scene and embarrass April, would you? I know how worried she was about all of her family members being here tonight."

"And how would you begin to know that?"

He smiles. "She told me. Don't you know? She's my cousin Connor's girlfriend. She's over here practically every day. Her and I are quite close, actually."

I know what "close" means to a guy like Colton. My body goes stiff. I am a rabbit he's just snared. How am I only learning this now? Auggie hasn't said a damn word.

"Hmm," Colton says, when he takes in my surprised expression. "So, what April told me the other day is true. You two aren't on speaking terms."

"Stay away from my sister." There is venom in my tone, determination.

He only smiles wider. "Don't worry. You continue to keep our old *friendship* under wraps from the public, and I'll be sure to take good care of April."

"If you so much as touch her, I swear to God . . ."

"You'll what?" he cuts me off. "Tell the cops on me? Go right ahead, *Jules Thomas*. Who you think they'll believe?"

I should tell him off, threaten to out his past relationships with both Kelly and me to his precious voters, but there's a sick part of me that cares too much about my career. I can't bear for him to jeopardize it.

A group of high schoolers take to the makeshift stage in the foyer to announce the tricky tray. They call out to Colton and Nicole to come up and introduce the event.

"Well, I better go. This is my show after all." He has the gall to lean over and place a hand in the center of my back. "See you around, Weaver."

I flinch as he descends the stairs to take the stage with his Barbie doll wife. A booming diatribe about being generous to our senior class follows, but it's a blatant campaign speech.

I'm grinding my teeth and moving back through the crowd on the main level, when Auggie catches my eye. He's leaning against a wall with Bridget, having witnessed Colton and my exchange, based on his scowl. I shake my head, too mad, and not needing him to make the situation worse than it already is. As April's closest confidant, I'm sure he knows all about April's relationship with the Davidson family and has purposely chosen not to tell me. I'll grill him for it later.

I'm looking everywhere for April, only to eventually give up and ask one of the preteens in the kitchen if they've seen her. The kid gives a noncommittal shrug, saying they think she went outside with some older guy. I tear out the door because Colton's no longer on stage.

But it isn't Colton I find sitting with my sister on the edge of that damn Dodge navy truck, but Gabe. Even more distressing is the fact that Gabe has April's hand in his own and she's wincing at his touch.

"What do you think you're doing?" I yell at him, storming to a stop before them.

"Relax, July." Gabe doesn't even look up from April's hand, which I realize he's wrapping in a bandage.

April flinches as Gabe turns the gauze a final time around her palm and tapes it in place.

"What happened?" I ask. "April," I demand again when neither gives me an answer.

"Chill," my sister says annoyed. "I burned my hand on a burner under a buffet tray. Gabe had a first aid kit in his truck."

Gabe releases her hand. "Good as new." He collects the bandage scraps and tucks them into the little blue bag I've just noticed behind them.

"April, go back inside," I say shoving my pointer finger in the direction of the house.

"Since when do you give me orders?" she asks.

"Now."

My look must sting, because she gets down and grumbles, "You suck," before heading in.

I grind my teeth. I will deal with her and her idiotic connection to the Davidson family later. I wait until she's disappeared inside before I whip back on Gabe. The driveway is abandoned other than the two of us; everyone is in the house watching the tricky tray raffle.

Gabe zips the first aid bag and hops down from the tailgate. "I was only trying to help."

"Yeah, well you tend to do a lot of that when it comes to Weaver women, don't you? What is it? The whole minor with a fucked-up family thing turn you on?"

Gabe squares his jaw, mad in a way I've never seen him. He shuts the tailgate and turns his back on me, heading for the driver's side door.

"What're you doing?" I bark.

"I'm done with this conversation," he says.

"So you're just gonna walk away?"

He stops, looks at me, unbelieving. "What do you want from me? When you're ready to have an adult conversation about everything that happened, you know where to find me."

He climbs into the truck and I go up to the open window. "Why would I need to? You made everything pretty clear when you were slamming the door in my face that night."

Gabe stares out at me. "You don't know the first thing about what happened between us back then."

I'm dumbfounded, but he doesn't give me time to respond. He's already driving away, leaving a trail of dust in his wake. I'm atomic.

As I march up the steps, I intend to get my keys and drive the hell away from this place, but Zoey catches me at the door. "Not to be a buzzkill on whatever that was, but your brother's looking for you."

"Which one?" I ask tiredly.

"The linebacker. Though I think it's the younger one you should be concerned about. They're over there."

Zoey points around the side of the mansion to where Pacific Lake cuts into the view over the hill. I catch sight of two figures stumbling in my direction. It looks like one is supporting the other.

Oh, God. I look to Zoey. She knows without me having to say a word and hands me my purse.

"Don't be a stranger," she says. "Come by the shop. I'll tell your fake fortune for free."

"Thanks, Z."

When I meet my brothers halfway down the drive, Auggie's holding up Deck. I don't need to be told what's happened. One look at Deck's drooping limps and relaxed expression and I know he's drunk.

"How much has he had?" I ask.

"Too much," remarks Auggie. His teeth are ground and he's clearly pissed off. "He made a whole scene. Got up on the stage and took the microphone."

"Oh God."

Deck waves his hands. "I just wanted to thank our lovely host, that butthole Davidson, for his hospitality and prickish good looks. I wished him luck in the upcoming election and his eventual trip to hell."

"He needs to go home," Auggie snaps. "Now. So I can do damage control. April's locked herself in the upstairs bathroom, mortified."

"Give him to me," I say, and take Deck's weight half onto my own.

"I can't believe you did this," Auggie hisses at our brother. Deck looks stricken. "I wasn't trying to . . ."

"He can't help it, Auggie," I say, defensive. Both for Deck and myself. "We should have known this was a bad idea, with the booze everywhere."

Auggie rubs his fingers over the bridge of his nose. "Whatever. Please just take him home. I have to go deal with April now."

I hoist Deck in the direction of my car. He's so drunk, I have to open the door for him and buckle his seatbelt. The smell of his breath makes my stomach roll and I push back the memories of my own similar fuckups.

"Man, I didn't want Auggie mad at me," he moans.

"Then you shouldn't have drank, moron," I snap at him, now in my own seat.

"I didn't," Deck whispers, his eyes already closing as I'm reversing out of the driveway down the hill. "I swear I didn't."

I don't respond. By the time we're winding along the main road that hugs the lake, he's already snoring.

15

Then

D ANTE WROTE THAT the path to paradise begins in hell. I wondered into the late hours of July 4 and the early hours of July 5 if that was true. Could life for my family ever go back to normal, let alone get better, with this perpetual void where May had once been? Would closure at this point change anything?

Divers dragged the lake first thing that morning. I didn't know if they would find May, but something told me that we were nearing the end of this thing, one way or the other. May Weaver. Laurel Dillon. Kelly Anders. The killer from the cabin. The gutted dear. *I am the king.* Whatever the police did or didn't find, it was all about to end.

I was one of the last of the Weaver tribe to arrive home, around one in the morning. My parents had heard the initial screams on the lake with April, and turned back for home; they'd known before any of us about the body. Harry would have run straight for the beach after dropping Kathy and April off, but by then, Kelly Anders was already halfway to the morgue. Mark was on a beach at the time, watching the fireworks with Nicole and his friends, when he heard the news. Auggie had been with Dan. When he appeared through the front door a little while after I did, he merely sat down beside me at the dining room table with his head in his hands. April had long since cried herself to sleep on my lap.

We Weavers knew our roles well after the last five months. All we could do was sit, worry, and wait. Everyone had entirely forgotten about Deck until he emerged from his room at eight AM to find us all congregated around the table, oblivious to the reason behind our silent vigil.

Detective Rafael arrived at the house a little after ten. When Harry led him into the dining room, he hesitated as he stared into the five faces of May Weaver's siblings.

Auggie and Mark were at the back window, the two of them having moved there to pace several hours ago. Deck fidgeted in his chair on the other side of Harry and Kathy, and April nestled into my shoulder like an infant. I should have given more thought about whether she should hear what was coming, but I was so wrapped up in my own anticipation, I didn't spare a second thought for her. But I guess, in fairness, neither did anyone else in that room.

Harry took Kathy's hand at the head of the table. "You can say whatever you've come here to say in front of them, too," he said. "It concerns their sister."

Some would construe this decision as irresponsible on the part of my father. But what I saw was acknowledgement of the fact that Auggie, Mark, and I had stopped being children the moment May disappeared last spring. Deck too was growing up too fast as a result.

Rafael pulled at the knot in his tie. I'd seen this man on some of his harder days and this topped them all. He looked like he hadn't slept in weeks, not hours, his suit rumpled and his hair out of place from its usual gelled comb-over.

He cleared his throat. "I think y'all should sit."

"We're fine where we are," said Auggie as Kathy mumbled, "Detective, please."

Rafael cleared his throat. He stared down at his shoes. I knew what he was about to say before he said it, and that was when I decided—hell must be an existence that some people never get to crawl their way out of.

"The body we found belongs to Kelly Anders. I know you're aware of her, as she was Mark's friend." My middle brother didn't so much as flinch. "She was last seen at a party two nights ago. She was supposed to drive up to Charlotte to visit her grandparents right after, but never showed."

"With all due respect, detective," Harry says. "The lake. Were any other bodies pulled out of the lake?"

"The divers are still out there searching, and likely will be for the remainder of the day and into the weekend," Rafael said. "They won't stop until we've dredged the whole thing."

"Did you find them or not?" Mark spat.

He stared at the detective like he wanted to lunge over the table and seize him by the collar. I knew the feeling.

Rafael cleared his throat again. "We found Laurel Dillon's body near Cypress Point an hour ago. She was weighed down with rocks the same way Kelly Anders's was." He looked directly to my parents, pure deflation on his face. "We found May about fifty feet from her."

Kathy let out a fierce guttural screech, the sound only a parent who loses a child can make. April looked at me, confused. "What does that mean? They found her?"

I couldn't answer my little sister, despite clutching her to my chest. I felt completely off kilter, dizzy. April must have caught on because she started sobbing again. There was shouting all around me. I vaguely registered Deck smashing a chair across the room, Auggie tackling him to the floor to restrain him, our youngest brother flailing. Mark left the room, not a word or look to the rest of our aching family. Harry and I were the only ones left perfectly still. Our eyes locked across the table.

All my life, I'd never seen my father cry. Maybe I was expecting it in this moment—at least for him to shed a tear for his youngest child, the one he'd been pursuing across the country over the last few months. But Harry sat stone-faced, unsurprised, unaffected. He wasn't even comforting his rocking wife, their hands having now dislodged themselves from one another. I never hated him more; I never understood him quite so much. My face was dry.

"I'm sorry," Rafael told us. "This was not the news I was hoping to bring y'all, but I hope it brings you some closure to know that she's found."

"And what about him?" I whispered.

"Pardon?" Rafael asked me.

I leveled my gaze up to the detective. I'm sure my expression was ice. "Are you going to find him now? The monster who did this? The 'king'?"

His eyes were sincere. "We're working on that now, Ms. July. I swear to you we are." He turned to Harry. "I realize this is a difficult time, but I'm going to need you to come on down to the morgue and identify the body when you're ready, Harold."

My father stood. "I'm ready now."

"Harry," my mother begged—a desperate plea not to leave.

All he did was offer her shaking form a solitary look as he circled her chair and followed the detective out without another word to us. I heard the front door slam, and we were alone—what was left of the Weaver clan reduced to shattered pieces. Nobody moved for a long time. April and Deck simply wept while Kathy shook her head and Auggie and I waited. We would fall apart in private once the others were put back together. That was how the two of us worked. Auggie had Deck sitting up now, Auggie's arms vining around our brother's torso.

It was Kathy who eventually broke the silence, her face linen but placid now; she scraped back her chair. Her attention was on Auggie and Deck, glaring with an intensity I'd never seen from her. Almost volatile.

"Kathy," I said.

Her eyes flicked to April and me.

"I need to lie down," she said.

April hopped up from my lap, wiping her cheeks with her palm. "I want to come with you."

"No," Kathy snapped. "Stay with your sister."

The little girl—a dam about to burst.

"Come here, Apes," Auggie urged, trying for damage control. He held out the newly freed arm that wasn't hooked around Deck.

April ran to our oldest brother and burrowed into his shoulder, a renewed sob. Deck, in turn, leaned over and enveloped her in a hug too. Auggie was so busy comforting the younger two in their pile on the floor that he didn't see it. The way Kathy stared at their cluster of three. The line in her jaw twitched once, with deep hate. It scared me.

"Kathy," I said. "I think you *should* lie down."

My mother jolted like I'd struck her. Whatever private moment I'd witnessed was gone.

"Please," I added.

I didn't need her to make the situation worse. She would have some form of a meltdown over this. I knew she would. I was simply attempting to delay the inevitable until Auggie and I could soothe our siblings.

Kathy seemed to sense that too. She left the room. Based on the creak of the door above us a few seconds later, she reached her bedroom.

"Someone needs to find Mark," Auggie said.

I turned to him, studied our youngest two siblings in his arms. The thought "youngest *two*" was a needle thread through my heart.

"Go," Deck said, still clutching April as hard as she was him. "He needs someone to check on him, too."

I somewhat doubted that Mark would want *me* to be the one to do that, but I searched the house for him anyway. I ended up outside the greenhouse. It was the only place he could be. The manor was empty, the boat still buoyed to the dock, Auggie's truck in the driveway. Unless Mark had gone for a walk or a swim, he had to be in here. Which was odd. I couldn't remember the last time I'd seen Mark Weaver step foot in Harry's greenhouse, if he ever had at all.

But I could see his form rippling through the transparent walls. I batted a regal fritillary butterfly out of my face as I entered. Mark had his back to me and was gazing down at the koi fountain.

"Mark."

My brother didn't move.

"She loved these koi so much," he said without looking up. "I used to find her out here at five AM before practice most mornings. She'd be sitting on the edge, with her feet in the fountain. Let the little fuckers nip at her toes as she threw them crumbs."

"I didn't know that."

I stopped beside him and looked down, too. The koi all congregated before us, one massive, shifting school of yellow, orange, white, brown, and black. It was as if by invoking the name of their favorite feeder, they were drawn to us, expecting their next meal. I caught sight of Melville's tail near the bottom, then his full form emerged from beneath several smaller yellow koi. He looked the worse for wear. Sometime in the months since I'd last really looked at him, the scales of his back right side had been scraped off. It left the snow-white fish with an angry pink gash that ran up his back fin. He must have been in a fight.

Mark's face was blank when I looked up, but I knew my middle brother. This was how he handled everything. The *Are you okay?* was not going to work with him. We were ironically too similar in that regard, too blunt. So I settled for, "Did you think she'd be dead?"

His eyes remained on the fish. "What does it matter?"

"I did. I knew she was dead the moment Laurel Dillon was reported missing."

Mark inhaled sharply. "Couldn't they have just stayed fucking gone?"

He turned from me and whipped open the greenhouse door, not bothering to stop two butterflies from escaping, and slammed it behind him, severing a monarch in half.

I stared down at the koi, wondering if I could ever look at them again without splintering, now that I knew their connection to May. That thought was halted by a cry. Mark screamed my name from the lawn.

Through the glass, I saw him sprinting through the back door into the kitchen, having seen or heard something within. I ran after him, nearly tearing the rusty hinges off the greenhouse door in my haste. Across the lawn. Tearing open the same door Mark just slammed.

I heard the shrieking first. Guttural. Manic. Familiar. But so much worse than ever before.

Kathy.

She was at the kitchen sink, whipping Harry's shotgun around the room, first aiming at Auggie, then Mark. A terrified April was plopped down on the basin mat beside her, screaming. Kathy looked as if she was attempting to shield the little girl from my brothers, her expression filled with abhorrence, but her eyes surprisingly clear. Both boys had their hands in the air, shaking as they stared down our mother—Auggie ten feet from her on the other side of the island and Mark a few inches in front of me by the table. I could see the piss running down the inner seam of Mark's leg.

Kathy yelled. Ordering her two sons to back up. Toggling the gun between them as targets, her finger dangerously close to the trigger. One slip and that would be it. My body froze. *Oh my God.*

"Kathy, please," Auggie begged. "Put down the gun."

He darted a worried glance at April. He was clearly thinking the same thing I was—that our mother had finally lost it. That one trip, and it would be a second baby sister bleeding out on the floor.

"Don't you dare look at her!" Kathy yelled. "I know the truth! One of you is the devil!" She moved the gun between her two eldest sons, but favored Auggie twice as much. Apparently, even crazy, our mother was able to properly risk assess. "Don't come any closer!"

I realized that I had to move. To somehow break whatever psychotic delusion she was currently inhabiting.

"Mama," I said, stepping around Mark like a timid cat, but pointedly blocking his body with my own. If Kathy was going to shoot anyone, it was going to be me or Auggie. Not one of our younger siblings. "Mama, it's me."

"July, be careful," Auggie warned.

I could see him stiffen out of the corner of my eye, like he was ready to pounce on our mother if she redirected the gun at me. I held a hand out behind me to stay him. Then I took another step forward, now in the center of the triangle made up by my two brothers and Kathy and April. Our mother's attention fixed on me. But I could tell that she was less alarmed by me than the two boys. Apparently, I wasn't in suspicion of being possessed by Satan. Good. I could work with that.

"You don't understand," Kathy muttered, the barrel of the gun now aimed at Auggie.

"I do. I do understand, Mama. You're just trying to protect everyone."

I took another step forward and she turned the gun on me.

"July," Auggie hissed.

"Shut up, Auggie," I said calmly. I tried to keep my face even, although my hands were shaking. "It's fine. We're fine, right, Mama? You won't shoot me. I'm your oldest daughter. Your first baby girl."

Kathy's brows furrowed, but I could tell that resonated with her. I stopped a foot away, the shiny black barrel aimed right at my face. I could feel my knees trembling, fighting every instinct of survival to cut and run. Maybe everything was leading up to this moment: my redemption. I couldn't save May, but I would save April.

"Mama, look at April. You're scaring her."

Kathy's eyes darted down to her youngest child. "I'm protecting her. I have to protect her better."

"Mama, please," April whined.

I gave April a warning look and she hushed.

"I understand," I said to our mother. "But I don't think April is safe in a room with a gun, now, is she? I think it would be better if we let her go upstairs and sit with Deck. She'll be safest there. Then the rest of us can figure this out. You don't want her to get shot trying to protect her, right?"

Kathy stared again at April, then the shotgun. She frowned. "April, go upstairs."

April sprung up, but hesitated to leave Kathy's side. I could see that she was scared to be followed by the gun.

"Move, April!" Mark ordered.

The shotgun turned back in his direction. Mark stilled again. His hands trembled midair.

"Keep the gun on me," I begged Kathy, a little too frantic. "Until April's out of the room, keep the gun on me. No one will move other than her. I promise no one will move except for April, who will leave the room."

The barrel winked at me again.

"Now, April," Auggie ordered.

And the little girl took off, sprinting out of Kathy's grasp and past Auggie. She rushed through the kitchen door, safely out of the line of fire. I couldn't help but sigh with relief. She'd go find Deck and they'd call the cops. I just had to buy the rest of us time until they got here.

"Now," I said to our mother. "I need you to let Mark go next. Okay?"

But my brothers had other plans. They must have communicated with a football signal or something behind my back, because all at once they were charging for our mother. Everything happened fast. Kathy screamed and flipped the gun. My brothers were on her then. I heard the shot. Mark seized the gun and skidded it across the floor, while Auggie pinned Kathy down, yanking her hands behind her back, as she howled and writhed beneath him. But our frail mother was no match for Auggie's might. I ran for the discarded shotgun and cleared the chamber, pocketing the rounds just in case Kathy somehow freed herself and made for the weapon again.

"You don't understand," Kathy screamed beneath Auggie. "You don't understand. He's the devil!"

"Auggie," Mark said in horror.

Then I saw what Mark had. The smudge of red that was rapidly growing on Auggie's shoulder, vibrant as a poppy bloom. It seeped through his T-shirt, then picked up momentum. Blood. So much blood.

"She shot you," I said, scrambling to my knees before him to get a better look.

"I think you better take her, Mark," Auggie said. "I might pass out in a minute."

My brothers switched positions, Kathy still muttering nonsensically. The blood was running down Auggie's arm and shirt as he leaned against a kitchen cabinet. I yanked dish towels from the oven and went to press them into his shoulder.

Auggie's hand came over mine. "I'm okay, July." His eyes were shiny. "Really."

"You're not okay," I snapped. "You've been shot."

The dish towels were soaking through too fast. Way too fast.

"The cops are coming!" I heard Deck yell from the doorway behind us. "Ambulance, too. They're five minutes out!"

"Come on, Auggie, I need you to hang in here with me," I said to him.

Auggie nodded, like he had any control whatsoever whether he bled out before then or not.

"Son of a bitch," Mark said.

We all heard the long-looped crackles of the sirens up the road. They grew preciously louder with every second.

"You're going to be okay," I told Auggie.

But he likely hadn't heard me. As I said the words, his eyes rolled back and he fainted.

*   *   *

It's easier to list what transpired over the next several hours—it's how the events blurred in my head. The police arrived and took Kathy away. Auggie was rushed into the ambulance and the rest of us Weavers piled into the back of his truck and tailed the emergency vehicle to Hazel General. Sometime after, Kathy was forcefully committed to the psychiatric floor, under around-the-clock supervision. Auggie went into surgery, and the four of us waited in the ER, so broken there was no point in speaking. A cheap clock ticked on the wall overhead and the paisley fabric chairs we sat in were fraying and smelled of mold. I closed my eyes, and for the first time in my life, prayed. I prayed for Auggie to be all right. I prayed for all of us to be all right. What I got instead was Harry.

My father hurried down the hall, cursing at any medical staff that managed to get in his way. When he spotted us, he stopped. Perhaps it was a shock to see his four unharmed children sitting there, two covered in the missing fifth's blood. We looked even worse than we had this morning. So did he.

"Go home," he ordered.

"But Auggie's still in surgery," Deck said.

"No, he's not," said Harry. "I just spoke with his doctor. He's in recovery. He's going to be okay. Go home."

"We want to see him," said Deck.

"He's sleeping," Harry said dismissively.

"We don't give a shit," said Mark.

I tugged on April's hand and woke her from where she had curled up on one of the couches.

"When are we going home?" she yawned.

"Now, sweetheart," I muttered. I turned back to our father. "After we see Auggie."

It wasn't a question.

Harry's jaw twitched, but he went back through the swinging doors. We all took our cue to follow behind. I caught up to my father's side and held him back while my siblings moved down the hall toward the room he pointed to.

"We need to talk about what's going to happen to her," I said.

"I have bigger problems to worry about than your mother right now," Harry said.

"Like what?" I snapped. "She just nearly murdered your first-born son."

Harry sighed, entirely drained. "Like rooting out who murdered your sister."

"God, do you see where we are?"

"I am very aware. Thank you."

I'd never been so furious in my life, which was saying something. "You don't even care that your wife had a psychotic break, do you? What, are you going to check her out again, pour a couple pills down her throat, and pop her in a rocking chair in front of Father Time again? We all just hope her schizophrenia goes away?"

There was a hard look on his face. "Your mother will recover. She always pulls herself out of these things."

I studied him, really studied the way he wouldn't meet my eyes. And then I knew. "You haven't been making her take her pills since you got home, have you? That's why this happened."

I can't believe I didn't notice it before. Sure, in the last few weeks Kathy had seemed more subdued, but she'd also withdrawn from the rest of us, more than I'd seen in a long time. Only there was so much going on, I hadn't been paying attention to her. How her delusions must have been building over the last few months, unchecked.

"I can usually manage her without them," Harry said. "Finding out your sister was dead was an extenuating circumstance."

I couldn't believe him. "What is wrong with you? In the midst of everything else going on, you thought that you could single-handedly manage what doctors and modern medicine have difficulty doing? All you did was hurt her by not getting her the help she needed. Look at us!"

Harry ground his jaw, that stubborn streak I hated. "I'm not in the mood for your reprimand, Livewire."

"Well, I'm not in the mood for the pathetic excuse for a father I have, yet here we are!"

Harry slapped me, hard. I didn't see it coming, and I fell, my back hitting the wall. I raised my hand to my stinging cheek. Tears formed in my eyes, but not in sadness. I was surprised. I was terrified, staring up at my father looming over me.

If there was violence in Harry's eyes, his skin flushed, or his fists balled in fury, it would have scared me less. But the man looking down at me was perfectly tranquil. Numb to the fact that he just hit his favorite child. Indifferent.

"Mind your place, Livewire."

And then he left me there on the floor. I forced myself to my feet, then followed him into Auggie's room.

My oldest brother was asleep in the hospital bed, our other three siblings congregated around him in silent vigil. Auggie had a bandage on his shoulder, an IV sticking out of his wrist, but otherwise looked no worse than I had seen him earlier. His color was chalky, but I guessed that was understandable considering he'd been shot.

"All right. You've seen him. Now run along home," Harry said.

I stiffened at his perfectly controlled voice. He wouldn't look at me.

"What about you?" asked Mark.

"I'm staying overnight," Harry said. "I'll be back at the house in the morning."

So we left Auggie to his drug-laced sleep, with the man who was supposed to be our patriarch. The four of us headed home.

I brought April to bed. It took a while for her to calm down, but the exhaustion of the day eventually won out and her gentle snoring let me know it was safe to leave her. I checked on Deck on the way by, but he was absorbed in his video game. Mark was the true surprise. I found him on his knees on the kitchen floor, meticulously scrubbing away Auggie's blood from the tiles, his pants drenched in it.

"You want help with that?" I asked.

"No," he said without turning his back from me. "I don't mind blood."

I thought about protesting, but I did mind blood, and the thought of being covered in any more of Auggie's today was enough to send me for the door. I stepped out into the night, and was pushed by the wind down to the lake. I stopped at the end of the dock, my feet an inch from the edge.

I just needed a minute of peace. Just one singular minute to end today, where someone wasn't dead or dying or losing their minds or threatening to kill someone else. Just a singular minute to stare out at the lake, its satin blue rivulets wrinkling across one another, the dark pines cutting above the surface's reflection of the moon. The quiet. I closed my eyes and listened to the gentle crash against the rocks. But even this feeling, along with the smell of mud and muck, took on a new, haunted flare. May had been left to rot under this lake, had possibly been murdered in it as well. It was no longer my refuge. It never could be again. The smell of it became her rotting flesh.

"July."

I turned, thinking the shadow descending the hill's shaky stairs was Auggie. But the form was wrong—slimmer, shorter.

Gabe.

Concern lined his face as he strode down the dock. I don't know why I reacted the way I did. I could blame it on the shock, the trauma of the day. But I think that was all just as excuse to run to him.

He caught me as I flung my arms around him. Desperate. He flinched only momentarily, but then gave into the embrace.

"I just heard about May, and then your mama . . . that she'd shot one of her kids," he said breathlessly. "I didn't know if it was you."

I pulled back and stared up at him. Maybe Kathy had gotten it wrong about which of her children was the possessed one. Because in an instant, I lost all agency over my own body. I kissed Gabe, and even more surprising, he kissed me back. It was heated, but brief. He broke it off as fast as I started it, but the damage was done.

I only wished I'd known then that someone else was standing at the top of the hill, watching our exchange. Maybe then I could have prevented everything. Maybe then, that final night of the attack wouldn't have happened.

16

Then

THE FLOWERS WERE pink. May hated pink. She said it was a girly color, preferring green, blue, brown, black, anything that wasn't remotely feminine. She was a lot like me at that age. She wanted to be a boy, to fit in seamlessly with our clan of brothers. But apparently the funeral florist hadn't gotten that memo. They heard eight-year-old dead girl and provided pink everything. Pink tulips. Pink roses. Pink carnations. Pink bows. The only thing that offset it all were the clumps of white baby's breath scattered in between. It looked like someone had puked bubblegum and taffeta all over the coffin and church altar.

I couldn't help but reflect on this—what I saw as a vital blunder—for May's entire funeral. It was easier to focus on the hideous display of flowers than the fact that what was left of May's little bloated body was in the wooden box in front of me.

The church was filled end to end. Apparently it didn't matter how oddball or crazy your family was when a child died. Every person in town seemed to cluster down the pews of St. Virgil's Church. We weren't even Catholic, but we'd needed to hold the funeral somewhere, and this was the only space big enough to accommodate everyone. The priest gave some worthless speech about life being ripped away too soon, as people who hardly even knew May wept in one collective wave, the only dry faces Harry Weaver and his five children lining the front row. We had no extended family. No grandparents left. So it was just the six of us. The younger three wedged between Auggie and me—a protective wall to shield them from the brunt of well-wishers.

May's second-grade teacher gave the eulogy. It probably should have been one of us, but with Kathy still in the psychiatric ward, and Auggie just out of the hospital with his arm in a sling, none of us had been able to sit down and put pen to paper.

I went up to the podium after the teacher was done, my hand wrapped around the neck of my guitar. I moved the microphone stand to the side, lowered it, and sat myself down on a stool. I had never performed in public before. I frankly didn't think I would again after this, but I needed to memorialize my sister somehow. I looked out to the shaken crowd, suddenly not sure I could keep myself together. It was one thing to keep my face straight when I was sitting, but it was near impossible to hide my emotions in my music. It was all too raw.

I heard a throat clear. Auggie. His non-bound hand was holding an arm around April, his gaze on me. Something about him telling me I could do this pushed the anxiety away.

I started to strum. "A lot of you didn't know this about May, but there was nothing she loved more than country music." I stared down at the strings of my guitar. "It used to drive us all in the house kind of crazy. Me, most of all—I hate country. But the last few months of her life, she was obsessed with this one song by Martina McBride. The irony isn't lost on me that it's called 'Wild Angels'."

I played the melody, slower, completely stripped down from McBride's version, but it somehow felt more right. I hadn't planned to sing along, but found myself doing it anyway. Reducing what was normally a sweet song, a woman reasoning that wild angels had to be what kept her and her partner together, into a melancholy love ballad, reverberating to the end of every note. It hurt for the music to end. I didn't realize I'd closed my eyes as I belted out the lyrics, until after it was over. No one clapped. There was only silence. I opened my eyes, and without looking out at the crowd again, I descended the altar stairs to resume my place in the pew. Harry didn't so much as look at me.

We buried May by noon, with more pink flowers thrown on top of her coffin as they lowered her into the earth. None of us spoke. The priest prayed. People wept. I was over all of it. I hid in the bathroom for most of the repast after, not feeling up to being confronted with condolences and well wishes over the buffet table. Eventually, Auggie sent Deck in after me, who huffed and complained about being forced into the women's room.

We had just exited, when I heard Rafael's familiar voice. "I don't care that it's her funeral. I told you that I wanted the results as soon as they were in. So do you have them or not?"

"I finished with them this morning," the man with his back to us said. He pulled a manila folder from his jacket. I knew exactly who he was—the coroner.

I grabbed Deck by the collar and yanked him back behind the corner and out of sight.

"What the hell?" he hissed.

But I gestured with my finger to be quiet. The two men were silent as I heard Rafael flipping pages in what had to be May's autopsy report. We'd been waiting all week for it, but Rafael said they were still testing particles for any sign of her attacker's DNA. Apparently, it was back. Though I doubted Rafael was going to volunteer that information to us today, with the burial going on.

"Cause of death?" Rafael asked.

"Drowning," said the coroner.

"So, she did die in the lake, unlike the others."

I peeked around the wall to catch the coroner shaking his head. "I don't think so."

Rafael put his hands on his belt, irate. "What do you mean? She drown in the bathtub?"

"You said the father has a koi tank in the back greenhouse right?"

"Yeah," Rafael frowned. "Why?"

"Because I found traces of fish scale cells under her left middle and ring fingernails. The nails were almost ripped off in some form of a struggle. Like she scraped her hand against a koi while she drowned."

My breath caught in my chest and Deck looked at me confused. Melville—the thick gash across his side—like something, or *someone,* had scratched him. Oh my God.

"Someone drowned the kid in that koi fountain," said Rafael. "In her own house."

I had to push Deck back as I heard their footsteps coming our way.

"Well, that clears up one thing near certain, then," Rafael went on. "Someone in that family killed her."

I held onto Deck until they passed out of sight down the hall. I didn't dare push off the wall until they were gone a solid minute.

"What the actual fuck?" Deck squealed. "May was killed in the greenhouse?"

"Look at me," I said, smacking him to focus. "You didn't hear any of that. Do you hear me? You play dumb, when and if Rafael tells us any of that."

"Why?"

"Because, idiot, every one of us are prime suspects." I stared around us. "Besides, no one else in our family needs to know about this yet."

Deck looked horrified. "You don't think any of us would hurt May?"

I grabbed his arm and yanked him toward the dining room. "I don't know anything anymore."

And the truth was I didn't. May had drowned in the greenhouse fountain, mere feet from where the rest of us slept. Was it so much of a stretch?

Harry was at a conference in Atlanta, but could have driven back in the middle of the night. Kathy was unstable, had proven only a week ago that she was more than capable of killing one of her own children. Without my knowledge, she'd been off her meds for months, possibly longer. Auggie was a steel trap of silence, a loner. Mark was clearly hiding something and hated everyone. Deck was viewed as an over-sensitive weirdo by the town. April fought with her twin half the time. I resented that I had to take care of everyone, hated my parents for having so many kids when they didn't bother raising any of them. It could have been any one of us. It could have been multiple members of the family, together. That's what the cops would say.

For the first time, I actually dared to consider the rumors, that a Weaver could have killed May . . . No, not only considered—believed.

* * *

He'd changed out his suit for sweats and an Army T-shirt. That was the first thing I noticed when Gabe opened the door to his Airstream. I liked the casual look on him better, even if it was accompanied by the troubled cloud to his expression.

"Hey," I said.

"Hey."

Gabe held open the door. I walked past him into the combined kitchenette living room. It was smaller in here than I remembered. I sat on a countertop. Gabe went to the fridge and pulled out a Sprite for me and a beer for himself.

"I buried my baby sister today," I said. "Think you could spare me the underage shit and hand me a beer?"

Gabe sighed, but did as I asked, popping open a second beer and handing it over. I took a long pull. It wasn't my first tonight. It had taken some liquid courage to get over both the funeral and the conversation Deck and I'd overheard. Also, a second one to pump myself up to come here. Gabe and I hadn't spoken since that night on the dock; this past week of funeral preparations had been insane.

"How you holding up?" Gabe asked.

"You know how tired I am of answering that today?" I took another sip.

Gabe leaned back against the fridge and drank, too. "Answer it anyway."

"I said goodbye to my eight-year-old sister, murdered by a serial killer that's potentially targeting me next, my mother tried to take the rest of us out with a shotgun last week, Auggie was shot, the rest of my siblings are melting down, and my father is AWOL, down at the station playing unwanted detective as usual. Also, the cops think it was one of us." I laughed humorlessly. "So you know, just another day being a crazy Weaver."

I could feel my own face crack at that last line. I was all out of tears after the last few months. All I felt now was numb—numb and defeated. That's why I'd come here tonight. For him to lift me back up like he always did. I chugged the rest of my beer.

"Can you grab me another?"

"No," Gabe said, taking my empty bottle and tossing it into the recycling under the sink. "Things will calm down. You just need to give it time."

"Sure they will. Once the day comes that I can finally leave this town, like you did."

"Well, I'm back, aren't I?"

My buzz helped me bring up what I really wanted to. "About what happened on the dock . . ."

He cut me off with a hand. "We don't need to talk about that tonight. Not after the day you had."

"I want to talk about it."

I meant it, too. Even if Gabe broke my heart here and now, it couldn't make this shitty day any worse. I couldn't live in awkward limbo with him. He'd somehow become a lifeline for me in the past weeks, arguably more than Auggie even was, who was busy going through his own shit.

"Fine," he said. "I shouldn't have kissed you. You were in a vulnerable place, and it was a mistake."

"I don't think it was a mistake."

Gabe frowned. "You're not even a legal adult yet."

He said it like it was that black and white. Like whatever current appeared between us the night of the drive-in couldn't exist because of one year.

"So you're saying the only reason you think it was a mistake is because of my age?"

"It's inappropriate." Gabe gestured around us. "Christ, July. You shouldn't even be in here alone with me. I've been too friendly with you the last few weeks, which isn't fair to you. I've led you on and I'm sorry."

I took a step toward him, annoyed. "The only thing you've been, Gabe Santana, is a decent human being. You've been there for me, seen me more than anyone else has this summer. You want to chalk the dock up as a mistake, because you don't actually look at me that way, then that's fine. But if it's just because of the age thing . . ." I shook my head. "That's dumb."

Gabe scratched his head. "You haven't seen what else is out there. You think you want me, the older guy, right now, but you really don't. It'll pass."

"Don't tell me what'll pass. And just be honest with me. Is there something here or not?" I was done with his evading.

Gabe sighed, put his beer on the counter. "I should take you home."

"I can take myself home. I drove."

"You also drank. And before you got here, too, I'm guessing. I'll drive." He grabbed his keys and went to the door, propping it open for me. "Come on."

But I stayed exactly where I was against the counter. This was the moment I thought tonight might come to. He'd forced me to it. "Do you know when my birthday is, Gabe?"

He looked weary. "You're a Weaver kid. All of you are . . . born into the same month you're named after." His face dropped. "Shit, July. Tell me your birthday isn't today."

I laughed. With everything going on, my family had forgotten. Everyone but Auggie. Not that I felt like celebrating the day of my sister's funeral. "Got to love Harry. He never can remember shit."

"I'm sorry. Happy birthday."

"Thanks."

"But that's even more reason I should take you home. You're only seventeen today." He looked even more mortified, if that was possible.

I took a step toward him. "No. My parents put Auggie and me in school a year late. That's why Mark and I are in the same grade. I'm *eighteen* today."

Gabe stood there, utterly dumbfounded. If his jaw could have landed on the floor like a cartoon character, I'm confident it would have. I could tell he had no idea what to do. He was paralyzed. So I stopped in the doorway he held open. "Still want me to leave?"

He blinked. "I'm still too old for you."

"Yet, here we are."

Feeling brave, I walked back to the kitchen. Pulled out another beer and popped it open before he could say another word, then leaned against the fridge to face him.

Gabe dropped his hand from the Airstream door and it slammed closed on its own. His eyes were on me with a longing he'd never allowed me to glimpse before. But still, he hesitated.

"Is it really all in my head, Gabe?"

I didn't think it was, but I'd been surprised plenty in the last week. I bit my lip. He walked over to retrieve his beer, downed the remainder of it, then smacked it on the counter.

"Christ," he muttered.

He came over to me. I took another swig off my beer innocently, and when I pulled it away from my lips, he took it from me with a hunger and put it down beside his own. Then he was leaning over me, his arm supporting his weight above my head, his face inches from mine. "If we do this, we go slow. I don't feel great about the age-gap situation, you legal or not. And you're gonna give yourself time to actually mourn your sister first. Agreed?"

"Yeah, I'm more of a dive head first into the deep end kind of girl." I grabbed him by the shirt and yanked him closer to me.

He caught my cheek with his hand to hold me back, but it was gentle. "I mean it, July. It's slow or nothing here. I don't want you to regret anything."

"Has anyone ever told you, you talk too much?"

I twisted my hand further into his shirt, and this time, when I leaned in to kiss him, he didn't stop me.

*   *   *

The cops showed up with a warrant to search the greenhouse again the day after the funeral. The four of us Weaver siblings (minus sleeping April) stood in our pajamas on the patio watching it all go down. We waited while they overturned the hothouse even more thoroughly than they had the first time in the days after May's disappearance—bagging plants, the chrysalis box, dead butterflies, fountain water, koi fish. Rafael netted out Melville and placed him in a water cooler to be transported along with the other koi back to the lab. Forensics took samples of everything. Drained and fingerprinted the entire fountain. A busted tile was uncovered that had somehow been overlooked during the initial investigation.

Harry returned home from his factory job halfway through the process and became belligerent. He threw himself at multiple agents as they trampled over the ecosystem it had taken him years to so painstakingly construct. He didn't understand why they were here again. No one did, except Deck and me. It was time to do some investigating of my own.

I went to my father, who was standing over a shattered pot of caladium. "Harry."

My father looked to me. We'd hardly spoken since the night in the hospital. I'd be lying if I didn't admit to still feeling a little nervous around him.

"They're wasting time here," he said. "I've told Rafael that. If they were going to find something, they would have during the first search."

"May had koi scale particles under her nails."

I wanted to gauge his reaction; Harry's face was blank. "Who told you that?"

"I overheard Rafael and the coroner at the repast. They think she drowned in the koi fountain."

My father's face paled and I tried to decipher what was running through his mind. He darted a glance back to the warped glass atrium, then his line of children several yards back. "Do the others know?"

"No."

Harry squeezed my shoulder. I flinched. "Good. Let's keep it that way."

Why? I wasn't done prodding him. "You know what this means, don't you? What the cops think?"

"If this is where you begin accusing me of murdering my own daughter, save it."

"Kathy was off her meds back then, too."

"Your mother didn't do this."

But she could have been in an episode, and you could have covered up her crime, I think. But that wouldn't explain Dillon and Anders.

He left me standing there, moving to the line of Caution tape to do his own visual scan of the crime scene. Ever the detective, barking complaints at the cops.

I returned to my siblings.

"Something you want to share with the class?" Deck asked.

The cops were packing up now, heading back to the station. Soon, Harry was the only one left at the entrance to the greenhouse dome.

"Deck and I have something to tell you both."

Auggie actually looked offended when I finished relaying what Deck and I had overheard. "How could you not tell us before?"

"We had one or two things going on," I said.

"So, she did die in the greenhouse," Mark muttered. His face was surprisingly alarmed.

Our brothers and I whipped to him.

"You say that like you already expected as much," I say.

"Never mind."

Mark moved to walk back toward the house but Auggie grabbed him by the collar. "You tell us what you know. Now."

Mark seized backwards. "I don't have to tell you shit."

"Mark," Auggie warned.

"Fine. When I got up to take a piss the night May went missing, I looked out the bathroom window and the greenhouse light was on."

"And you didn't think to mention that to the cops during our initial interviews?" I snapped. I wanted to throttle him. Why would he conceal that?

"I was still drunk from the party at Nicole's. I didn't know if I imagined or dreamed it."

"You moron," I said.

Mark squared his jaw at me, infuriated. "Oh please, like I'm the only one whose been keeping things from the cops."

What did that mean?

"You should go into the station, Mark. Tell them now. It could help," Deck said.

"Or they'll think he kept it to himself because he did it," I spat.

"Watch it," Mark growled.

Auggie took a step between us. He glanced around. "No one's going anywhere. If what July and Deck overheard is true, that means our entire family has moved to the top of their list of suspects. We need to act normal."

"Why do we need to act normal when we have nothing to hide?" asked Deck.

"Because," Auggie said. "Everyone has secrets."

17

Now

I ANSWER THE KNOCK at my door at nine AM, still in my robe, and am ready to throttle whoever has chosen to wake me up this early on a Sunday. I was up most of the night nursing Deck through the worst of his drunk-turned-hungover vomiting, and had hoped to sleep in. No such luck with Mark in my doorway. Great, the last person I want to see. The Laurel Dillon video is a knot of tension between us.

"When did you get in?"

Mark shrugs. "Last night. You were locked in the bathroom with Kurt Cobain at the time. Sounds like I missed one hell of a fundraiser."

I squint at him. "Is there a reason, then, other than the fact that you're a masochist, that you're standing in my doorway this early?"

Mark frowns. "Of course. It's Sunday morning in the Weaver household. The cops are here."

I groan. "Please tell me you're not serious."

Mark shakes his head and goes to bang on Deck's door, then sticks his head in. "Wake your drunken ass up. The cops are here to arrest you."

Deck must have sat bolt up in bed, because I hear him smack his head against his headboard and curse. Mark rolls his eyes.

I catch sight of April at the top of the stairs. She's already fully dressed.

"Do you know why they're here?" I ask.

April appears genuinely shaken; she's not numb to the stream of dysfunctional events like the rest of us are. "Someone tried to burn down the Davidson house last night. I just got off the phone with Connor."

I freeze. "Is anyone hurt?"

"No. Colton and Nicole got their kids out in time."

I thank God for that, even if I don't care for the Davidson couple one bit—it's not like I wish anyone harm, especially not kids. "That's a relief, I guess. How bad is it?"

April's eyes are wide. "Bad. Half the house was gone before the firefighters could contain it. They think it was arson."

"Shit." This means nothing good for our family, especially if the cops are already at our door.

Mark pushes between us down the stairs. "Hurry up. They won't wait forever."

Great. Here we Weavers are again. Prime suspects in another investigation. At least this one is only attempted instead of actual murder. Silver linings and all.

Auggie heads a triangle of Mark and April in the foyer by the time I get Deck downstairs. The three of them are standing in front of Father Time, a miniscule shadow to the tree, as they face off two detectives I don't recognize. I thank the saints that Rafael's probably retired by now.

"Please calm down, Mr. Weaver," the frumpier, balding detective says to Auggie. He looks to be about Kathy's age and crusty around the edges.

"I'm calm, detective," Auggie bites out, his hands on his hips, which suggests he is anything but. "What I'm not, is understanding of why of all families, you've shown up to question mine this morning."

Mark appears bored to April's nervous, at Auggie's flanks. It's all a ruse. We Weavers know our parts when the authorities come a-knocking.

"We're simply here to speak to you and your siblings, Mr. Weaver. July and December in particular. It won't take more than a few minutes. They home?"

"You really suspect either one of those numbskulls started the Davidson fire?" Mark asks. "I mean, look at them." He gestures back to us on the stairs.

The detectives turn. The two of us must be a particular sight: Deck with the dark circles under his eyes and hungover squint, me in my robe with my hair unbrushed. Not very convincing arsonists.

The second detective pulls out a notepad. "Good morning, Ms. and Mr. Weaver. My name's Ellie Schick and this's my partner George Ruble." She's younger, probably a rookie, and clearly the more with it of the two. "We'd like to speak with y'all one on one. Is there somewhere we can sit?"

"Standing here in the foyer is just fine by us," says Auggie.

Schick nods her head in forced acquiescence, but Ruble scoffs.

Schick glances at her notepad. "What about Mrs. Katherine Weaver? We'll be needing to speak with her, too."

"That's not happening," Auggie says. "Her mind's in a fragile state and I don't wanna upset her. She's asleep upstairs."

I walk to Auggie's side, pulling my robe closer around me.

"Listen, detectives," I say. "We heard about the Davidson fire and I'm sure you know this isn't this family's first interrogation. So, what hours do you need the five of us to account for last night when the fire was started?"

"That's not how this works," Ruble says angrily, but Schick holds up her hand to silence him.

"One AM to one forty five AM," she says.

I appreciate her willingness to get on my level.

"Right," I say. "One AM to one forty five AM." I look to my middle brother. "Mark's plane got in late from LaGuardia, so he wasn't even at the Davidson fundraiser last night. What time did you get in, Mark?"

Mark feigns indifference. "Landed at eleven thirty. But didn't get home until, I don't know . . ." He thinks about it. ". . . about twelve thirty, twelve forty five. Passed out soon after."

"So that accounts for him," I say. "What about you, April?" I look pointedly back to the detectives. "She's dating the Davidsons' cousin Connor, by the way, and is a close personal friend of the family."

At Auggie's nudging, my little sister speaks in a timid tone, then clears her throat, louder. "I went out with Connor and our friends on the lake after the fundraiser. He dropped me off at the house at about three AM."

"Three AM?" Auggie frowns at her.

That's a curfew lecture waiting to happen. April only rolls her eyes.

"Will Connor and the others back you up on that?" I ask her.

April nods.

"Good." I say. "Auggie. He was at the fundraiser with his fiancé Bridget. Auggie, whereabouts one to one forty five AM?"

Auggie clenches his arms across in chest. "We felt bad that Deck made a scene at the event, so we stayed and helped clean up. I drove Bridget home around ten, and I stayed over."

"Something Bridget will also confirm, I'm sure—that you were with her all night?" I ask.

"Yes," says Auggie.

"This's ridiculous," Ruble says. "This isn't procedure."

"Fuck your procedure," says Deck.

"Watch it, young man," the older detective warns. "I can arrest you for interfering with an investigation."

"Oh, I'm genuinely terrified," Deck says.

Mark has the wherewithal to whack Deck in the stomach. That shuts him up.

"Now," I say, my attention once again fixed on the detectives. "You're really not here to question those three, though, like you said. Or Kathy, who was home all night, by the way. You just wanted to cover your bases. Who you really want to talk to is Deck and me. Deck, because he made a scene at the fundraiser. But why me?"

Schick looks up from her notepad she's been scribbling in. "You were seen having what looked like an altercation with Mr. Davidson on his landing at the party."

I squint, curious. "Did Colton Davidson confirm that?"

Because I was pretty positive he hadn't. Then he'd have to explain that he's blackmailing me.

Schick lifts her eyebrows. "No. It was two third-party witnesses who came forward. When we asked Mr. Davidson about it this morning, he claims he was only directing you to the bathroom. But our witnesses insist that the conversation took place for several minutes. That it looked like the two of you were arguing."

I can sense Auggie stiffening beside me. And I'm sure I'll get an earful for it later, right after he's done reprimanding April for breaking curfew.

"Well, what can I say?" I feign indifference. "Davidson and I have a history. We were catching up. That's all."

"Why'd you threaten him to stay away from your sister, then?" Ruble asks.

He's smiling because he thinks he's caught me in a lie. I don't look back at April.

"He knows why. But that's not relevant to this conversation. You're asking me these questions because you want to establish if I have a motive for starting the fire."

Schick shrugs.

I puff out air. "It's no secret that I can't stand the man. That's easy enough to admit without me having to elaborate on personal conversations the two of us would rather remain private. My alibi however, which we all know is the important part here, is as ironclad as my moronic hungover brother's back there. After he made his little drunken speech at the fundraiser, Auggie handed him off to me and I took him home around nine PM. We spent the remainder of the night on the bathroom floor, as Deck puked his guts out. Went to bed late. So, as you can see, we're each other's alibis."

"And can anyone else verify that the two of you were in fact home at the time?" Ruble asks.

Oh, right. Because now we've leapt to the possibility that Deck and I could have done it together.

"That would be where I come back in," Mark pipes up. "Heard them when I got home. My bedroom is unfortunately directly next to the bathroom, so I might as well have had a boom box blasting Deck's upheaving against my wall all night."

The detectives are rendered silent, because what else is there to say? We're a hostile bunch and we've left no room for them to wriggle their theories into. Unless we're all lying.

"This is the part where, if you don't have a warrant, I'd kindly ask you two to get off my family's property," Auggie says.

There's a collective exhale after Mark leads the detectives out of the house and their cruiser disappears down the drive.

"Well, that felt like a throwback," says Deck.

Our four glares turn on him, and Mark smacks him across the back of the head.

"Ow!" Deck shrieks. "What was that one for?"

"You think those dicks would have shown up here if you hadn't made such a scene last night?" Mark accuses.

"Hey," Deck says, genuinely outraged. "My drink was spiked. I swear to God!"

Auggie and I raise dubious eyebrows at that.

April pinches the bridge of her nose. "I can't handle this damn family." She struts off in the direction of the kitchen.

"Hey, wait a minute," Auggie says going after her, and I'm following. We stop in the jungle hallway. Deck and Mark are yelling at each other in the background.

"You're not going anywhere near the Davidsons anymore, do you hear me?" Auggie says.

April pauses at the kitchen door. "If you're about to tell me that I need to break up with Connor, you can fuck off."

Auggie's expression hardens. "Excuse me. You want to walk that back a step?"

"Yeah, about that," I cut in. "I don't give a rat's ass that you're dating Connor Davidson. But this whole you spending time with his family, *Colton* Davidson specifically, ends now."

"Why?" April asks. "You jealous that a Davidson would actually choose to date me, when you were just looked at like a town whore?"

Auggie's between us, his face beet red. "You apologize for that, right now."

I put a hand on his chest as a sign to calm his blood pressure, and step in front of him to face our teenage sister. "You're not a baby anymore, April. You want to know the truth about what Colton Davidson said to me last night?"

April stills with her hand on the door. She's curious at least.

"That man you admire so much, the great patriarch of the Davidson family, Pacific's future mayor—he threatened to seduce you if I didn't keep my mouth shut."

"Seduce me?" April says, confused.

"Are you kidding me?" Auggie asks me.

"It means . . ." I start, but April cuts me off.

"I know what it means," she snaps. "He wouldn't do that. He cares about me. He's always been kind to me, ever since May."

"Sure he has," I say. "He was kind to me once too. Until he got me in the back seat of his car, got what he wanted out of me."

"I don't believe you."

The words are a knife.

"That's not what he's like," she continues. "What would he even want you to keep your mouth shut about?"

"The fact that he was hooking up with Kelly Anders the final summer she died. And that he was the last one to see July alone before she walked off into the woods the night of her attack," Auggie says.

I'm glad he says it, because it's too hard for me to.

April shakes her head, venomous. "No. I don't believe any of that."

"I don't give a damn if you do or not," I say. "But do us all a favor and stay away from Colton, all right? Go be with Connor, go freaking ride off into the sunset on the lake, and into the backs of pickup trucks with him, for all I care. But stay away from Colton. He might be nice to you, but make no mistake—you're a pawn to meet whatever end he's after. I promise you that. He probably thought it would help his damn mayoral campaign to look like he took the local murdered girl's lost twin under his wing. Now, he thinks he can use you to keep me quiet, when the irony is, I've never had any intention of reliving that night."

"Did you set fire to his house?" she demands.

"No. I didn't."

And it's the truth.

April is as much a pot of water about to boil over as Auggie is now. She looks to me in anguish. "I hate you. I wish you never came back here."

"April," Auggie says.

But April stomps a foot like a petulant child. "No. For once, I get to make the scene! I get to be the one who admits how much I hate this family. I hate being a fucking Weaver!"

She sprints from the hall, immediate tears ricocheting. I guess she was entitled to her own tantrum at some point.

Auggie looks back at me, inhaling sharply. I can see the hurt plain on his face, his fists release at his sides. He's dying to go after her.

"Let her cool off," I tell him. "She doesn't mean it."

He sighs. "Yes, she does."

"Maybe the family and being a Weaver part. But not you."

He fixes his annoyance back on me. "When were you going to tell me about Davidson threatening you?"

"When I felt like you needed more ammunition to want to kill him. Besides, I handled it."

"He threatened our baby sister."

"No, he threatened *me,*" I correct. "The bastard would never risk his campaign by going after April. He just wanted me to believe he would."

"You still should have told me."

"We have bigger problems on our hands currently."

I nod to where Deck and Mark are still arguing beneath Father Time. They're apparently unfazed by April's outburst; they're too busy having one of their own. Mark is cursing while Deck shakes his whole body in protest.

This is a headache neither Auggie or I are jumping to take on, but into the frying pan we go. I knew this would be a conversation the four of us would need to have this morning. Deck is attempting to pretend that nothing has changed.

"Wrong. Wrong. Wrong," Deck insists. "I didn't do it. I don't remember drinking!"

"Right," says Mark. "Just like you don't remember shooting up before you decided to hurl yourself off the Hazel Bridge."

"Enough," Auggie commands, and both of our brothers' heads pop up.

"I didn't drink last night, Auggie," Deck says more insistently. "You've got to believe me."

It breaks my heart to see the desperation on my youngest brother's face, because I've been there. He wants so badly to believe the words he's saying—that he hasn't hit bottom again so soon. Hell, I want to believe him too—but I was the one holding him up last night, vodka breath and all.

"You were drunk, Deck," I say. "If anyone is familiar with the look, it's me."

Deck flails his arms at his sides. "But *I* didn't drink. I . . . I don't know. Someone must have spiked my soda. It didn't taste right, but it didn't taste like booze. And it was only one. Definitely not enough to get me drunk, even if it was." He is retrospective. "Someone must have roofied me, then gotten me drunk." He thinks harder, his brow a hard line. "I remember being in the bathroom, someone forcing a lot of fluid down my throat from behind me. They said it was water. Then they pushed me out of the room."

"Oh, good. We're back to goddamn Delusionville again," says Mark. "Just when we thought we got rid of the Kathy crazy."

Deck shoves him. "Don't you ever call me crazy!"

"Hey!" Auggie yells, forcing himself between the two of them.

I push on Deck's chest to urge him back a step. "Sit down."

Deck listens because he knows my look. He plops down in one of the wicker chairs, gripping the arms.

"July, come on," he says. "Think about it. This all has to be part of it. Me not remembering getting high, and all of a sudden I'm drugged on that bridge in June. Last night. Someone is doing this to me. Someone is setting me up."

I run my hands over my face, because I feel as if I'm in both a time capsule, reliving the worst of my childhood with Kathy, but also multiple adulthood moments in Nashville with Deck.

"Have you been forcing yourself to puke up your pills after I make you take them?" I ask.

It would be a first, but not out of the realm of possibility.

"What?" He looks outraged. "No!"

"He's losing it," Mark says.

"I'm not losing it!" Deck says. "It doesn't make sense. None of it makes any goddamn sense!"

"Well, what the hell are we supposed to do with you, now?" Auggie remarks, running an anxious hand through his hair. I haven't seen him this exasperated in years. "I mean, fuck. This summer was your final shot, D. I had to blackmail July and Mark to come back here."

Deck seizes forward and grabs Auggie's arms. "Look. I know. I know. I know. But I didn't intentionally do this. Please, Auggie. Please. Don't put me back in the hospital or rehab. Don't put me back."

But Auggie has turned his head away. He won't even look at our younger brother, and I know what they are both feeling then. I've been on both ends of it before: the disappointed and the disappointing. I don't know which is harder.

"We don't have any other choice," Mark says. "Clearly this whole summer recovery kumbaya has failed. We need to figure out how to fix you."

The word "fix" strikes me in the gut, but Deck flips to me before I can get defensive with Mark. I am our youngest brother's last stop.

"July, please. I'll go back to Nashville with you. I'll do the meetings. I'll work the damn program. But I'm not sick again. I haven't been puking or hiding my pills. I swear to God, I'm not Kathy. I've never *been* Kathy."

I have his heart in my hands. But I take it and crush it in my fist.

"You and I both know that nobody can forcibly commit you right now." I say. "But this—us playing house—the plan in two weeks after Auggie's wedding for you to stick around here or move back to Nashville with me, it's over. You messed it up, Deck."

I watch him deflate. Hopeless. Completely and utterly hopeless. He sits on the floor crisscrossing his legs and puts his head in his hands. For the first time, I think he's doubting himself.

When he looks up to me, there's desperation. "You actually think I'm losing it again? My mind, I mean, not just my sobriety?" He's asking me and only me, the person who knows him and his disease better than anyone. Sometimes even himself.

"Yeah, Deck. The way you're talking, I think you might be heading in that direction." I kneel down in front of him and take his hand. "I don't want it to come to another bridge."

And there is understanding in his gaze. It's his love for me that makes him open his mouth once again. I already know what words are about to follow.

"All right. After Auggie's wedding next week, I'll go back in."

He stands up and storms from the room. I try to follow after him but Auggie grabs my arm. "Now, let *him* cool off."

I whip on my oldest brother, tormented. "This never should have happened. You should have just let me take him back to Nashville when I wanted to."

"And that is my cue to be anywhere else," grumbles Mark and he too is gone.

"What do you want from me?" Auggie asks, equally irritated. "Every other time you've been in charge of Deck, he's fallen flat on his face. Forgive me if I thought maybe Mark and I being around this time would help."

"Oh, because you're so great at managing the mentally ill?"

"What's that supposed to mean?"

I gesture to the empty couch stationed beneath Father Time before the projector. "How about the fact that your overmedicating has basically reduced our mother to a shell? She either needs a medication readjustment or a new goddamn psychiatrist!"

Auggie turns red, the veins at his neck pulsing. "You don't get to come in here and bark orders at me on how to handle Kathy. You weren't here for her second breakdown after Harry was convicted. I was the one who agreed to take care of her."

"Right. Take care of her. Not strip her of all agency over her own life. I mean, Jesus Christ, Aug. Have you seen her?"

"You've only dealt with the front end of this disease. I've been dealing with the back end. All those meds eventually catch up to them. We're lucky she's as good as she is."

"That's bullshit, and you and I both know it. She's overmedicated." I jam a finger up in the direction of the stairs. "Something has to change there!"

Auggie scoffs. "Funny that you've spent basically the entire summer with her, and only bring this up now, right before you go back to Nashville. Unless you're suddenly offering to take her with you?"

I clench my jaw and he knows he's beaten me. I am a hypocrite.

He backs for the front door. "In that case, I don't want to hear another goddamn word about how I'm taking care of this family."

*　*　*

I toss in my sleep. Guilt, and the feeling that I have somehow failed both Deck and Kathy washes over me like a tidal wave. I'm remembering it all. I'm drowning in the past, my mind churning and scraping over memories like currents. May's death. Kathy's breakdown. Gabe's heartbreak. Harry's conviction. One second I'm at the drive-in, punching Colton in the face, only to hurtle into the kitchen as Kathy aims the shotgun. Deck is on my bathroom floor after his first opioid overdose, we are sitting in an office days after as a doctor informs us that Deck has inherited Kathy's illness. Auggie is helping me down from flying in the truck, then throwing Mark into the porch wall. I see the cabin, I'm on my knees trembling before it. I'm getting in Colton's car the night everything happened, numb to the world. Mark is screaming at me in the driveway about his relationship with Laurel Dillon. Then I'm on my back in the woods, fighting, scratching, anything to get away. I'm in the psychiatric visitor's center, turning my back on Kathy in goodbye. Kathy is yelling at me to wake up, to see that Harry isn't guilty.

It's like a slideshow of erratic images, of words and promises and pain, and I bolt awake, my heart and mind throttling beneath my skin.

I need oxygen. Cold air. I trip getting out of bed, then dash down the hall like a glimmer. Father Time haunts me as I run past, the split antlers of a hanging deer. The jungle swallows me, then spits me out whole. I'm on the lawn in the moonlight, the land gray and soft beneath my toes. The night is hot, balmy, the air sweet with life and fresh mowed grass. Fireflies everywhere, mosquitoes. Cicadas in the trees. But I'm still running. Barefoot, hurtling open the door to the greenhouse to charge inside. I land on my shins, my knees scraping the side of the koi fountain that held my baby sister's last thrashing breaths.

I'm back on my feet, hurtling pot after pot, plant after plant, across the room. Glass and ceramic smashes. The butterflies launch into an uproar, little black shapes taking for cover every which way. It's a massacre scene. I see Harry's chrysalis box full of empty and immature cocoons. I can't believe Auggie has kept it. I can't believe he has kept any of this. All I see when I grasp the box between my fists is my father bent over it. Harry. My attacker. May's murderer. So attached to his precious little winged creatures. So willing to take his own Livewire's life.

I hurtle the box through the air and it lands on the other side of the atrium with a crash. I'm not done with it. Not done destroying my home that has so thoroughly wrecked me. So I go to it, I lift it up to throw it through the damn window, but something small falls from the bottom into my hand.

I lift my palm, realizing it is an earring. A simple gold dangling star. I pry the chrysalis box open, not knowing what I'm expecting. It's full of previously breached and failed cocoons, but there are also other things rattling around at the bottom of the box. Five more earrings. I pull them out. Not a single matching set.

The next four additions aren't remarkable. A silver hoop. A blue plastic stud. A pearl. A feather. But it's the last one that makes my heart still in my chest.

A long dangling red bow—one I've seen before. It's too unique not to remember. I've seen it a million times over the last few months in the photo plastered across the news. Adrian Bennet, the mom from Alabama. She's wearing it in her missing photo.

PART III

18

Now

I'T'S COINCIDENCE. IT has to be coincidence. Granted, it's the same red bow earring, yeah it's pretty unique looking, but it's hardly the *only* red bow earring out there. A lot of women other than Adrian Bennet have a pair like this one. At least that's what I keep telling myself.

Because what other explanation is there? That Adrian Bennet is somehow related to the murders of nearly a decade ago? That Deck's original ramblings to Auggie were right? But Harry has been in prison for years, and Adrian Bennet only missing for a few months. That would mean that Harry wasn't the killer back then, *that I had gotten it all wrong.* Or just as disturbing, that there's a copycat keeping evidence in our family greenhouse—in a place no one but a Weaver would go. *Fuck.*

As I study the earrings in my palm, I realize how crazy my line of thinking is. There has to be another reasonable explanation for why the earrings are in here and that the red bow is not in fact Adrian Bennet's. Kathy could have stuck them in the chrysalis box during one of her delusions. Or April stashed them away years ago to play dress up. Or April and Auggie use them for some bizarre practice to do with the butterfly cocooning, maybe the colors attract the caterpillars to the chrysalis box—I don't know how this stuff works. I think of Harry bending over the box, Mark standing in here night after night staring into the koi fountain, the few times I caught Deck sneaking a joint in here. All of which occurred that final summer.

Reasonable explanation. I'm looking for a reasonable explanation. I'll ask April the next time I catch her alone. She's in here the most frequently; she's the one who tends this greenhouse. She'll have a perfectly reasonable explanation for why I found earrings, one uncannily similar to the pair in Adrian Bennet's photo. April will know.

So in the early hours of the morning, before the fog has a chance to burn off our yard with dawn, I right what took only minutes to destroy. I place the chrysalis box back on the bench where I found it, door slightly more dinged up than before, earrings replaced inside. I turn back over pots. I replant those ferns and *Ficus* I orphaned in a sea of shattered ceramic. I hose soil down the main drain, sweep up the pieces, and by the time Mark and Auggie appear at the kitchen door at half past six, I'm walking across the patio, caked in sweat and earth.

"Did you and the cacti get into a sparring match?" Mark asks.

"Something like that," I mumble. I look to Auggie. "I did some repotting. If anything's too fucked up, I'll pay for it."

I didn't give either of them a chance to respond, pushing between them to head upstairs for a shower. It's only as I am standing under the water, the drain swirling brown between my toes, that it occurs to me that Deck might not be the only one losing it.

*   *   *

The wedding is a bigger affair than I thought it would be. It seems like Bridget has invited the entire county, and paying for it, too. "Our family comes from money," a cousin tells me over the mandated breakfast buffet for the two families and bridal party the morning of.

I get what she's saying, as we sit on the patio of the Belfry Estate. There are waiters in formal dress serving our party's every need (despite the buffet), with a setup that could better feed an army. The twenty of us sit around white-clothed tables overlooking the back English-style gardens where venue employees are setting up a battalion of folding chairs facing a gazebo.

Mark's wife Lindsay has arrived with all the pomp and flair of a New Yorker, donned in sleek black, and a rapid way of talking that relegates her to the fish-out-of-water status I expected. Every other word is a complaint: about the mosquitoes buzzing about her head, the wet August heat, the fresh mowed grass that has stuck to her two-inch heels. It takes only a look between Mark and me for him to scowl at me. He knows I'm amused. There's nothing more he would like to do than wipe the smirk off my face as he fusses over his city heiress wife. I try not to think about what I know about him and Laurel Dillon. *Could he have killed her?* I feel ill even thinking it.

April has been cornered into conversation with Bridget's parents—them asking the usual questions every rising upperclassman in high school loathes: *What colleges are you looking at? What do you want to study? Let me give you some advice—don't go in undeclared, you'll party too much.* I watch her obvious misery at the other end of the long table, but am powerless to prevent it. I've got my hands full on this end between our other siblings and mother.

Deck isn't here, having chucked a pillow at me when I attempted to wake him in our shared room this morning. He's barely said a word to any of us since we told him he needs to go back into treatment after the wedding. Mark and Lindsay are going to fly him to New York with them tomorrow afternoon. Mark apparently has an in at some fancy city hospital that specializes in treating individuals with both mental illness and drug addiction.

I should have forced Deck out of the room with me earlier. I know I should have, as I stare at the second-floor windows of the hotel behind me. He could be getting drunk or high as we sit here. I just didn't have it in me. The earrings are still bothering me, and getting April alone over the last week has seemed impossible.

That isn't what my attention is on right now, either, however. No, that would be Auggie, seated at the center of the table beside Bridget (they've forgone the whole "don't see the bride before the wedding" thing). He's several people down, but I can see his face. There's panic there. He hardly responds to Bridget's attempts to loop him into conversations; his gaze is fixated on his plate. I know what he's feeling. My older brother's face has always been an open book to me. He wants to run, but knows he can't.

Our eyes connect, and he realizes I know.

Breakfast begins to clear. Bridget and the bridesmaids head off to get ready. April and Kathy return to their room. The groomsmen, Auggie, and I follow soon after. We're heralded by Bridget's eccentric wedding planner up the stairs into suites. The planner pauses on the landing in an attempt to push me off in the direction of the women, but Auggie holds up his hand.

"She's my best man, she's with me."

The planner doesn't look happy, but has my dress moved into the room next door to the men.

I'm hardly changed into my navy sundress, strapping on my heels, when the knock comes at my door and I let him in. Auggie's in his suit, his tie out of place.

"I'm sorry," he blurts out.

"For what?"

Words rush out of him like a current. "Our fight about Kathy. I didn't mean to shut you out on it. I'm just used to managing her on my own. But I think you're right. I think I've neglected her over the past few years to take care of April, and not always listened to what she needed or wanted. If you think the three of us should revisit her dosage with the psychiatrist before you leave, I'd be open to talking about that."

My mind is so not on Kathy right now, but Auggie doesn't need to carry my suspicions or fears today. "That's all I'm asking. But for the record, I'm sorry I overstepped. You're right. I should have come to you with it at the beginning of summer, not right before I was about to leave and dump it all on you as usual."

And I do plan to revisit this topic over the next few days with Kathy, just after I've finished reassuring myself that we don't have another serial killer on our hands. *Priorities*.

Auggie exhales in relief.

"Now, you want to talk about why you're panicking?" I ask. This is a problem I can actually solve right now.

Auggie sits on the bed, his head in his hands. He looks like he's about to set off for a funeral, not his own wedding. "What if you were right? What if I rushed into all of this?"

I sigh. "I'm never right. You should know that by now."

"I'm serious."

"So am I," I say, knocking him in the shoulder. "Look at me."

He raises his head.

"It's okay not to love her yet," I say. "They say that's the biggest thing, if you love someone, right? Well, I think that's crap. Respect. Companionship. Those are just as important for someone you're about to spend every goddamn day in and day out with, and you have that with Bridget."

"I started seeing her to prove you wrong." He can't look at me when he says it. "After our fight in Nashville."

Well, shit. I'd figured as much, but it's another thing altogether to hear it confirmed. Also not another one of my finer sister moments.

Auggie had shown up to my house four hours early for a weekend visit. He discovered me with a married guy, a songwriter I'd just written another useless single with—something about driving in a truck with the right girl. We weren't literally in bed, but the guy behind me as I answered the front door in my bathrobe was incriminating enough. I wish I could say I'd given a thought for the guy's wife, or any of the others before, but I didn't, not at the time. Jules Thomas: homewrecker—at least I never had any repeat offenses or expectations. Not that that made it better.

It was a side of myself I buried deep and rarely acted upon. I couldn't put my finger exactly on why I did it. But a therapist probably would have said it was a way to punish myself—to become the "slut" my hometown had once accused me of being.

Still, I would rather have kept that self-loathing to myself. But Auggie saw the guy, saw the ring he slipped on his finger before heading out the door. That was all it took.

Big brother lecture about getting my life together. A screaming match. Auggie saying I should come home to Pacific for the millionth time, me telling him to get lost, that I never wanted to see him again, him saying it was mutual. He left, and the next several months had been crickets on both sides. When I finally reached out, Auggie hadn't answered. Then Deck had gone up on the bridge.

But I knew why my actions had bothered my brother that day. I read it on his face as he pulled his truck out of my driveway. Auggie had sacrificed everything—college, a potential football career—to stay in Pacific and take care of the rest of our family. All so that I could go and have this other life, and this is what I chose to do with it.

"It gutted me, what you said," Auggie says, "that I was too obsessed with you and our brothers' lives, that I'd always used it as an excuse not to find my own."

"I didn't mean that," I say. "I was ashamed, and pissed off."

Auggie drops his hands to his lap. "You were right, though. And now Bridget's pregnant."

"And now Bridget's pregnant."

He can't back out. We both know that. He looks so sad as I make him stand and straighten his tie for him.

"You've always wanted a normal family, Aug. This is your chance."

He nods, inhaling. "Promise you won't push me away again?"

"Never."

The ceremony and reception go fast. I'm proud of my big brother. I only hope that Bridget and this baby will eventually make him happy. Gone are the reservations I'd seen earlier on his face, fake joy plastered on instead. He looks like a man never gladder, pushing cake into Bridget's face as they cut it, drifting across the makeshift floor for their first dance. I never knew Auggie could be such a damn good actor.

I feel off walking around the reception. I tell myself that I'm only uneasy about this entire summer and the family's failed attempt to pull Deck back from the deep end. When I find my youngest brother at the bar, I fully expect for him to be plastered. There seems little point in not being so, as he is destined to go back into treatment tomorrow anyhow—a lot of addicts/drunks choose to go out on a bang before walking back into rehab. But Deck is sober as a monk, perched on his corner barstool as he overlooks the dance floor. He's nursing a club soda when I try to talk to him. He kindly tells me to fuck off, then stumbles off to sulk at our table. I don't bother following him. He's an adult, and besides, I spot April out on the patio talking to Connor, and see my chance.

"It's soda," Connor mumbles when I spot the flask he's slipping into his inner jacket pocket.

Both teenagers look guilty as hell.

"I don't care if it's lighter fluid," I say. I turn to my sister.

She's pretty in her blush-colored sundress, her hair in twisted ringlets like the other bridesmaids.

"I have a weird question for you," I say. "Are you missing any earrings?"

"Earrings?" April knits her eyebrows together.

"Yeah, earrings. I found one on the floor of the greenhouse earlier this morning. I thought it might be yours." I figure this is probably a better explanation than that I found a whole hoard of them in the butterfly chrysalis box, none of which match, and it kind of freaked me out.

April shakes her head. "I don't even have my ears pierced."

My eyes dart to her earlobes and she's of course right. April had a fear of needles when she was little. Guess that carried over.

"Hmm," I say, forcing nonchalance into my voice. "Well, did you have any of your friends over to hang in the greenhouse?"

April scoffs. "You really think I would ever let anyone actually see that place?"

"Maybe it's Kathy's," I mumble.

"Unlikely," April says. "She doesn't wear earrings much anymore."

"Maybe it's Bridget's or Lindsay's," offers Connor, clearly trying to suck up to me.

"True," says April. "Ask Mark. He's been out in that greenhouse every freaking night when he comes home on weekends." She makes a face. "Pretty creepy, actually. He's always just standing in there, no lights on, half the time staring down at the koi pond or at that stupid chrysalis box."

"In the chrysalis box?" I ask because my heart has momentarily stopped beating.

"In, at, I don't know," April says annoyed. "Do we really have to keep talking about earrings?" She grabs Connor's arm. "I want to dance."

Connor offers me an apologetic smile as April tugs him to the dance floor. I watch them join the other partygoers jamming to the beat of some pop song I can't remember the name of, but then it switches to a slow song, Fleetwood Mac's "Landslide." I watch my baby sister be taken into the arms of the boy she maybe loves, the two of them slowing to the vibrations of Stevie Nicks's voice. I can't help it; this song has always reminded me of May.

The couples sway on the floor: April and Connor, Auggie and Bridget, and soon after even Mark and Lindsay join the ten or so pairs.

I watch my middle brother rock his wife. Mark has his usual stiff air, but is actually smiling. I wonder if he loves Lindsay like he loved Laurel Dillon. There are so many unanswered questions with him. Why he never told the police that he'd known Laurel, that she had an affair with an older man. Now, why he spends so much time in that greenhouse—hell, I'd caught him once or twice in there myself, but hadn't given much thought to it until now. Why he told on me and Gabe. There are pieces missing to Mark's last year we all lived together: reasons and truths.

"It isn't fair he gets to be happy," Kathy says.

I hadn't realized she'd come to stand beside me. "Who?"

Kathy's eyes stay on the dancing couples. "Him. Not after everything he's done."

I realize she's looking at Mark and Lindsay. "I know you know more than you're saying, or at least suspect it. You wouldn't have warned me to leave or shown me that video of Laurel Dillon and Mark otherwise. So can we just stop with the cryptic messages, please? What do you know?"

Kathy's eyes are bright, but her head doesn't turn from the couples. "If you refuse to leave here, you need to go see your father."

She attempts to back away, but I grab hold of her arm. "No. Talk to me. Does someone have you scared? Did you see something?"

She cups my cheek, a tender smile on her lips. Kathy does love me, I think. I've always felt that, even in her harder moments. I wish I showed her more that I do love her, too. "I can't," she says. "I have to protect my little girl. I failed the first time. I can't be the one to talk to you."

It hits me with a force just how right my developing theory is. I've been watching my mother over the last two weeks since my fight with Auggie. Is she overmedicated? Definitely.

But she's also deliberately playing into that image; it's strategic. I can see it in her movements when she thinks no one's watching. She knows more about what happened back then than she's letting on. She's hiding, but from what, from who?

"What are you talking about?" I demand. "May's dead. It's too late to protect her."

But Kathy frees herself from my grasp. "Go. See him. He can tell you."

I try to stop her again, but she's moved out of range, back toward the main reception. I know without following her that I won't get her alone again tonight.

I have to act.

I don't say goodbye to anyone at the reception; I know I won't be missed. Could this wait for tomorrow, sure, but I'm too amped up. After the dead end with the earrings and Kathy's warnings, I need some form of answers tonight. So I get in my car and drive to the north end of the lake.

His porch lights are on when I pull into the drive. He must hear my tires on his loose stone driveway, because by the time I'm out of the car, he's standing on his porch, his hands on the wooden rail.

"What are you doing here, July?" Gabe asks.

19

Then

As LATE SUMMER arrived, the Weaver family was locked out of the investigation of the three dead girls more than ever. Rafael returned to the house only once after the greenhouse search, and that was to confirm what we already knew: May died the night she disappeared; her head smashed against one of the tile walls while she leaned over the koi fountain, the killer held her under until she drowned; she flailed her arms during the drowning and scratched Melville's tail; the fountain water particles matched what were found in her lungs and the koi scales the cells under her fingernails; her body had no sign of sexual trauma; she was wrapped in construction-grade trash bags and duct tape, weighted down with rocks, and disposed of in the lake out by Cypress Point.

We weren't given details about Laurel Dillon or Kelly Anders, but something about the way Rafael relayed everything, I got the impression that May had been the lucky one—"lucky" being a subjective word, apparently.

After that visit, as far as we were informed, the investigation might as well have come to a standstill. But I knew that couldn't be true. Cops had doubled on every corner of Pacific and Hazel over the final weeks of July and into early August. Eyes were constantly on us Weavers, along with the families and friends of Laurel Dillon and Kelly Anders. I often caught an unmarked car outside Pickens when I walked in and out of work. There was a cruiser stationed in plain view of the house at all hours of the day and night.

We five siblings did our best to return to our normal routines—that meant Auggie, Mark, and me our summer jobs, and Deck relegated to watching April in our absences. Harry was home, returned only to his nightly foreman job since school was still out for another two weeks, but his every free minute was spent in the hospital visiting Kathy. He'd originally intended to bring her home, but then child services showed up. Our father was given two options: either Kathy could be transferred to a long-term psychiatric facility for the next few months, then be reevaluated, or his three minor children would be put into foster homes, potentially until they all turned eighteen.

Auggie balked when he heard that. If Harry was stupid enough to lose custody of our younger siblings, he and I would find a way to get it now that we were nineteen and eighteen respectively. It would only be a matter of coming up with enough money to pay for a place to stay. I knew Daniela would take us in temporarily, if it came to it. Just in case, Auggie took a job as a day laborer at a construction company in Montgomery. Going to college was officially off the table.

As I mentally prepared myself to start my senior year in the wake of the discovery of May and the other girls, my only respite became my guitar and Gabe. Playing at May's funeral had returned my music to me. No one was more surprised than me that when my fingers re-met the strings, it was country ballads I was suddenly writing. These songs were how I grieved her, but also how I kept her alive. I spent hours on end finessing the melodies locked away in my room. Then, when I ran out of excuses for why they weren't done, the person I rushed to play them for was Gabe.

I don't know how to characterize exactly what we were. Gabe was still tense about our relationship, let alone willing to put a label on anything. We were taking things slowly, as he'd dictated, spending almost every night after I got off from Pickens, and him from his brother-in-law's sawmill, curled up in the bed of his truck somewhere remote. Sometimes we overlooked a patch of uninhabited lake, other times an empty field. We didn't dare spend time at his Airstream. Daniela would give us both an earful if she found out.

The emotional piece was easy. We spent hours lying on a blanket in the bed of the truck, sometimes side by side, sometimes leaning against the indents of the back wheels. My favorite was when he held me. It took a lot for him to let me kiss him on those first few nights, a hell of a lot more for him to be the one to initiate. He wanted to wait on further intimacy—he worried I was in too vulnerable a state, that he was taking advantage and I would regret it later.

When we finally did have sex, it was mostly fumbling. Me inexperienced, him trying to make sure I was actually sure and comfortable. It felt strange, but right, opening up an entirely new piece of world for me . . . one I clung onto the more times we were together. All I wanted was to be with him. That first moment when he arrived at our meeting point every night was the best of my day. In a year that had otherwise been hell, I'd found this one sliver of light.

It was what made everything that happened after so devastating. To have it all ripped away.

On a morning in mid-August, a man got out of the unmarked car that sat outside Pickens. I was startled to see him coming toward me as I stepped out of the diner. At first, I thought he was maybe the killer after all, finally approaching me. But then he flashed his officer's badge. I'd seen the guy before. He was at the hunting cabin the day of the search—the cop who'd looked like he wanted to kick Harry in the face. He said that Rafael wanted to talk to me. I got into the back of his car.

The last thing I expected when we arrived at the police station was for Gabe to be standing in the middle of the hall. I didn't understand why he was there, why he had that anxious look on his face. Unless . . .

I ran for him, bypassing the cop who tried to stop me, and flung myself at Gabe like his touch was vital for me to breathe. I cupped his face with my hands.

"Gabe," I begged.

But he pried himself out of my grasp, stiff as a corpse, and pushed me back. He was a different man, his expression cold in a way I'd never seen before. He couldn't even meet my eyes.

"I'm not supposed to talk to you until after you've spoken to Rafael."

Daniela appeared out of a room at the end of the hall, where Detective Rafael stood in the doorway. My boss furrowed her brows at me with simultaneous pity and anger, then walked up to pull on her brother's arm. "Come on. We've got to go."

"Daniela."

"Not now, honey," she said as she towed her brother toward the station entrance.

Gabe looked back as they reached the door. I only turned when Rafael cleared his throat behind me.

"Come on in."

I followed him into the interrogation room and he shut the door. We sat in flimsy metal chairs facing one another, a matching card table between. Most people would feel intimidated, knowing they were about to be interrogated by a detective. But I'd been interrogated one too many times over the last six months—most of the time by Rafael. This scene didn't scare me for myself. I worried what it meant for Gabe.

"Does my father know you dragged me in here?" I seethed.

Rafael pushed down his ballpoint pen and tilted his legal pad against the table so I couldn't see it. "You're not a minor anymore, Ms. July. I no longer legally have to include your father in our interviews."

"But you do legally have to include my lawyer if I request it."

Rafael narrowed his eyes up over his glasses. "That would be your prerogative. But I would think you and I have a decent-enough relationship after everything that you know I'm not out to get you."

"Then what do you call that?" I gestured to the door. "You clearly know about Gabe and me, or you wouldn't have dragged either one of us in here. What? Are the police interested in teen relationships now?"

"We are when it's potentially related to a murder investigation, and one of the parties was a minor when it began."

"I wasn't a minor. Gabe and I didn't start a relationship until I turned eighteen."

"Only a month ago? Not before?"

"You want real specifics? It started on my eighteenth birthday. Besides, the age of consent in Georgia is sixteen, last I checked."

Rafael scribbled something on his legal pad. "It's still questionable. Especially in this context where all the murder victims were underage."

I crossed my arms on the table. "Gabe was reluctant to even be my *friend* when I was a minor. I was the one who had to convince him when I turned eighteen to give us a shot. Even then, he was hesitant because of the situation and the age gap. So if you're even considering that Gabe Santana could be capable of hurting underage girls, you're out of your mind."

Rafael dropped the legal pad on the table and sighed. "Here's the thing, Ms. July. I know that you're lying to me about the timeline."

I bristled. "Excuse me?"

"I've spoken to a reliable source that says they saw the two of you kissing on your family's dock the night your mother shot Auggie."

Panic seized my chest. I hadn't counted on the detective knowing that—otherwise I wouldn't have purposely omitted it. Had Gabe told him? "Who?"

"Your brother, Mark."

I sank in my seat. I didn't believe him. I knew there was a part of Mark that hated me, but this? He'd never betray me like this. He'd never go to the cops to rat me out.

"I don't believe you."

Rafael shrugged. "Believe what you want. But your brother came into the station this morning to file a report. He believes you two were carrying on an affair since the beginning of summer. Wanted me to look into Santana for the murders."

His words sunk in. But why would Mark sit on that kind of information for over a month, only to report us now? It didn't make sense.

"July," Rafael prodded.

"I was distraught. I'd just watched my mother put a bullet in Auggie's shoulder after you'd come to our house and told us you found May. I was the one who kissed him, not the other way around—and he pushed me away. It was just a kiss, a one-time thing."

Rafael began writing again. "And what was he doing at your house in the first place?"

"He was checking on all of us."

That sounded weak even to me.

"Checking on all of you, or checking on *you*, a seventeen-year-old girl he was attracted to?"

"He didn't do this. So unless you want to start throwing accusations around of me being a suspect, I think we're done here."

Rafael tapped his pen. "No. I know for a fact that it wasn't you."

"How's that?"

His eyes bored into mine, with an intensity I'd never seen from him before. Was it care? "I saw you that day at the hunting cabin. Your reaction, having that panic attack on a rock, with Santana standing over you. Any chance of you being the murderer or even an accomplice was null and void the moment I saw your face. Not even the greatest actress in the world could fake that. But I've got to be honest, this Gabriel Santana variable's got my hackles up."

"Why, exactly?"

The detective sighed. "What I'm about to tell you is not public knowledge. And it's going to remain that way. Understood? It doesn't leave this station, not a word to Santana or your father or anyone else in your family. I'll deny it if it does."

I nodded, crossing my arms tighter across my chest. I could always break that unspoken promise later, as I saw fit. As far as I was concerned, I owed this prick nothing.

"As I've relayed to your family already, May's murder seems sloppier than the two that came after, like the killer refined his craft the more he went along." The way he seemingly equated the killer to an artist unnerved me. "Laurel Dillon and Kelly Anders—well, for one thing, they were both involved in sexual encounters right before they were murdered."

"You say that like they were consensual."

"Their injuries do not correlate with sexual violence."

"What kind of violence do they correlate with then?"

"Our best guess . . . the women had consensual sex with their attacker, and shortly after, they were strangled to death."

My stomach rolled. I thought I might puke. "But you said May wasn't?"

The detective shook his head. "No. Not May. I hope that gives you some comfort."

It did. Then I felt guilty that I was grateful it had been the other women, and not May.

"And you think that Gabe could be the killer because 'the king' had sex with two of his minor victims before killing them?"

"It's a possibility we need to consider. That hunting cabin scene was set up with precision. Someone with military training could easily fit that bill. Not a fingerprint left over."

"It's a possibility with little to no evidence," I snapped back. "If you spent more than five minutes with Gabe Santana, you would see he isn't remotely capable of that. It took me weeks after I turned eighteen just to get the man comfortable with kissing me."

"But isn't it a little coincidental that he appeared back in your family's lives around the same time that May went missing? Come on, July. You're a smart kid. Even you can see that it looks like he targeted and groomed you as a minor to begin a sexual relationship. We think the same could have happened to Dillon and Anders. The last thing I want to see is you as the next girl at the bottom of that lake."

I could tell by Rafael's blotchy face that, in his own way, he'd come to feel protective over me. He wanted to find this killer, badly. He'd even convince himself of the guilt of an innocent man.

"Gabe wasn't even in the state when May disappeared. But I'm sure he told you that already. So why are we actually here?" There was another reason. I could feel it.

Rafael sighed, like he was preparing to lay all his cards on the table. "Because I don't know what your connection is to all of this, but something in my gut says that you're at the center of it, July. The murders started with your family. One of the other victims was your year at school. You found the cabin. Your face was on the wall. You had a hostile run-in earlier this summer with Colton Davidson—yes, I know about that too; a relationship with Gabriel Santana; you interact every day with half of the people on my suspects' list, several of which are your own family members. So I need to ask you for something."

"What?"

He puts down his legal pad. "Your help. I'm an outsider. You've been here from the start, witnessed how people in town, people in your own family, have acted in the wake of all of this. You can help me determine whether this was the work of some deranged killer or if it started with someone trying to cover up an accident that first night in the greenhouse, or even if it's a pair working together."

"You still suspect my parents."

I knew that the main theory around town—especially after Kathy shot Auggie—was that my mother drowned May, my father rushed home to cover it up, then after getting a taste of blood, he killed Laurel Dillon and Kelly Anders on his own. It was absurd.

And unlikely that Kathy or any other woman was involved in the Dillon or Anders murders, given the sexual components to the killings.

"I suspect everyone," Rafael said. "Except you and your sister, at this point. So will you help?"

I thought about all of the people he mentioned that I came into contact with every day: my family, friends, every kid I went to high school with, every townie I had spent my life growing up around, the cashier at the Piggly Wiggly, the bank teller at Wells Fargo, the old Presbyterian minister, McNeil's dive bar owner. When I really thought about it, any of them could have had an opportunity to kill May and or one of the other women. I couldn't trust anyone male.

"What do you want me to do?"

Rafael leaned forward. "Simple. Watch. Watch them all."

* * *

The last thing I expected was for Mark to be leaning against Auggie's truck when I walked out to the station parking lot. I charged past him; I didn't trust myself not to kill him if I confronted him now.

"July," Mark called. "Come on. I had to."

Oh, fuck it all to hell. I was too mad. I swung around on him and shoved him against the truck. He held his hands up, horrified. I'd never been physically violent with one of my brothers in my life.

"Did you have to?" I yelled, slamming my hands against him again.

I wanted to punch him. I wanted to kick the living shit out of him. I wanted to punish him for risking the one goddamn good thing I had left in my life. I settled for balling my hands into fists and backing up. I could feel my body vibrating with rage. I'd never hated a single being more than I did Mark in this moment, and I'd spent most of my adolescent life actively hating Harry.

"He took advantage of you," Mark shouted. His face was crimson, embarrassed, furious, defensive. "All of this started when he showed back up. May disappears, then Laurel, and he's suddenly around you all the time? What if you're his next dead whore?"

I slapped him so hard my palm stung. I could see the shock as he brought his hand up to his cheek. I didn't care. I hated him.

I stumbled backwards, far enough away that I couldn't reach him again. "Gabe didn't come back to town until June, Mark. Four months after May died. He was on an Army base. You just nearly ruined an innocent man's life for nothing."

But my brother's face hardened. "And you expect me to care?"

That was it—the final straw. I was through looking out for him. "If you need anything, you go to Auggie. I never want to see your face again."

He didn't come after me as I stormed out of the parking lot. He didn't even yell my name. He knew. He knew we were done.

*   *   *

I banged on the door to the Airstream like my life depended on whether it opened or not. Passing Daniela's house, she'd tried to tell me to go on home, but I ignored her, looping around to the backyard and the firepit to get to Gabe's door. I was banging for a full minute before it opened.

Night had descended. We were standing out beneath a curtain of stars, on one of the prettiest nights of the summer, the warm breeze jostling my curls. I hardly noticed. I was too fixated on Gabe's face, his hand clutching the door to bar me from entering.

"Can we please talk?" I asked.

"I don't think that's a good idea."

His expression was the same hard rock it had been at the station, his eyes unreadable. I wasn't used to this callous version of him. I didn't like it one bit.

"Please," I begged. "I explained everything to Rafael. That nothing happened before I was eighteen, and that you weren't even in the state when May died, so you're not on the suspects' list anymore. I'm so sorry. My brother Mark . . ."

"He saw us that night on the dock."

"Yeah. I told him off—"

"You should go home, July."

He tried to close the door in my face, but I threw my hand in the frame.

"Gabe, please. I fixed it."

He closed his eyes and exhaled, like he was trying to contain his own anger. When he looked at me again, he was hard, determined. "You fixed it after your family broke it. It always comes back to your insane family."

I felt that last jab in my gut. No other person could have hurt me more with those words than him. Mostly because I never thought he'd be capable of them.

"I'm sorry. I'm sorry about all of it. I never meant to drag you into my family drama—"

"Well, you did," he said. "And now my family, too."

"What are you talking about?"

"You need to go."

"Please."

"I said *go*." His tone was like a smack. Forceful. It jolted me.

"Gabe." I clung onto the doorway like it was the only thing separating me from a condemnation to hell. "I love you. Please don't send me away."

His body sagged and he sighed. "You were just an easy fuck for me, July. That's all it was ever about."

I shattered. Pain welled up in my chest. I pushed off his door, and fled, tearing across the lawn and making for the woods. I'd walked there and would have to walk all the way home through the dark.

I was sobbing, uncontrollably, deep guttural wailing in a way I'd never before. Not when May disappeared. Not when May was found dead, or at her funeral, or when Kathy shot Auggie, or when my siblings and I stood around time and time again throughout our childhoods and adolescent years all thinking the same thing but not daring to ask it out loud—why we'd been born to these parents, why we'd been born to this fucked-up life and situation, and damn it all to hell, I needed a drink. I needed to be drunk.

I ran down the road, Pacific Lake chasing me along my right the entire way, taunting. There was a part of me that contemplated just jumping in, letting the water take me before the town's serial killer had a chance to. That thought alone was enough to slam me to a stop, realizing I was at least a full two miles from Daniela's house. Another mile from home. I'd been running for longer than I thought. Probably a half hour at least.

The moon was out, a sharp peel curved off a knife, refracting off the billows of the lake. The air smelled of pine and I thought how masochistic Mother Nature had to be to allow such a glorious night to also be one of the most devastating of my life.

It wasn't just Gabe. I realized that even in the state I was in. It was everything. Everyone. May. Kathy. Harry. Mark.

This whole summer. My whole life. It was finally catching up with me, as I doubled over and clutched my knees, forcing air into my lungs.

When I started back again for home, I was calmer. Resolute, my entire body almost entirely numb. I think I was just trying to keep moving forward, which to do so meant flipping a switch. A switch not to feel.

That's the only way I can explain why I slowed when Colton Davidson pulled up beside me in his Jaguar, top down, a sneer on his face.

"Bit dark to be out here walking alone, ain't it?"

I kept walking.

"What? Fresh out of your usual barbs now that your family's been outed as the trash it's always been?"

I stopped and stared at him. This man had assaulted me at the beginning of the summer, had tried to do so much worse at that drive-in. Yet he didn't even make the top five of the list of horrible things that had happened to me over the past few months. And as I thought on it, there was something so minuscule about the boy in his flashy car. It was a relief, I realized, now that I had come face to face with him again, to find that he had no power over me. In fact, I felt nothing when I looked at him. Nothing but a way to hurt myself more. Which was exactly what I was after.

I sidled up to his car. "You stop just to gloat or you gonna give me a ride?"

He seemed taken off guard. I still didn't think that he was used to anyone daring him; he didn't know how to handle it.

"Now, why would I do that? The last time you socked me in the face."

"What if I actually gave you something you wanted this time?"

Colton squinted. "Meaning?"

I was leaping fully from that tightrope of my own volition, finally plunging into the bottomless abyss that was my own tormented agony. I didn't want to see up. I wanted to pull that final thread that was July Weaver and unwind her until she was completely undone.

"What you wanted from me in the first place."

Colton grinned. He popped open the passenger side door, and God forgive me, I got in.

20

Now

"WHAT ARE YOU doing here, July?"

Gabe's question echoes through my bones, a forgotten song. My name on his tongue, with all the history and love and pain it has wrought me. I've avoided reliving these emotions by pushing him away since returning home. But now I feel the force of them all at once, staring up at him on his porch landing.

He isn't happy to see me. I can tell that from the way he crosses his arms. After our fight at the fundraiser, I don't blame him.

"You said I didn't know the full story about what happened between us back then," I say. "I want you to tell it to me now."

"Last time I tried to talk to you, you accused me of lusting after your teenage sister."

I stop at the base of his porch steps, take hold of the bottom railing. "I know. I'm sorry."

Apologizing has never come easy for me and he knows that. His face twitches. If the man is anything like who he was nine years ago, he won't hold a grudge.

"I feel like I'm going crazy being back in this town," I say. "There are missing pieces to that final summer I'm trying to sort out. One of which you have."

He groans. "You want a cup of tea?"

"I want answers."

"I'd forgotten how blunt you are. Impatient, too."

"Yeah, well," I say, losing steam with every word. "I've heard it's part of my charm . . . or curse, depending on who you ask. Now, please tell me."

Gabe shakes his head. "You want to hear, it's on my terms this time. You're not going to demand it out of me."

I realize that our roles have changed in the near-decade that has passed. I was used to Gabe rolling over, giving in to everything I asked for in our friendship, then relationship. But this isn't that Gabe, any more than I'm that July. The man before me is resolute, jaw set, and holding open his front door for me. There are only two options: enter or go. I move up the stairs and pass him into the house.

I look around me, attempting to gauge the type of life the former love of my life has lived in my absence. It's unsurprising—Gabe's ranch-style log cabin is simple, masculine, with no knickknacks to line the walls or plants hanging from shelves. There are a few books, some photos of Daniela and his other sisters' kids, a statue of the Virgin Mary on his mantel; otherwise the space is all shaggy carpet and neutral-toned furniture. The place smells like him—mahogany and sawdust from the shop next door. I feel calmer. Safe. Warm.

"Earl Grey okay?" he asks, leading me into the cramped kitchen.

"Fine."

I decide now that a memory is easier to despise, especially when that memory is living hundreds of miles away in another state, nine years removed. It is so much harder to hate Gabe when he is in front of me, removing a whistling tea kettle from his stove.

I perch on the edge of my chair at the kitchen table while he pulls sugar from the cabinet and milk from the fridge.

"Aren't you supposed to be at your brother's wedding? You're dressed for it."

His back is to me. It bothers me slightly that I'm pleased he noticed I'm dressed up at all.

"I won't be missed," I say.

I take in the few photos in this room. One of Gabe and two other officers in their fatigues. And a three-generation snapshot of the Santana family—Gabe the only male above ten years old in the lot, his mother and grandmother standing at the center.

"How's your family?" I ask. Maybe if I play into his game of chitchat, we can get this over with. My body's buzzing being this close to him.

Gabe pours the hot water into mugs. "Angela moved with her husband to Alabama a few years ago. Daniela and the kids are good. She got divorced. Rose runs the cleaning company now." He pops one of the mugs down for me and sits across the table with his own. "My mom died two winters ago," he says, his face drawn. "Abuela a few before that."

"I'm sorry."

Gabe shakes his head. "Ma had been sick a long time. Cancer."

There's fresh pain there. Like her ghost still haunts him. I get it. Nine years later and I still see May everywhere I look.

"I'm sorry." I'm a broken record.

"So am I . . . about your family."

That one's probably a murderer and the other's in jail taking the blame for it?

I get up, suddenly too claustrophobic in this tiny room. "Can we go out on the deck? I can't sit right now."

What I can't allow myself to do is get distracted over why I'm here. Gabe's presence is too heady. He seems a little unsteady himself, as he leads me through the house and onto the back deck. It's not screened in, which is rare for these lakefront houses because of bugs. But the view of the north end of Pacific Lake is gorgeous. Any further up and we'd be staring into the less glamorous breeding pond. I inhale the damp breeze as it drifts up from the water and evergreen trees. I taste wild air in my mouth.

"You always were calmer outside," he remarks, leaning over the railing beside me.

I sip my tea and stare out. Someone's radio is blaring out on the lake. Probably some kids hanging out. They shouldn't be out there in the dark, but I did it at their age, too. Country music, something I think by Rascal Flatts, calls back to us from their boat.

"You ever write for them?" Gabe asks.

I look over; he's hard at work studying me.

"No," I say. "You know about my songwriting?"

Yet again another member of Pacific knows about my career. I guess I should assume everyone does. I've kept my end of the deal, and my mouth shut, so hopefully Colton leaves it within the town limits. Unless he believes my family burned down his house. Then my career's screwed.

"I've heard every song you put out." Gabe places his mug down on the railing. "Though if I'm being honest, I like your earlier stuff better."

"Yeah, you and everyone else apparently."

"Wasn't exactly fun hearing the ones about me, though."

I offer him a pointed look. "What makes you think anything I wrote was about you?"

He raises an eyebrow. "'The Crime of Youth'? 'So, Thank You'?"

He has me there. Heartbreak ballads. "All right, maybe those were about you."

We're silent for a minute. I'm about to ask him again to tell me what he meant in the Davidson's driveway, but he starts talking again.

"I never thought you'd come back here," he says. "I thought that when you left, that you were gone for good."

"I could say the same about you. I'm not the one who reenlisted." My tone's more brusque than I mean it to be, and he stiffens.

"I didn't have a choice."

"That's a load of shit."

His eyes bore into mine. "I didn't. Not after what happened. I couldn't stay here, be around you."

Something new flashes in his eyes. Regret? Longing? Maybe I'm not ready for his confession yet, after all. I move down the railing, putting distance between us. I'm getting pissed.

"Sorry it was such torture to have to deal with seeing your puppy dog ex-girlfriend around town."

He shakes his head. "That's not what I . . ."

But I cut him off. "Why'd you bother coming back then? You finally realize I skipped town?"

Gabe inhales, annoyed. "No. After two tours in Afghanistan and a divorce in between, I didn't feel like I had anywhere else to go but here."

His near decade-long highlight reel hits me like a brick. Gabe was married. In the war. I don't know that I can fully breathe over either.

"Why'd you come back?" he asks, when I don't respond.

I shake my head, trying to play it off. "One addict brother and another who thinks he can fix everyone isn't enough of a reason?"

But Gabe isn't laughing. "You never came back before. That's why I was so surprised to see you that day in my shop."

I had for Harry's trial, but I hadn't stayed in Pacific then—I hadn't been able to bear it at the time. I didn't even want to testify, but the DA said it was the only way to ensure my "monster" of a father would stay behind bars for good.

Monster.

The word bothers me now. The question of whether the title fits.

"I wouldn't have come if I'd known it was yours," I say. "I wouldn't have wanted to mess with your life."

There is such hurt in Gabe's eyes when I say that. Too familiar. Suddenly we are back in time, leaning against his pickup truck out in a field somewhere. I'm eighteen years old and all I want is for him to kiss me. I shake off the thought. What is wrong with me? What is wrong with him? He's looking at me the same way.

"The last thing you could ever do is mess with my life."

This was a terrible idea. I startle back a step.

"I should go," I say, moving for the stairs that lead around the house. "I don't know why I thought bringing any of this back up would help."

"July." Gabe's voice stops me before I step down. "You clearly came here for a reason. Something's bothering you. I've seen it on your face since the moment you got out of your car."

I flip around. "Don't pretend you can still read me, that you know who I am anymore."

Gabe rests one arm on the railing. "I did once. I'd argue, better than most people. And I think you're here because you know that you can trust me with whatever it is."

"I thought I could once, too. But that was clearly a lie like everything else."

His eyes light. "None of it was a lie to me."

"Right. Not a lie. *Just an easy fuck.*"

Gabe's face collapses. "I hate that you remember that."

"Kind of emblazoned on my memory."

"I didn't mean it."

"Sure you didn't."

This pisses him off. I can see it in the set to his shoulders, like a hornet's nest that only requires one final, agitated kick. "Can't any conversation be easy with you?"

"I don't know why you try," I snap. "You already got what you wanted from me. As you so kindly pointed out then—I meant nothing to you. So why are you messing with my head now, with this bullshit about me not knowing everything that happened?"

He strides toward me, stopping directly in front of me at the top of the stairs. "*Goddamn it*. Because you don't. Because I made you believe that night that you meant nothing to me." His eyes are dilated. "But I loved you."

I'm too shocked to speak. Our faces are illuminated beneath a flickering lantern. Moths clink against it, launching their precious dusty wings against the glass in the hope of reaching the light. My light back then is standing right in front of me. I would have thrown myself against the glass for him once, too.

"You broke up with me," I say. They're the only words I can manage to stumble out, as stupid as they sound. "You broke my heart."

Gabe's expression is tormented. "He made me do it. He made me turn you away and never so much as look at you again, or he threatened to report Ma and Abuela to immigration. I had to protect them."

"What are you even talking about?"

"That day at the police station," Gabe says. "I was planning to come see you after, to figure it all out, but your brother was on Daniela's porch when we got home. He said that if I didn't break up with you, and not tell you he was there, he'd report my family to immigration. My Ma and Abuela would have been deported to Ecuador."

My heart stops. I can't think. I can't feel. I'm reliving that night. It all rewinds like a VCR tape. Gabe's words and how they'd gutted me: *Just an easy fuck.* I startle back.

Mark. All of this has been because of Mark.

"I didn't have any choice," Gabe insists. "I had to protect my family."

But I can hardly process what he's saying. "You were so cold. I believed you."

Gabe looks anguished. "It gutted me how quick you did. I didn't even have to convince you. It was so easy for you to believe that our entire relationship meant nothing to me."

"I walked home through the woods because of that conversation," I say. "I was attacked. Pinned down. He was going to kill me. I was only there because I was so devastated by what you said."

"I know. I know."

There are no tears from me, only fury. Fury at Mark for forcing us apart, fury at Gabe for letting him, fury at myself for being so goddamn naive and making the choices I did that night. Because I don't really blame Gabe. He was as much a victim of the Weavers' web as anyone. But I am angry at the universe.

"You should have told me," I whisper.

"How could I?" Gabe asks. "That's why I had to reenlist. I couldn't stay here and see you every day around town and keep lying. Not with how I felt about you. Plus, there was always the possibility that he would change his mind and go to the cops anyway, for the hell of it. I figured the best way to keep my Ma and Abuela safe was to just leave."

This rewrites every brokenhearted love song I've ever written about Gabe. Redefines all shades of the last near-decade of my life, the affairs, the drinking, the unwillingness to give anyone my heart again. Gabe's rejection has been part of my excuse for all of it, part of the narrative I have so painstakingly written for myself. Now to find out that our downfall was the work of someone else entirely—well, that makes it all the more tragic.

"I'm sorry," Gabe says. "I'm so sorry I didn't keep you from walking into those woods that night."

Guilt. He feels like Harry's attack on me was his fault. Maybe it partially was. But it was also Colton's. And my own. And Mark's. And Harry's. No one present that night is entirely innocent.

"You couldn't have known," I say. "I've never put that on you."

"Well, I do." Gabe inhales. "I wanted to go to the detectives after and tell them about everything, but by then they'd already arrested your father. I didn't want to add to all the pain you were going through, so I stayed away until I left. I didn't even hear that you'd dropped out of school and left town until after my first tour. I thought I was doing the right thing by leaving."

"So did I," I say, meaning myself.

"I'm relieved at least I can finally tell you the truth now that Ma and Abuela are gone."

Yeah, but it's not like I know what to do with it. Now I only have more reasons to suspect Mark of being the real Pacific Lake Killer, or even Harry's accomplice. And somehow, where I thought Gabe's confession would give me the closure I once so desperately sought, I feel as if my world is a gaping wound. What passed between us had been real.

"Thank you. For telling me," I say.

"Maybe now you can stop writing songs that make me want to rip my heart from my chest."

I laugh. "Come on. I highly doubt they affect you that much anymore. You've been married, for Christ sake."

Gabe's eyes are on me, a window. "I never loved anyone like I loved you, July."

I feel my breath catch in my throat, then I train my eyes back out on the lake, my hands gripping the railing for balance. "You can't say things like that to me. Not now." Somehow, of everything tonight, this is the most offensive.

"Why not," Gabe asks from behind me, "when it's the truth?"

And in my heart, his words on the wind, I know it is. Because it's the same for me. I've loved since Gabe, but never as much as Gabe. Losing him was like losing the moon.

He places his hands on my arms and turns me. I don't know whose mouth finds the other's first, but we interlock. Our kisses are long and deep. We drift off the deck and through the house like two swaying phantoms. Clothes falling and limbs touching, until we're in his room, against one another over his comforter, reliving everything from before, and carving a new present.

* * *

Later, I envy Gabe's ability to sleep. It's not something I'm capable of, staring up at his bedroom ceiling as he snores on his stomach beside me. My mind is too busy swirling. About him, about the past, about Mark's role in all of it.

What I know: Mark was closer to May than any of us. Mark was in love with Laurel Dillon and didn't tell anyone that she was also apparently seeing an older man; Mark was friends with Kelly Anders. Mark hated me; Mark turned Gabe in to the cops so they would suspect him of the murders, then threatened him to end our relationship. Mark was often in the greenhouse where May died. Mark left town at the time Harry was convicted and the murders stopped; I found the earrings, including possibly Adrian Bennet's, only after Mark returned to town. What if I had gotten it all wrong back then? What if this entire time my father has been sitting in a cell, when my brother is the actual murderer?

What I want to do is run home and throw Mark up against the tree and force him to convince me I'm wrong. Because no matter how cruel he can be, no matter what he's done, I still don't yet fully believe that he was capable of killing those women and framing Harry. But what if they were in on it together, and now Mark is carrying on the tradition alone? I'd be a fool not to at least consider that possibility, right?

Another memory crackles across my consciousness. Kathy standing in the kitchen the day they found May, her waving the rifle at my brothers. She said he had the devil in him. Was it a delusion, or did she know something? Is that why she said he didn't deserve to be happy? Why she feels the need to keep silent now? Is she scared of him?

There's only one other person I can go to for the truth.

I stare at the clock. Five AM. If I leave now, I can drive all night and be there when visiting hours start.

I find my dress on the floor of the hall along with my heels. I trade them in for one of Gabe's plaid shirts, an oversized pair of jeans, and a pair of boots by the back door. This isn't goodbye to him, though I'm sure he'll be pissed as all hell when he wakes and finds me gone. I just can't wait. Not when all the answers are on the tip of my tongue.

It's raining hard when I back my car out of his driveway, so heavy I can hardly see the road. I plug my destination into the GPS and drive. It's three hours away. I clean myself up in a bathroom stall of a McDonald's halfway there.

When I reach my destination and pull up to the massive gate, a guard gets out of his stand and asks why I'm here.

"Visiting hours," I say. "I'm July Weaver, here to see my father, Harold Weaver."

The wire gate parts, and I drive onto prison grounds.

21

Then

I LAID MOTIONLESS IN Colton's passenger seat, waiting until he was finished. It was fast, sloppy, and I was so far gone I didn't even feel like the dirt I wanted to when I got in his car. Only empty.

I turned my head away, trying not to picture Gabe. A part of me had done this to erase all traces of him from my skin, but it only brought him up more. That thought alone made me want to cry. But I bit my lip and forced myself to sit up when Colton flipped off me. I wasted no time in yanking on my underwear and jeans. He nipped my shoulder and I shrank away from him like he was made of hot embers.

"Touchy," he said, but there was a laugh in his throat.

I threw my tank top over my head and pitched open the Jaguar's door. My Converses were in my hands.

"I thought you wanted a ride," Colton called after me.

I didn't answer him.

"Suit yourself, if you want to walk home in the dark."

But I was already gone, my feet crunching over gravel as I put distance between that creep and me. I didn't look back, less because I didn't want to give him the satisfaction, and more because I frankly didn't give a shit. I'd gotten what I wanted from Colton Davidson, used him in the same way Gabe had used me. *Just an easy fuck.* I didn't feel any lighter.

Colton had parked us in the middle of an abandoned field, but I didn't follow his tire tracks back to the main road. I knew exactly where I was—a mile or so from my house. If I hefted it on foot, I'd make it back by dawn. After that, I wasn't sure about the order of things. I would shower, I would sleep, and sometime before this time tomorrow, I would be on a Greyhound bus out of this town. The events of the night had decided that for me: I was leaving Pacific, and I sure as hell was never, ever, going to come back.

I wove among the trees, my shoes I had since pulled on snapping on branches and mold-caked leaves. There were bats and owls shrieking in the distance, the vague cuffing of water against the shore far to my right. It was harmony, a chorus of air.

But the night also carried my name on the mist. I heard the call. It sounded like a hawk's screech, and at first I thought I'd imagined it.

But then it came again, "July."

This time more distinct, robotic, like one of those handheld, voice-changing megaphones Deck used to love as a kid. I flicked my head around, panicked, my hand going for the pocketknife I'd taken to carrying around since that day at the hunting cabin. But I couldn't pinpoint which direction the voice was coming from.

After a moment, I convinced myself that I must be tired, my body run down and paranoid after everything that had happened that day. Still, I picked up my pace. Something was gnawing at my stomach in addition to my resolve, some instinct that urged me to run, despite my mind trying to reassure me.

I am the king.

I was close to home, maybe half a mile to go. I veered closer in the direction where I knew the road would be. I'd feel better when I was out in the open, jogging down that dotted gold line.

A hand came over my mouth. A man emerged behind me, his forearms becoming a vise around my core. I tried to scream, to kick back against him, but he caught me firm and something smashed against the back of my skull. Maybe a rock.

The world turned hazy. I saw only shapes in the dark, branches tilting overhead, blurry stars. I smelled dirt and moldy leaves and damp around my hair. Then there was him, his body hovering over mine on the ground. His cologne burned my nostrils—cedar and sweat. Distinct, pungent. That combined with my headache made me want to be sick.

I panicked, realizing I was about to be *the king's* next victim. I thrashed, yelling for help, my reality refocusing with my fear. But the man pinned my hands, pressing his body into mine, his elbows digging into my chest. Then his hands wrapped around my throat.

The body's instinct to survive is a remarkable thing—it overcomes all sense, all desire. Where I thought my mind had all but departed me mere seconds ago, my body was now grappling to stay alive. With my attacker's fingers digging into my throat, he may have been able to stifle my scream, but he couldn't stop my now free hand from reaching out to my side and grabbing hold of a piece of driftwood. It was thick, heavy. I doubted it would do much in the way of inflicting damage, but it did surprise him when I rammed it across his temple, then kneed him in the groin.

The killer jolted back. I took my one shot, half stumbling to my feet. I still felt off kilter, but forced myself to move, launching myself from tree trunk to trunk as I regained my footing. When I caught my equilibrium again, I took off sprinting. My attacker wasn't in sight when I dared to look back at the hollow of trees he'd forced me down in. He'd vanished—a shadow in the wood.

I didn't dare scream again in case he was looking for me. Instead, I forced myself through the bracken toward the road, my lungs fried and my legs aching by the time I reached the blacktop. I tripped, but forced myself to keep stumbling down the centerline. Mercifully, headlights shimmered on the horizon, careening down the hill. A car roaring toward me. No, not a car—a truck—and a familiar one at that.

The driver slammed on his brakes. I went to my knees in the middle of the line. I'm confident I must have looked like a wraith—the ghost of our dead sister come back to haunt him.

Auggie rushed from the truck, my defiant rescuer haloed like a deity in the high-beamed headlights. "July?"

I latched onto his arms like a woman possessed. I reeked of the cologne. I reeked of *him*.

"Daniela called," he said. "She said you took off on foot. I've been driving up and down this road for the last hour looking for you."

Auggie attempted to hug me but I pushed him away with my palm. I felt wild, unhinged.

"It was him, Aug," I huffed, out of breath. "He tried to get me, too."

Auggie looked up around us in alarm, his eyes darting to the woods. "Him?"

Our very survival depended on this moment. We needed to move, fast.

"I know who the killer is," I said. "We have to get out of here. We have to go, now, before he finds us."

I tried to get up on my own, but Auggie didn't need more convincing. He lifted me into his arms and carried me to the passenger side of his truck and slammed the door after me.

"We need a phone," I said once he climbed in.

Auggie pushed the truck seventy miles an hour down the thirty-mile back road. He whipped us curve for curve, the lake kissing the shoreline immediately to our left. We were lucky he knew these roads or we might have gone over the edge entirely.

"What we need is to get you to a hospital," Auggie said.

"No," I yelped, grabbing hold of the handle overhead at a particularly jolting turn. "We need to get to the police station. To Rafael."

Now Auggie appeared the unhinged one. "July, you're hurt. Look at your neck."

I popped down the passenger side mirror. Dark welts were already beginning to form in the shape of finger pads along my collarbone.

"I'm fine," I said, snapping it closed. "Cops now. Hospital later."

Auggie released something resembling a growl.

"Auggie."

"Fine."

He turned left at the juncture where the lake road split in two. We sped opposite of Hazel General, bearing straight for the center of town—where the police station waited.

*   *   *

We were at Hazel General, Rafael having forced us here after I relayed every detail of the attack, him fearing I had a blood clot or brain injury once he saw the bruises on my neck and gash on the back of my head.

"I'm not taking any chances with you," he said, and Auggie agreed.

So I found myself in a hospital bed with an unnecessary IV in my arm, an ice pack for my head, and a full body scan behind me. I'd already been scavenged for DNA: my clothes taken, my skin scraped. But I had drawn a line at a rape kit. I told the detectives and hospital staff that it wasn't necessary. Although I did have to relay that I'd had consensual sex with Colton earlier in the night in case they found his DNA on my skin. Auggie stiffened at that, but I wasn't up for his judgments. He'd been as absent as the rain over the last few weeks.

My brother did insist on staying with me through all of the exams. My neck and vocal cords would recover, my voice was only raspy to show for it, and the spot on the back of my head was hardly even bleeding.

"Where is she?"

I heard my father's voice before I saw him.

Rafael and the other officers weren't in my room at the time. I'd wanted it this way. Just me, and Auggie in the chair beside my bed. The cops crowded the outer corridor as Harry burst into the room.

"Livewire," my father huffed. "Thank God."

For once he actually appeared the picture of fatherly concern. His eyes were bloodshot and he was sweating head to toe. He'd been outside, supposedly on his way home from his foreman job, but Rafael had called the tire factory beforehand. Harry hadn't shown up for his shift earlier that night.

His gaze darted between Auggie and me. Auggie was a wound spring, his knuckles knit over his lap. I could tell it was taking every ounce of strength he had not to tackle Harry to the floor. Our father, as usual, however, was oblivious to this, or chose to ignore it.

"Well?" Harry waited. "Tell me what happened. What did he look like?" He noticed the bruises at my throat. "Jesus, Livewire." He made a move to touch them.

Auggie got up. "Not another step."

Harry froze, his hand still outstretched toward me. He looked to his eldest son, all authority. "Sit down, boy."

Instead, Auggie balled his hands into fists at his sides. The two of them were the same height, build—it would be a close fight with Auggie's shoulder still healing, but he did have twenty years on the old man.

"It's all right, Auggie," I said.

I leaned forward and Harry brought his fingertips to trace the outline of one of my bruises, only to draw back when I flinched.

"What happened?" Harry whispered, his eyes glimmering with unreadable emotion.

"I think you know already."

It wasn't a shot over the bow. It was a hole blown through the goddamn heart of the ship.

Harry's gaze moved to my face. "What did you say?"

"She said that you know already," Auggie said.

Outrage appeared on Harry's squinted brow. "Don't tell me that the two of you have allowed those detectives to convince you that I had anything to do with this?"

I shook my head. "I couldn't see the man in the dark. But I knew his build. I knew his hands as they wrapped around my throat." I practically choked out the last words.

Harry stumbled back a step. "You . . . you think I would *ever* be capable of harming you? You, Livewire? Or your sister . . ." He spat the words, disgusted. "You're my daughters, for Christ sake . . ."

"Cedar," I said.

Harry shook his head, confused. His entire world was crumbling down around him. "What?"

"The killer, when he held me down. He smelled like cedar. It was your cologne. I'd know it anywhere."

"A lot of people wear cologne."

"Do a lot of people lend their working gloves to serial killers, too?" Auggie asked. "Because the cops found this one left behind at the scene."

He threw the evidence bag with the tan leather glove on the bed between us. Harry gazed at it, then looked up.

"That could be anyone's glove."

"It's full of your DNA," I said.

Harry shook his head. "Then someone is trying to set me up. They planted it. They—"

But I never got to hear how my father intended to finish that thought. Rafael clearly believed he had given Auggie and me enough of a grace period. Multiple officers entered the room, the detective at the lead with a pair of handcuffs.

"Harold Weaver," Rafael said. "You're under arrest for the murders of May Weaver, Laurel Dillon, and Kelly Anders, along with the attempted murder of July Weaver. You have the right to . . ." He read off Harry's Miranda rights, but my father wasn't listening. His attention was solely on me.

An officer handcuffed him. Harry looked as broken hearted as the morning he'd returned home from Atlanta to discover his youngest daughter gone. Just as stunned. "You're smarter than this, Livewire. You know I'm not responsible. I'm being set up as the fall guy, and you're helping the real killer do it."

But I turned away from my father, my once bright speck on the dark lake, my protector from the lightning. I couldn't look at him, as they hauled him out. He bellowed down the hall, yelling back at me to *think*. To really think.

I stared out the window at the sidewalk, the poorly illuminated bus stop cube and flickering EMERGENCY sign on the nearby lawn. A hand cupped my shoulder and I flinched. It felt so like his that I thought I was back in the woods again. But it was only Auggie, trying to comfort me as always. I leaned into him, releasing a harsh guttural wail.

He held me as I clutched onto his shirt, the balance to our relationship restored. He was my own personal Atlas, straining beneath the weight of my crumbling world.

"Auggie. July."

We flipped around. There, standing in the doorway to the hospital room, were our three younger siblings. Deck, wild-eyed and anxious; April, beaming and relieved; Mark expressionless and cold.

I had no words for them. For what was left of our fractured family. The sibling I still vowed never to speak to again. The other two I had fully intended to abandon until two hours ago. I didn't have the strength to go to any of them, to hold out my arms and tell them everything was going to be okay.

I couldn't. Right now, I couldn't even take care of myself.

Auggie slapped on a fake smile. Painful to no one but me.

"It's going to be okay," he told them. "It's over now."

CHAPTER

22

Now

I DON'T KNOW WHAT I expect when the prison visiting room door buzzes open, but I guess it's this. What strikes me first is the quiet. Apparently not a lot of people come to visit detainees at nine AM on a Monday morning. I nod to the six or so guards I pass lining the walls, careful to weave through the circular tables jammed at awkward angles throughout the all-white space. Three orange jumpsuits stand out, the inmates mirrored at their designated tables by men in various forms of dress, a couple in suits.

I sit down at one of the empty tables and make a show of staring at my hands. I'm all too aware of being the only woman in this room. It's hard not to be, when I feel all sets of male eyes on me. My foot taps nervously of its own volition. I've been dreading this; had almost chickened out of coming altogether.

Before I can rethink that, the door on the opposite wall buzzes and another orange-clad inmate enters the field. My father is a giant in comparison to the others, the corded muscles that run from his neck to his wrists glaring in his short-sleeved prison shirt. He looks different from how I remember him—old and ragged, a near decade inside having aged him twice as many years. When his gaze locks on me, he takes a visible inhale of breath, as if he didn't actually expect me, despite what he'd been told.

He sits down and I force myself to meet his eyes.

"Hello, Livewire."

His voice is gravelly like I remember it. I feel overcome. Nostalgia for who he was, rage for who I've believed him to be, and uncertainty for who he actually is. I don't know what to think. All I keep staring at are the crow's feet crinkled at the corners of his eyes and his large palms on the table that display his veins. I wonder if I have done this to him—if I have single-handedly facilitated the incarceration of an innocent man. It's selfish, I know that, but a part of me has come to reassure myself that he is guilty. That would make everything so much easier.

"Harry."

"I knew you'd come. One day."

"I don't know why you thought I would, after everything that happened."

Harry's lips go into a hard line, resigned. "I'm not going to sit here and try to convince you that I'm innocent. Once, I would have done that, would have been desperate for you to believe me. But after all these years, I'm only happy you're here. Even if it's to hate me."

I inhale sharply. I was expecting anger, his old eccentrici-ties even. What I was not expecting was this resigned version of my father, forgiving. I try to figure out how to phrase what comes next. For all my driving through the middle of the night, I didn't once give a thought to how I was going to start this conversation.

"I've heard your songs," he says.

"Don't," I say. "I'm not interested in the father-daughter reunion special. I came here to ask you questions."

Harry straightens up. "All right. I'm listening."

"If you didn't murder May and the other girls, then who did?" The words are out of my mouth like a snap. Apparently, I'm not going to warm up to it.

Harry's eyes study mine, two fiery coals. He's now curious, but calm. "Why? What's happened?"

"I never said anything's happened."

"But something has. Otherwise you never would have come here and asked me that. I can see it on your face. You're finally questioning everything."

Damn biology for making it so easy for my kin to read my emotions. But who am I kidding? I've never been a good liar.

Harry's a lit spark. "I knew you would. I knew one day you'd be the one to figure it all out."

"I haven't figured anything out," I snap.

Harry laughs, jabbing his pointer finger in my direction. "Maybe not yet. But you're close. I can see it. Things are starting to fall out of place about what happened back then."

I stick out my jaw. "What is it with you and Kathy and the cryptic messages? Why doesn't anyone in this family just come out and say what they actually suspect?"

"Tell me *who* you suspect."

I knit my fingers, and lean over the table, deciding this second that I do need him as much as he needs me. *Prove to me that I wasn't wrong all these years. That you haven't been rotting in here while my baby sister's murderer is out working on Wall Street or running for Pacific town mayor, killing more women.* "You tell me who you suspected back then and why. Maybe then, if I feel like sharing, I will."

Harry taps his fingers on the table, thinking. "I only had suspicions. Never any proof."

"You were gone half the time on wild-goose chases looking for May those first few months. What did you learn then?" He'd never shared anything with us.

"Nothing. I was tracing serial killer cases across the country. None of them ever matched your sister. After a while, I realized it had to be someone close to home, not random. Dillon and Anders' bodies showing up confirmed that."

"That's why you stuck around after Laurel Dillon disappeared."

I'm still not totally buying his story, but I'm willing to go along with it for now. Maybe then I can find a hole in it—the proof I'm desperate for that he is the Pacific Lake Killer and I've only become paranoid.

Harry goes on, "I thought it could be one of the heroin addicts or migrant workers that started popping up around Montgomery County. That theory was reinforced when you and Deck found the cabin in Dewey Meadow, where they all used to camp. That felt weak, though.

"I considered other possibilities—neighbors, friends, May's teachers. But also no one in town fit for having connections with both May and the two older girls. Dillon and Anders likely crossed paths with the same people, but an eight-year-old? The twins hardly left the house aside from a playdate.

"I then wondered whether it could've been two killers. May's death was different—a drowning, as opposed to a sexual encounter followed by strangulation. But then, they wouldn't have all been found disposed of in the water the same way next to each other. No, Rafael was right about May being a prototype for the king's later victims. What I can't to this day wrap my head around is why not a less-sheltered child. The killer could have taken any handful of young girls off Main Street without anyone noticing. So, why May? Unless . . ."

"It was personal."

"Someone close to her," Harry offers. "It's no secret that, with your mother's condition at the time, we weren't exactly friends with many folks in town. I'm not fool enough not to have seen how our family was looked at. But that also meant that May's circle was small."

"Just say it," I growl. "You think it had to be one of us."

Harry nods. "The narrative fits too well. That was why it was so easy for the police to pin it on me. They always look at the family first, especially the male relatives."

"Kathy tried to kill us all once," I point out. "She could have lost her mind, drowned May in a delusion. You could have covered for her, then decided you liked it, and gone after Dillon and Anders on your own."

My father looks bored, almost annoyed. "Now you're repeating the crap Rafael fed to you."

"I'm still not convinced he was wrong."

"Your mother wasn't capable of killing one of the twins. Besides, based on the angle that May was held down and the other women strangled, the killer had to be a man over five eight. That left me and any one of your brothers that summer."

"No chance," I say. "The three of them adored May. None of them were capable of harming her."

"Deck did not love your sister. She tormented him and April. Your mother and I saw that. Auggie cared *too* much about all of you. And Mark spent the most time with May alone—he bonded to that little girl more than he ever did the rest of you. They were constantly in that greenhouse together."

There, I feel my stomach sink like a rock. That last sentence. I'm sure it's obvious on my face because of how Harry studies me.

"You are questioning one of them."

"No."

Harry sits back in his chair, frowning. "Why did you come home, July?"

"Who said I did?"

"Stop evading my questions," Harry says. "You've been home, at least for a while, if you were brought to the point of coming here. And you wouldn't return to Pacific unless something made you. You wouldn't come for your mother. So which of your siblings crashed so epically that you had to come back?

I swallow. "Deck tried to throw himself off Hazel Bridge in June. He has drug problems, and schizophrenia."

Harry nods. "I suspected if any of you would inherit your mother's disease, it would've been him."

Excuse me? "Why?"

"He agitated easily as a child, was moody. He also had difficulty at times distinguishing his dreams from reality. I didn't know for a fact, but I knew it could be a possibility."

I'm furious. There are many forms of monsters in this world, not all of whom are murderers. "And God forbid you actually have him diagnosed and medicated before he hit a tipping point, right? Let's ignore the problem, and hope it doesn't exist, as usual?" I smack my hand on the table. "Do you have any idea how many years it took me to get him regulated in Nashville? Hell, he'd already turned himself into a heroin addict by the time he was finally diagnosed, because he was so desperate to figure out how to cope on his own."

Harry's jaw clenches with that stubborn willfulness I know well. No, of course he wouldn't take care of Deck when he first noticed the warning signs. He wouldn't get his own spouse, the love of his life, help for her mental illness. Why would he address the same problem potentially in his son?

"He could have been having delusions back then . . ." Harry starts.

But I hold up my hand. "Deck's never been violent to anyone but himself. Besides, it couldn't have been him. That night in the woods, my attacker was too big, like you. Deck was scrawny."

Harry shrugs. "It was the oldest two I suspected more anyway."

I laugh without humor. "You really think Auggie could hurt a fly?"

"Who else could you confuse so easily for the shape and feel of me, other than Mark or Auggie?" my father asks. "Who would know to put on my shoes and gloves, my cologne so you would smell it?"

I shake my head, not wanting to believe it. Everything my father is saying, it is only leading me closer to Mark. The killer can't be Auggie. He was the one to find me on the road afterwards.

"Both of your brothers knew Anders, for all I know, Dillon too."

I allow seconds to tick by before I answer. I debate whether to reveal all that I know. Because if I do, and I'm wrong about this, if Harry's only using me for leverage to try to escape from prison a guilty man, I'll only be giving him more ammo to do it.

I can't help it. My instincts twist, like ribs snapping, telling me to trust the man across from me I've spent the last decade despising.

"Mark did," I say. "He was in love with Laurel Dillon."

Harry's eyes widen, and I see that I have provided a missing piece he too has been searching for.

"How do you know?"

"I suspected it back then, but Kathy showed me a home video where he and Dillon were together. I confronted him about it. He hid the relationship because he was embarrassed by her. But he also claims that she was seeing an older man on the side. I assumed that meant you."

"Or, so he wants you to believe," Harry says. "He never told the cops any of that. He could have invented that the moment you confronted him, to throw off your suspicions."

"I know."

"He also was the one to report your relationship with Gabriel Santana to the police."

This floors me. "How do you know about that?"

Harry scoffs. "I know every detail about this case, Livewire. Down to everywhere you were the night you were attacked. I looked into both Santana and the Davidson boy my first months in here, with my lawyer—despite Davidson's father redacting his son's name from the final report because of his sexual encounters with both you and Anders. But Santana was on an army base when May was killed and Davidson was in Chicago with his family for the weekend. I could have connected either of them to the older girls or you, but again . . ."

"Same killer," I finish.

"Same killer."

"There's something else," I say, then hesitate to get the words out. They sound more damning than when I asked April about them. "I found earrings in the chrysalis box in the greenhouse. All unmatching. One is exactly like what a missing woman from Alabama is wearing in her news photo."

This, of all things, Harry has not been expecting. He looks almost frightened. "You're sure?"

"It's pretty distinct. Unless I'm following in the family footsteps, and losing my mind, too."

It wouldn't be out of the realm of possibility, but Harry shakes his head. "Where are the earrings now?"

"I put them back in the box. I didn't want whoever put them there to know I'd seen them. I thought maybe they were April's, but she didn't know anything about them and I don't think they're Kathy's, either. Auggie never goes in the greenhouse. The only people ever in there are April to take care of the plants and Mark when he's in town. According to April, he's spent almost every night he's visited out there at all odd hours."

"As I said, he had an odd attachment to your sister," says Harry.

"But he's so normal, the most of any of us," I say. "That's what I'm struggling with here. But I just found out that he threatened Gabe to stay away from me or he'd report his family to immigration back then. And on top of that, Deck swears he was drugged, both when he relapsed before the bridge and at the Davidsons' fundraiser a few weeks ago, like someone has been setting him up. The Davidson's house was later set on fire that same night. Mark said he got home around midnight, but we have no way to prove that."

"What would burning down the Davidsons' mansion accomplish?" Harry asks, attempting to follow my logic.

I shake my head. "I don't know. It just feels like too much coincidence for it not to be related. And all the rest of us are accounted for at that time, but him."

"These are all speculations at this point," Harry warns. "You need evidence."

"Fuck the evidence. My teenage sister has been living in the same house with a potential murderer for weekends all summer, and there's a missing woman's earring in the fucking butterfly box."

"Settle down. We need to think."

I feel as if I could reach across the table and strangle him in this moment. The irony isn't lost on me.

"I am thinking," I snap. "All I've been doing all god-damn summer is overanalyzing and thinking. Now, I wonder if I should have just stayed out of Georgia and left this family to rot. Maybe I still will."

But Harry shakes his head. "You can't do that."

"Oh, because I'm supposed to think you're completely unbiased here?" I accuse. "Because we both know it's in your best interest for Mark to be the killer so that you can walk free."

"This isn't about that. Listen. You say you've been home all summer with all of them. That Deck's been potentially put off the rails by Mark, that April is exposed to him every day. You need to get your younger siblings out of there. Take a picture of the earrings in the chrysalis box, then make an excuse to pack up Deck, April, and your mother, and go. Don't stop at Nashville. Get as far away as you can off the grid, then call the police. I will handle it from there."

"You're a convicted felon in prison."

"A convicted felon with the truth on his side," he points out. "What we really need is for Adrian Bennet's body to show up, to connect her to the earlier murders."

The irony that my father is hoping for another woman to show up dead isn't lost on me. Only Harry.

"Good luck with that," I mutter. "They've been looking for her for five months."

My father thinks hard. "If she was taken by 'the king,' then she'll be close by. In the meantime, you need to move. Go home. Call me when you're somewhere safe."

He stands, but I do not. I am perfectly frozen, exactly where I am in this seat, my mind whirling.

"July," my father urges.

"You actually didn't do this, did you?" It's only sinking in now.

Unless Harry is the greatest actor in the world, he is not the Pacific Lake Killer.

He smiles, sad. "I really didn't, kid."

It's difficult to get the words out. "It was me who put you in here."

But Harry shakes his head. He reaches out his hand and offers mine a squeeze. It is the first time we have touched in fifteen years.

"No, Livewire," he says firmly. "You didn't. Your brother put me in here to punish me. And I put me in here with my own foolishness. I should have seen it clearer. I was just so overwhelmed, the same as all of you, that I missed it. I mean, even your mother saw it better."

"What do you mean?"

"Running around saying there was a devil in the house. Her waving that gun in the kitchen that day—your mother knew. I think she saw her son was evil and didn't know any other way to tell us." There are tears in my father's eyes

"I don't know how I make this right," I say.

My father offers me his hand again, but I don't take it when I stand up.

"Start with the picture," he says. "Then get Deck, April, and your mother out. The rest will follow."

As my father steps back, I feel simultaneously hollow and filled to the brim. I watch him as he heads toward the inmates' door, only to stop in front of the guards buzzing it open. He looks back. "Livewire?"

"Yeah?"

"Be careful."

*　　*　　*

I've already been on the freeway for twenty minutes, when my phone rings. I stare at the caller ID, unknown, but quickly realize there are four other missed calls from this same number, starting ten minutes after I walked into the prison at eight-thirty. Shit.

I answer, knowing it's Gabe before he breathes a word.

"Hi."

My mind is elsewhere, mostly on the accelerator I'm currently pounding into the floor. My car encroaches on ninety.

"Are you serious?" Gabe asks. "You sneak out in the middle of the night and leave a note with your number on my pillow, and all I get is a hi?"

"I had somewhere to be this morning."

"Yeah. Where?" Gabe sounds pissed and doubtful.

"Prison."

I hear the coffee pot slam on his counter. "Say that again?"

I take a deep breath. I wasn't sure before if I was going to share any of this with Gabe, he's already been in enough of my family shit, but I don't see that I have much of a choice. Someone needs to know.

My speed reaches ninety-five. I hope there are no cops on this freeway.

"I went to see my father."

Gabe hesitates for only a second before he asks, "Why?"

"Because something hasn't been sitting right with me since the beginning of this summer. Ever since coming back here—the story back then, Harry being guilty. It doesn't add up. Something isn't right. And then I found an earring in the greenhouse chrysalis box and Mark has been acting weird and was connected to both Laurel Dillon and Kelly Anders . . ."

"Slow down," Gabe says cutting me off. "What about an earring?"

"There's a stack of earrings in the damn butterfly cocoon box in my family's greenhouse. One looks exactly like one that that woman from Alabama, Adrian Bennet, is wearing in her missing person's photo. And Mark's apparently the only one who spends any time in there, and then after what you told me about how he came to your house and threatened you back then . . ."

"Wait, stop," Gabe says. "You think Mark killed May and the other two girls? Not Harry?"

"Yes," I say, not believing that I'm actually saying those words out loud, let alone believing them.

"But Mark wasn't the one who threatened me on Daniela's porch that night."

I'm nearly cut off by a truck who attempts to swerve in front of me, but I accelerate and blare my horn. Not today. "What do you mean?"

"Mark was the one who saw us that night on the dock and called the cops," says Gabe. "But he wasn't the one to show up to Daniela's and threaten to call immigration on my family. That was Auggie."

I feel my heart rap against my lungs. "Auggie?"

"Yes."

"That's not possible," I say. "Auggie would never do that. He would never threaten anyone."

"July, he pinned me up against the side of the house and told me that if I so much as looked your way again, that he would 'murder me and make sure my family was on the other side of the border only after they watched'."

Auggie.

I want to call Gabe a liar. But then my mind flashes to that night on our own porch after the drive-in incident. To Auggie choking Mark, to him pounding his fist into the shingles while he snapped at me for going out with Colton. The wide receiver who should have been a linebacker. The reserved sibling with all of the power and none of the words that kept our family together. My protector.

A litany of other moments come rushing back in an instant. Auggie's continued hovering in my life. His disdain for both Gabe and Colton whenever they showed up around me. Him lying for Harry at the hunting cabin. His declaration that he would find a way to bring me back to Pacific, no matter the cost. My pulse rises in my ears. What if Deck and Kathy had been the cost?

July, come on. Think about it. This all has to be part of it. Me not remembering getting high, and all of a sudden I'm drugged on that bridge in June? Last night. Someone is doing this to me. Someone is setting me up. Those had been Deck's words the morning after the fundraiser.

No, I can't believe it.

It's not possible. Auggie found me on the road moments after I'd been attacked in the woods. He'd claimed he'd been out looking for me, but what if he'd simply changed his shirt and jumped in his car?

"Gabe, I have to go."

"What? Tell me what's going on. Where are you?"

"I'm on my way home. An hour out. I have to go back for Deck, April, and Kathy."

"Why?"

"Because one of my brothers is the real Pacific Lake Killer, maybe both."

I hear him grab his keys. "I'll meet you at your house. I'll head over there right now."

"No," I insist. "You want to help, you go down to the boat loading zone and find April. She's supposed to be working there today. Get her and drive her to Nashville. I'll text you my address and meet you there once I get Deck and Kathy."

"I don't want you going back to that house alone. I'll call the cops."

"Not yet," I say. "April first. If one or both of my older brothers is anywhere near Deck or her, I don't want to spook them yet. Whoever it is doesn't know that I know."

"I'm calling you every fifteen minutes. If you don't pick up, I'm calling the police."

"Fine."

I end the call and return to punching the gas. I urge the car over a hundred. Willing it to make sure I'm not too late.

23

Then

ALL BEGINNINGS NECESSITATE endings. That was something Harry told us children when we piled into his and Kathy's bed on early childhood nights. The beginnings of his bedtime stories always began the same way—there once was . . . once upon a time . . . there was a time when . . . — while his endings were never concrete, always shifting. The same stories begged for night after night never had the same ends. When Mark, Auggie, and I once asked why, Harry said it was because the future was never finite. We always had the capacity to alter what came next.

But I had already decided on my ending to this story. It was simply a matter of tying up the loose threads. That began with a trip to see Kathy at the psychiatric facility. Auggie and I went together to break the news of Harry's arrest to her. Sitting on the facility's garden patio, nurses standing by in case our mother reacted poorly, Kathy took the fact that her husband of twenty-three years had been convicted of murdering three women, one of which was her baby daughter, surprisingly well. She simply sat there in her metal grated chair, her chin resting on her knuckles, absorbing the words as we relayed them.

I'd worried when coming that the new cocktail of drugs pumping through her bloodstream would leave her more out of it than before, but that thought was quickly dispelled when I looked into her clear eyes. It hurt after eighteen years to finally see my mother so utterly sane, when if Harry had only allowed her to be institutionalized before, or even just properly treated, she could have reached this point years ago. Reflecting on what we knew now, I could only assume that had been intentional on his part. A certifiably insane wife would never be believed if she cried serial killer husband. Another of Harry's manipulations.

"Kathy," Auggie said, bringing his hand to rest on our mother's.

Kathy shook her head, like she was attempting to shake off a dream. "I don't believe it. I don't believe a word of it."

"He attacked me," I tried to explain. "I saw him myself. It was his cologne on me, his glove found at the scene, his DNA."

But Kathy crossed her arms, defiant. "I don't believe it. I know your father better than anyone. He isn't capable of this."

Auggie and I exchanged a look, knowing that in our mother's unmedicated state, it was entirely possible that she'd had no freaking idea what her husband had been capable of. But Kathy was a proud woman. She would never admit that fact.

"You'll see," she went on. "The truth will come out eventually." She fussed with a tissue between her fingers, ripping it. "When can I see him?"

Auggie glanced at the nurses behind us, one of which nodded their head. "I don't know about that. But we're pulling you out of here at the start of next week. The docs say you're about ready to come home."

Kathy scuffed her chair back, and stood. "Good. We'll begin to clear this up then."

I stood too, pressing my palms against the table to lean over her. The power had flipped in this dynamic; she just hadn't realized it yet. "Sit down. We first need to discuss the conditions of you coming home."

Kathy narrowed her eyes, confused. "Conditions?"

"Sit down."

Kathy lowered herself into her chair.

"We don't need to do this now," Auggie said to me.

"Oh, yes, we do," I said, then turned my attention on our mother. "Auggie is worried that you'll snap again if we don't wear kid gloves around you about this, but I don't agree. If you expect to come home, you need to know what's actually been going on over the last week and a half since Harry's arrest. Child services has been showing up. Auggie and I have been going through hell trying to convince them that the house is still a safe environment for Mark, Deck, and April to live, in between Harry's arrest and you coming home."

Kathy went pale. "They're taking them away? The government?"

"No," I said. "Auggie was granted emergency custody of the three of them in the wake of everything that's happened. But after shooting him, you being brought back into the house could jeopardize that."

"I told Auggie how sorry I am," she said, offering a horrified look to her eldest son. "I was out of my mind."

Auggie, the saint, squeezed her hand. "I know that."

"Well, child services isn't as forgiving as your son," I said. "So if you want to come home when you're released next week, you're going to do everything he says."

Kathy bobbed her head. "I'll do whatever you want."

"Good." I nodded. "You can start by staying on your medications. No more of any of what you've pulled over the last few years. Flushing them. Claiming they're lost. Throwing them in the damn lake. You'll take your pills every day, see a counselor every week, you'll go to your psychiatrist's appointments. And if Auggie thinks you're drifting again, and need a medication readjustment, you'll go back into the hospital without question or fight. You'll do whatever Auggie says, or not only will you be without a house, but you'll be without a family. I mean it, Kathy. If you don't keep your shit together this time, Auggie and I'll take Mark, April, and Deck from you, and you'll never see them again. You understand me?"

My words were iron: harsh, but I believed necessary. I wasn't trying to strip her of all her agency. But after everything we'd just been through with Harry, I was determined to be sure that Kathy was not going to be the reason that we lost the rest of our siblings.

She didn't cry as I expected her to; the corner of her lip merely trembled. "I understand."

I saw it in that one look—she felt like a failure as a mother. I had to turn away. I had to wall myself off from feeling compassion for her in order to say what came next.

"Good," I said. "By the way, I'm leaving town."

* * *

After leaving Kathy, I knew I was going to have a panic attack. I sprinted down the hall and through the two security checkpoints until I was out of the facility's visitor center and spilling into the parking lot. I darted for the strip of grass along the barbed wire fence, my knees hitting the ground as I forced air into my lungs. All I saw was hot white static. Panic: Emotional, physical. I felt nothing, but also everything.

Livewire. Harry's little Livewire.

"You okay?" Auggie said, coming up beside me.

Hot tears flowed from me of their own volition. I felt like I couldn't breathe. It was the strongest reaction I'd had since that morning at the hunting cabin—months of agony billowing to the surface in one prolonged anxiety attack. I hadn't even allowed myself to process the attack on me until now. Why did I feel like I was drowning?

Auggie sat down on the grass beside me, but didn't move to touch me. He knew better in these moments. "Just try to breathe."

He stayed with me until it was over. Fifteen minutes must have passed before I no longer felt like I was having a heart attack. Then he was holding out his hand to help me up. "Come on. I'll take you home."

I took the boost, and we walked across the parking lot. My gaze drifted to the sky: gray, with the final remnant of summer just past. It was strangely cool out. The quiet facility grounds made it all the more eerie as the two of us climbed into his pickup truck.

I studied my brother as we rode in silence. The two of us had always been mistaken for twins. While the younger three Weaver siblings were born with the sugar-light hair of our mother, Auggie and I'd been the only two to inherit our father's sandy curls. We had the same nose, the same thin lips. No one would have guessed that Auggie was eleven months older. We'd certainly never acted like it. On the day I was born, he'd appeared at my side, and it felt like he hadn't left since. But if I was being honest with myself—I realized that despite what I'd always believed, there was a part of Auggie that had always needed me more than I did him. That's what made what was coming next so hard.

"You don't have to leave," he said.

"I can't argue with you too, Aug. Please don't make me."

He gripped the wheel tighter. "I'm just saying. You don't have to go if you don't want to. No one's making you. You could stay, and not drop out of school."

"And you could leave." We'd done this dance already. Multiple times.

"They need me."

I shook my head. Auggie might as well have been Father Time, with roots stretching all the way beneath Pacific Lake. He never would leave. Staying to take care of our younger siblings was just the excuse.

"I give it six months before Mark is on a bus out of town too," I said.

"That's his prerogative. He's too old for me to father. The other two are going to need me, though. Kathy too."

"I give it six months before Kathy has another break-down, too."

He inhaled. "Then I'll be here for when that happens."

I pounded my fist into the dash. "Damn it. The more you cast yourself as the martyr, the more I feel like I'm abandoning you to do it."

He veered the truck off the side of the road and put it into park, before turning on me. "Please stay. Please don't leave me."

I stared out at the tree line ahead. It was hideous along the side of this highway compared to Pacific. Half the pine trees were bare and orange.

"Don't ask me that again."

"Why not?"

"Because . . . it's you, Aug, and if you ask me to stay again, I will. And I can't."

Auggie smacked the wheel, exasperated and angry. "Why not? You haven't given me a real answer why not. Why do you have to leave?!"

"Because . . ." I wanted to scream. "If I stay in this town, it'll kill me. Can't you understand that? If I have to look at that damn greenhouse day after day, take care of Kathy, hear about Harry's trial every time I go into town, have to live with Mark, or run into Gabe, or have to be Harry's Livewire one more goddamn day—it'll kill me. There will be nothing left of the sister you love. I'll throw myself into the lake."

"Santana's gone."

I didn't process his words at first. "What do you mean, Gabe's gone?"

"He reenlisted. I doubt the prick will ever be back."

I didn't know how to feel about that. I hadn't seen Gabe since the night of my attack.

"That doesn't change anything. I'm still going."

Auggie sagged in his seat. "So that's it, then."

I took his hand in mine and squeezed. "For me, in Pacific, yeah. But not for you and me." I would not lose my brother over this. "I expect you to visit me in Nashville all the time. Bring April with you."

Auggie sighed. "What about Deck?"

"About that . . . I told him he could come with me."

Auggie's eyes widened. "You what?"

"He doesn't want to stay here any more than I do. Besides, it's not fair to leave you with all three of them and Kathy."

"He's fifteen. He's going to need somewhere to sleep, a place to go to school."

"They do have those things in Nashville you know."

"You'll have no way to support the two of you," he argued.

"There's this thing I could get called a job."

"You won't even have a high school diploma."

"I'll get my GED along with the job." I would too. I was stubborn like that. I didn't tell him I'd already decided on a new name—Jules Thomas.

"I'm being serious."

"So am I," I said. "Let Deck come with me to Nashville. Mark will be gone God knows where once he graduates in a year. That'll leave you with only April and Kathy."

"Our family divided."

"That's the only way our family's going to survive right now."

He contemplated it.

"You can't just quit," he said after a minute. "If Deck gets tough, you can't just ship him back. If we do this, we're striking a deal."

"And what do you propose?"

"We promise each other. If I take care of April and Kathy . . ."

"Then I take care of Deck?" I finished for him. "One of us is getting the more rotten end of that deal."

He shrugged. "If one of us needs help, the other calls. But without the other's permission, we can't quit on our respective siblings. This family is run by you and me now, indefinitely."

"You want to pinky promise on that?"

Auggie held out his hand. "A handshake will do."

I took my eldest brother's hand, and shook, the deal bound. He went to pull back, but I held onto him.

"I'm going to miss you, Auggie Weaver."

There was a set determination in my brother's eyes. "Don't worry. I'll find a way to get you back here."

CHAPTER

24

Now

Because honey we can't fight nature
And mine's killer
So you better stay back
I'm a live wire ready to react
                    —"Live Wire," written by Jules Thomas

DECK IGNORES MY first five calls, then the five after that.
I'm frantic at this point, only fifteen minutes out, calling and calling, as the green exit sign for Pacific, Georgia,
comes into view. I rip the car off the exit ramp, slowing only
enough so that I won't be pulled over.

Pacific Lake taunts me when I turn parallel to it and
whip along its shoreline. I don't think I've taken these turns
faster in my life. It's gloomy out. About to storm. With my
window cranked down, I can feel the electricity in the air
like a hiss. The smothering humidity. It will be a bad one.
The waves crashing against the bordering rocks is a rhythm
of wallops and smacks.

I'm going to need to move fast. Take the picture of the
chrysalis box, and go. Find Deck and Kathy, then call Gabe,
who will hopefully have April by then. We'll all be okay.

Auggie was leaving for his honeymoon in Fiji with Bridget first thing this morning. Mark and Lindsay are supposed to head for the airport with Deck in an hour. My heart thunks. With all that has been going on, I've forgotten. Mark changed their flights. They're at the airport already.

I call him.

"Nice of you to see us off," Mark says.

"Where are you?" I snap.

"Where do you think I am? Our flight boards in twenty minutes."

"Is Deck with you?" The panic rises in my gut. I still don't know who to trust.

"Of course he is," Mark says. "Why wouldn't he be?"

"Put him on the phone."

Mark mutters to someone in the background. Then his voice returns to me. "He says he doesn't want to talk to you, and to stop calling his phone."

"Put him on now," I demand. "Unless you want me to fly up to New York and ensure you can never have children."

"Bitch," he mutters, but there is shuffling.

"What part of I don't want to talk to you do you not understand?" Deck asks.

"Walk to the other end of the terminal. Away from Mark."

"Why?"

"Just do it."

I can hear voices in the background, flights being called. Deck grumbles. "Okay. I'm pacing here, but Voldemort and his wife's eyes are on me. You want to tell me what's going on?"

"You were right," I say, taking a particularly windy turn that causes the car to clip branches. A weak limb tumbles down in my rearview mirror. "About all of it. Harry's innocent. I think either Mark or Auggie are responsible for the murders back then, and murdered Adrian Bennet too. I think whoever did it drugged you before your relapse, and the night of the fundraiser."

"Are you serious right now?" There's fear in my youngest brother's voice, but also validation.

"Yes. And I don't know which of them it is yet, or even if they're in on it together. Which means you need to get away from Mark right now."

I know my brother. Deck's a master at slipping away from places unnoticed. He'll find a way to get out.

"And go where?"

"I'll pick you up. Just get out of the airport and somewhere in Atlanta. Call me, and I'll come for you. I'm going back for Kathy and evidence first, then meeting Gabe with April. The five of us will get the hell out of the state."

"Roger that," Deck says. "But July?"

"Yeah?"

"You're sure it's one of them?"

Your father keeps the devil away when he's home. Kathy's words. She'd known all along. We'd just attributed it to her madness.

"I am."

I reach the bottom of the hill, where our driveway starts. Father Time sticking out of the roof is the only part of the house visible through the densely packed fog.

"I have to go," I say. "I'm here."

"Be careful," Deck says.

"If you can't reach me, find Gabe."

I end the call, praying that Deck makes it out and Gabe has already located April down at the boat launch. My job is the only one left.

I park my car in the empty driveway, wondering where Kathy is. It's early, so I assume still sleeping. I'll get the pictures first, then go grab her from her room. I try to calm myself down. My brothers are both at the airport or on a flight already. My younger siblings are about to be safe and far away from both of them. I am alone. All I need are my mother and the photos.

The manor has never felt so haunted as I hurry around it through the mist. It's gothic, uncanny. The worn brown shingles have witnessed more than one act of evil. I never realized quite how many until now.

The dome of Harry's greenhouse isn't visible until I'm directly in front of it, shoving open the door. It's heavy, slams, and I'm grateful no one else can hear it. As usual I'm greeted by heat, only it feels balmier because of the humidity outside. The interior walls are coated in droplets, keeping anyone from seeing in or out.

The hothouse hardly comes alive with my arrival. A few butterflies are startled by the noise of the door, but all the rest keep their wings pressed together atop their flowers, nectar trays, and orange slices. The fountain is the dominating sound of the room. I can't help but stare into it—at the school of koi that instantly congregate in front of me. I see the crack in a side tile where my sister's skull met it.

Hurry, I order myself, and move to the chrysalis box. I pull out my phone. I even contemplate taking an earring or two as evidence in case one of my brothers' fingerprints are on them, but then I open the box. The six earrings, which had been there only last night when I rechecked, are gone. Including Adrian Bennet's.

Shit.

"July."

A rag comes over my mouth, clamped down by a large hand, restraining me until I breathe the chemicals in. The last thing I see is the chrysalis box tilting sideways, along with the rest of the world.

*   *   *

It smells like fuel and fish guts. That's the first thing I register through the pounding in my head and the vibrations of something moving below me.

I snap my eyes open. I'm on a boat—our family's troller, my hands bound behind my back, my cheek pressed into the damp carpet. I turn upward and see gray skies, feel the mist against my skin. It's lightly raining, storm clouds rolling in from the south end of the lake. *It's gonna be a big one.*

"You're awake," he says, and my body is righted up.

My brother pushes my back against the side of the boat so I can face him at the wheel. He looks happy to see me, but there is also anxiety in his expression, like he's afraid of how I will react.

"Are you all right?" he asks. "The headache will fade soon. Don't worry."

There's a part of me that has known it's him since my phone call with Gabe. I just didn't want to believe it. Somehow it was easier to imagine Mark a murderer.

But Auggie is the Pacific Lake Killer.

"Where are we?" I ask.

"Out on the lake," Auggie says.

We course correct, moving north. His long hair flips to the side with the wind.

"Where's Kathy?"

"I left her tied up in her bedroom. She'll be fine."

Thank God. Gabe will find her when he comes looking for me.

"Where are you taking me?"

"Away," Auggie says. "Somewhere safe, don't worry."

"Don't do this," I say, picking up my nerve. "Don't kill me."

Auggie looks horrified, then offended. "You really believe I'm capable of hurting you? That I would ever hurt you?"

"You attacked me in the woods."

I can see it perfectly now. Auggie's shape is the same as Harry's. He'd donned our father's boots, his shirt, his cologne. Then, when I got away, he ran back to his truck to change. He'd found me on the road in minutes. I smelled the cologne still on him when he hugged me. I only thought it was me.

"I was never going to hurt you," he says. "Don't you think that if I wanted to kill you, I would have any other time that summer? Or this one? You hardly even grazed me with that log that night. I planned it all. I needed you to escape so that you would tell the cops it was Harry."

"It felt pretty damn convincing to me. Were you planning to rape me first, too?"

Auggie grimaces. Like I have said something entirely out of the realm of possibility. "Don't be disgusting. And I never raped anyone. Laurel Dillon and Kelly Anders gave themselves to me willingly. Anders practically threw herself at me at that party." He smirks at the memory. "She wanted to hook up with the star wide receiver. It was all too easy to herd her out into the woods."

I don't want to hear the rest. How he likely strangled her with her clothes still off.

"But you can't blame me, July," he says. "She was cruel about May. I saw the way she taunted you, taunted our family. She wasn't a good person."

"And Dillon?"

"Dillon was more complicated. Did you know that she had a thing with Mark?" He doesn't wait for me to respond, his eyes on the dark lake in wonder. With the rain escalating, it's minutes from becoming a tempest out here. "I saw the way he looked at her when I picked him up from tutoring, the way she adored him—but he just ignored her. That's when it started between her and me."

"You were the older guy she told Mark about."

Another missing piece slides into place. I try to be subtle about looking around me for a weapon, evaluating my options for escape off this boat. The answer is nothing, and none.

"It was only a few times," Auggie says. "I liked her because . . . well, she let me give in to certain urges. Be in control. But then I grew bored. I didn't . . . I didn't want May to be alone down there at the bottom. So I decided to give her

Dillon to keep her company, then Anders. I would have given her more if the boat traffic from the Fourth hadn't brought Anders back up again." He shakes his head. "It figures that stubborn bitch wouldn't stay down."

I can hardly breathe at how horrific it is. Of the fear I'm sure Dillon and Anders felt in their final moments as Auggie's fingers gripped around their windpipes. Of how scared May must have been when her own brother, the boy who was supposed to be her protector, bashed her head against a tile and drowned her with her precious koi.

"Why May?" I ask, a tremble in my voice. "Why start with May?" I feel anger inside of me building—no, rage. I want to drown him in this same lake he buried those women in.

Auggie inhales. "I never meant . . . she wasn't like the others. May was something that never should have happened. An accident."

"Then how did it happen?" I snap.

"You asked me that day in the tux store if she was mean. And I lied to you. I knew she was. May was also a rat. Remember how she used to listen in on our phone calls? The kid would go running to the nearest parent if one of us stepped a toe out of line. The only one of us she liked was Mark."

I'd forgotten this about my sister. Both twins were busybodies, but May was a hundred times worse than April. Nothing stayed secret.

"She overheard me on the phone that night with Dillon." Auggie exhales, but his eyes are hard. "It was late. I thought everyone in the house was asleep. Dillon and I had just started meeting behind Mark's back. I walked into the kitchen and caught May listening to our whole conversation on the other line. You know how close she was to Mark. She would have told him—and the six of us needed to stick together, with everything Harry and Kathy were putting us through. Mark didn't need any more reasons to resent me. So I tried to talk to May, but then she ran."

I can't breathe. He looks like he's relaying the story of another person's memories, cold and detached.

"I chased after her out into the greenhouse. I just had to explain that it wasn't what she thought it was. But when I found her in front of the koi pond, she told me she was going to tell all of you about Laurel. Then she kept saying that I was dirty, over and over again. And, well . . . I just wanted her to be quiet, so I slapped her. It wasn't hard, but she tripped back, fell into the pond, and smacked her head on the tile. There wasn't any blood, but she was unconscious, and I was about to pull her out, but . . ."

"You drowned her," I say, and I can picture it.

That violent urge taking control of him. A desire to kill.

Her face in the water, unconscious, but her body's survival instincts kicking into gear when it started, her arms and legs flailing, her fingernails scraping Melville's scales as Auggie held her tiny body down by the neck. How she must have screamed beneath the surface. How she must have screamed for one of us to come help her.

I gag, and Auggie has me turned and bent over the starboard of the boat, holding my bound body as I vomit into the water. It happens a second time. He pushes hair out of my face like I am a broken child. I hate him. I've never hated another human being so much in my entire life. How sudden it happened.

When it's clear I've finished, he lowers me back into my seated position against the boat wall and takes his seat opposite me at the helm. He looks spooked, panicked. "Here, take some water," he urges, unscrewing a bottle and attempting to tip it into my mouth.

It's a joke, because the rain is full going now. If I wanted water, it is all around us. Our clothes are soon soaked, my hair plastered in wet clumps against my neck and shoulders. We need to get off this lake. I haven't heard the crack, but my instincts say it's coming—lightning.

"You killed our baby sister."

His expression is haunted. "I had to, July. I'm sorry, but I had to. She would have lied to the cops and said I beat her, or tried to kill her when she hit the tile, and they would have taken me away. They would have taken me away from you, from all the rest of our siblings, and you needed me. You needed me, with Kathy off the rails, and Harry being a worthless father. How would you have survived if you were the one expected to take care of everyone? I had to choose: her or the rest of you."

He's shouting because it's the only way to hear each other over the thrashing rain. It beats against my skin like fists. I half contemplate jumping into the water, bound hands and all. But I'm not done yet. A sick part of me needs to hear everything he has to say before I go.

"And what about Dillon and Anders?" I yell. "Were they accidents, too? Or did you kill our baby sister, and get a taste for it?"

His lack of response is the only confirmation I need. Auggie had killed—only to discover that he liked it. So he kept doing it.

"What about Adrian Bennet, and the other five women those earrings belong to in that chrysalis box?" I continue. "Did they die for a reason, too, or just to satisfy your own sick urges?"

Auggie's jaw twitches, his grip hard on the wheel, to keep the boat straight in the tumultuous waters. "You were never supposed to find those. You hate that greenhouse."

"Where are the others, Auggie? Where's Adrian? Are she and the others at the bottom of this lake too?"

Auggie has the audacity to appear smug. "Harry's in prison. Who would expect to find bodies at the bottom of the same lake twice?"

I want to vomit again, but I have nothing left. "Why? Why do you do this?"

Auggie's unraveling. I can see it. I've cut him open, to expose his true self.

"Why do you do anything?" He lashes out. "Why are you an alcoholic? Why is Deck schizophrenic and a drug addict? Why are Mark and April as damaged as they are? We were raised like this! We were raised to be this way!"

"You don't get to blame Kathy and Harry for turning into a murderer!"

Auggie huffs. "Because you're so much better? What you've done with your life in the last nine years? Was what you found in Nashville worth what you abandoned me here for?" He shakes his head. "I thought by getting rid of Davidson and Santana that I would be setting you on the right track. That you would see that it was still me," he beats his chest, "our family, our siblings, that were the ones who had your back. Just like always. The five of us."

"Is that why you set fire to Colton Davidson's house? Nearly burned his wife and children alive? To have my back?"

"And April's," said Auggie. "She was getting too close to that family. After everything Davidson put you through that final summer and him threatening you at the party. The same with Santana. At least him I was able to handle back then. I thought pushing Mark to go to the cops about your relationship would be enough, but that piece of shit was too in love with you. I had to take matters into my own hands." He looks to me. "But I did it. I protected you like I always do."

Auggie, the puppet master. He'd been pulling the strings all along.

"And the hunting cabin?"

"A way to build suspicion against Harry. I wore his clothes so the drifters would provide his description to the cops. I lied about Harry's whereabouts to Rafael that day, so I would have an excuse to go into the station and retract my statement the next morning. I told that stupid detective that Harry threatened me, that we were all keeping quiet because we were terrified of him, that I was convinced that he was the murderer, and gave facts to back it up. I needed to set Harry up to take the fall. Especially after Kathy went into the hospital, getting more regulated by the day."

"You're the devil she talked about."

"She called me that constantly when none of you were around—suspected from the beginning that I killed May. That's why she brought the shotgun into the kitchen that day. I was fortunate that Mark wasn't inside when it started. She kept screaming that she knew it was me. Mark, bless his dense head, didn't think she was making any sense, and you didn't get there until she was pointing the gun at both of us. It wasn't coincidence that I was the one she shot."

"That's why she's so drugged up now," I say. "She was fine when I left, better than ever, but then you messed with her doses. What? Did you convince the doctors she was worse than she was, to keep her from revealing it was you?"

Auggie smiles. "Poetic justice that the one who screeched the loudest then is the one rendered speechless now, don't you think?"

Little does he know just how loud our mother still is, even subdued, biding her time, while Auggie's written her off as incompetent. She's known, and has been trying to warn me all along.

"You're a monster," I say.

He shakes his head. "No. I love my family. More than anything. I love you, more than anyone. That's why I needed you back. Everyone else I could get, but you? You've always been so stubborn on never stepping foot back here."

"So you drugged Deck in Atlanta to get me here?"

Because I already know that's what happened. Deck was right.

Auggie sighs. "It was the only way. Can't you see that? After our fight in Nashville, our promise was the only way I could think to get you to come back home. I even dropped him in that stolen pickup off on the Hazel Bridge to make sure he'd end up at Hazel General."

"So why drug him again at the fundraiser?"

"So you and he would have an alibi for the Davidson house burning. Don't you see? Everything I did before you left, everything I've done since then, it's all been for the four of you. It's all been to keep us together." He begins listing off. "I chose Dillon because Mark was turning away from us—Nicole never had that same pull over him. I chose Anders because she taunted you all through school. I got rid of the men who hurt you. I got Kathy under control and put Harry in jail so they wouldn't bother any of us anymore. I paid for Mark's school in New York, so he'd always feel like he was beholden to me and had to come back, too. Hell, I raised April and kept our home ready for when you all decided to come back. But you, Deck, and Mark weren't coming. *You* just weren't coming. So I had to push you. I had to push you like I always do."

"Where's Bridget, Auggie? Tell me you didn't murder your pregnant wife."

Auggie laughs. "She's sitting at an airport gate waiting for me, probably. Don't worry, by the time she realizes I've stood her up, the three of us will be long gone."

"Three of us?"

Auggie nods, annoyed. "You've forced my hand. I can't trust you to leave things be, now that you know, so we have to go away. To be a family—where no one can tear us apart again. Maybe not all of us. But the two of you were all I could manage right now."

He leans back toward the motor. There's a large black tarp there. We've always used it to cover fishing equipment to keep off the rain, but I should have noticed how bulky the pile beneath it is now.

Auggie yanks the tarp off, and there is April on her side, her hands bound behind her back like mine. She's awake, with a gag over her mouth, but she's attempting to scream. Thrashing.

"April," I shriek.

"Don't worry," Auggie insists. "I won't hurt her."

April's eyes are huge. She's clearly heard everything.

"Auggie," I say, my fear spiking tenfold, not only for myself, but for my sister. "You need to let us go."

Before, I'd been prepared to jump from the boat at any time, storm be damned, but with April? That's no longer possible.

Auggie shakes his head. "I can't. I wish I could, but you know too much. Coming home, you started to figure it out. I thought we would be fine if Mark took Deck back to New York temporarily and maybe I could convince you to stay on by yourself. But then April told me last night that you were asking about the earrings in the greenhouse, and I realized you knew. I waited for you to come home, but you didn't. I was surprised as anyone when I called the prison this morning and they said you'd been there to see Harry. So, you knew the truth, or at least part of it. I had to act."

"You need to let us go," I repeat with more steel in my tone. "The two of us won't tell anyone. Hell, we'll let you run off in the sunset and make for Canada or Mexico. But you need to release us."

Auggie shakes his head. "I can't do that. Haven't you been listening? I need you. I've worked too hard the last nine years to get you back."

"Then take me, but let April go."

I mean this. I will let him kidnap me and fight back later. Based on the way Auggie's talking, I don't expect him to let either of us live long.

It's as if he can read my mind. "No. She belongs to us, July, the same way we belong to her. But I promise, I'll keep you both safe. I have a cabin waiting. We'll be a family. The three of us."

I can barely hear him, hardly even see him through the rain. I hear the first crack. It's from the south end of the lake.

We're almost to the northern edge. I keep blinking, trying to clear the rain from my eyes, only for it to be replaced.

"What about Bridget and your baby?" I ask. "You really want to leave that family behind?"

"I never wanted that family," Auggie says. "That pregnancy was a complication. And the wedding became part of getting you all back this summer."

The sky's near black. The rain's pounding, so torrential and thick, it's painful. I count Mississippis. Two miles. The heart of the storm's close, the crashing deafening. We're now at risk from Man and Nature.

"Auggie, we need to get off this lake!"

"We'll be there in ten minutes! Trust me!"

Auggie has pivoted his eyes ahead. There are no boat launches this far north, nothing else but woods and the breeder pond, until you hit road. I know without a doubt that if Auggie manages to get us to the northern shoreline, there'll be no more chances for escape.

My eyes lock on April's. She's terrified. I can see that in her expression. But she darts her eyes down and to the left, trying to catch my notice. I follow her gaze as she squirms an elbow out at an angle that she shouldn't be able to if she were bound. My clever, brilliant sister has spent this time under the tarp rubbing her roped wrists against one of the boat's sharp edges behind her. She's free. She can swim. What she's waiting for is a way to get to me.

I hear the whack of thunder on the Georgia mountain peaks. It the chorus of a god, angry and malevolent. The zig of white snaps the center of the lake behind us, as if a movie on mute. There is only the smacking of rain, then the crash comes, delayed. The tides of water jutting off in all directions. There are no Mississippi's left to count. We are in the heart of the storm. Out on open water in the middle of lightning. Flash.

But we have no choice. April and I both see that, as the northern shoreline comes into view.

"I don't want you to worry," Auggie yells, barreling straight for it.

Another god's bellow. White static somewhere behind us.

"I'm going to take care of you both. I know you can't understand that right now. But you will."

The shoreline's only a hundred yards away. I somehow make out Auggie's truck parked on the beach. We're out of time.

Flash.

"April, go!" I yell, throwing myself up and lunging my body into our brother, at the same time he springs up to restrain me.

I vaguely catch sight of April jumping into the water off the bow, but my attention is on Auggie as he backhands me across the face.

He grabs me by the shoulders, shaking me. "Stop! God-damn it, July! Stop it!"

But I'm thrashing, even if it's useless with my hands behind my back. I kick and I head butt him and he undercuts me across the jaw. I can taste blood in my mouth, a tooth knocked in.

He has me in a bear grip, pressed against his chest. The biggest comfort of my life, once, being hugged by my brother. Now it's wet and cold, tainted by violence.

I hear the screaming of the wind. The storm overhead. It's impossible to see anything through the downpour. Only thunder, lightning. Pounding. Flashing.

Auggie's expression is darker than I've ever seen it, as he strikes me again, this time in the gut. I double over.

"Why did you make me do that?" he demands. "Why do you always have to make everything harder?"

He punches me across the jaw again, and I land on my side hard on the floor. A rib snaps, and I scream.

"For the love of God, stay down!" Auggie shouts, turning the boat around. "We're almost there!"

But I don't. If I'm going to die, it's going to be on my terms. That's who I've always been.

A live wire.

I tackle Auggie from behind. Had he been expecting it, he could have easily caught me. But he thought I was down. The force of my unexpected spring knocks him off balance and we both fall into the water.

The shock of the cold makes me gasp, which is a mistake because my lungs are full in seconds. My hands bound behind me, I'm fighting to tread the choppy waves against the current. My head's above water, my legs kicking beneath me, but it's sloppy. I keep going under. Keep swallowing water. I'm going to drown. I might have made it on a normal clear day with my hands restrained, but in the heart of the storm, I'm as good as dead.

One Mississippi. Clap. One Mississippi. Clap.

Auggie's screaming for me. He's thrashing through the water toward me, then pushing me back up into the boat. My body flips up onto the floor, my lungs gasping to expel water. Then Auggie grasps hold of the side of the troller with one hand, about to lift himself up, too. But I act on instinct, go for the wheel, and push the accelerator with my elbow as high as it will go. Close to twenty knots. The boat takes off, and Auggie is thrown backward off into the heart of the storm.

I can't see him through the sideways rain in my wake as the boat bounces frantically, smacking and jamming against every wave chop. The wind carries his scream of my name and then the world goes temporarily white.

The lightning strikes somewhere behind me around the center of the lake. Not directly next to, but definitely in the vicinity of where I have left my oldest brother to tread through the current.

Oh my God.

It is silent, that initial white, a breath of release.

Too late to turn back.

Then there is the crash, the wave, me hurtling forward as the boat does.

I must fall overboard at some point. I am drowning again.

Then, nothing.

*   *   *

I hear her voice. May.

No, not May. April. She's screaming at me.

"Breathe, July!"

There's pounding on my chest. Air in my lungs.

I'm choking. Up on my side, coughing up water. Over and over again.

April sags, relieved, holding me sideways.

I take my time, clearing all the water from my lungs. They ironically feel on fire. Like the water will never leave even after it is long gone. I'm rasping breath. Shivering.

April leans over me, her red hair pinned to the sides of her face and neck. She shivers as much as I do.

The skies are clearing over her head. A typical Georgia summer storm. Here, and rolling out just as fast. The Mississippis are spacing out. The dark clouds and soaking earth around us the only evidence that it had been here at all.

The lake is behind me. I sit up when I can manage it and stare out. The still-beating waves are dying down. The troller's close, but there's no sign of anyone in it.

"Where is he?" I rasp.

April shakes her head. "I don't know."

I don't know why this devastates me. I don't know why I don't trust it either.

I don't truly believe he's gone until Gabe and the cops arrive and fish him out of the water about a quarter mile up shore. They try to stop me, but wrapped in a wool blanket, I'm among the first to meet them when they pull him in.

They flip his body over on the sand. His eyes and mouth open, his skin blue. Electrocuted. Drowned. What does it matter?

I've been here before. I know this feeling. A sibling—the devastation of it. Only this time, I am the reason why.

I am the reason Auggie is dead.

25

Now

> There's no such thing as peace
> For people like you and me
> Only reveries and should have beens
> We carry it
> Our curse to bear witness
> That's our punishment in the end
>   — "Survivor's Guilt," written by Jules Thomas

I DON'T UNDERSTAND WHY I'm not dead.

I was in the water, too.

Electric shock drowning. That is Auggie's official cause of death. Where your body in paralyzed by an electric current passing through a body of water and then you drown. I fell in later, after the initial strike, I was so much further away down the lake by that time—this is the best explanation the medics can offer me for why I am not dead, too. It is a miracle, that is what they call it.

A miracle. That I'm alive and Auggie is dead.

April saved me. After she jumped from the boat, she reached shore, and saw when I went over for the second time after the strike. She risked further lightning, dove under the wave chop again and again to dive for me, then hauled me out. She, too, is a miracle.

Kathy, as it turns out, is the reason the cops arrived so fast. Apparently, my willful mother managed to slam her chair into Father Time hard enough to break it, then crawled her way through the hall jungle to reach the kitchen phone. With the risk of both her daughters' lives on the line, she finally told the cops everything. The women of my family are resilient, I will give them that.

April and I hardly spoke to each other in the back of the ambulance on the way to Hazel General, hardly glanced at one another as we were checked in and examined by doctors. But when one nurse attempted to relocate me behind a curtain, a mere bed away from my baby sister, I threw a fit. She will not be taken from my line of sight. Not for a long time yet.

I hear the full story of how April ended up on the boat when Schick and Ruble come to question us. Auggie picked her up early from her shift at the loading dock, claiming a family emergency. Once out of sight down the road, he'd pulled over and drugged April the same way he had me. She'd woken up under the troller's tarp shortly before I did.

The truth about Auggie's secret life has devastated her. I can see the betrayal on her face. I have to remind myself that his loss will be different for her than the rest of us. Auggie was in essence her father, the person who raised her. To have him do this to her, to kill her twin, for him to be dead—I make a mental note to find her a therapist wherever we end up after this. One heck of a good therapist.

Kathy is wheeled in on a bed shortly after and set up beside us. She for the most part appears unharmed, other than rope burns on her wrists to match April's and mine, but she's also shaking.

"Thank God," she whispers.

I lean over and squeeze her hand. "It's okay. We're okay because of you. Thank you. For trying to warn me."

Kathy shakes her head furiously. "I . . . I couldn't tell you everything. He threatened me. He said he'd kill April . . . when you and Mark left. He convinced the doctor to up my dose."

All this time I have underestimated my mother, but the tenacity it must have taken to live every day of the last nine years under the threat of a monster, while battling her own mental illness—I've never admired her more.

Mark is a screech down the hall, demanding from nurses our location in his normal gruff tone. When he enters our room, pushing past the stationed cops outside, he has Deck at his flank. While Mark stops mid-doorway, Deck barrels in and throws his arms around April, Kathy, and me, one by one. I don't push him away when it's my turn, but I don't have much to offer in the way of physical affection at the moment. The shock's still wearing off.

"You scared the shit out of us," Deck says.

I look to Mark. His arms are crossed and he's scowling, but there's something so vulnerable in the way he stands, like he doesn't know where he fits in this scene. Hell, I hardly do either.

"I'm glad you're all all right," he says, then fixes his gaze solely on me. "Although it would have been nice if someone had clued me in before I had to chase Deck through half of Atlanta airport and tackle him on the sidewalk."

"I'm sorry," I say, choosing to be completely honest. "I thought there was a chance it could have been you."

Mark's face twitches in a way that reminds me of Harry. I'm half expecting him to scream at me, but then I realize he's choked up.

"I'm sorry," I repeat.

But he shakes his head. His next words are hoarse, fighting everything not to cry. "I would have believed me before him, too."

Devastation. That is what passes among the four of us remaining Weaver siblings and our mother. Auggie fooled every one of us. And now, our former hero, the best of us—is revealed to be a lie. So which do we mourn? The real man or the illusion?

"When can we go home?" April whispers.

"Define home," Deck says.

Mark and my eyes lock, the role of family leaders having been bequeathed to us in a lightning strike.

But Kathy surprises us, taking that responsibility: "Soon."

* * *

The greenhouse is blocked off by the time we arrive home, a thick CAUTION tape line crossed over the door. I'm standing in front of it beneath a cloudy night sky. There's rumbling, another storm having just departed, and my feet are bare on the wet grass.

Deck steps up beside me with his hands in his pockets. He stares up at the night, then at the dark greenhouse.

"You know, my whole life, I don't think I've ever seen the lights fully off," he says. "It just looks eerie."

"We should have knocked it down after she died," I say.

"That'll be up to Harry and Kathy now, won't it?"

I nod. I haven't talked to our father, but I suspect he's been told everything by now. I don't begin to know how to feel about any of it. I aided in him being locked up for years for a crime he didn't commit. A near decade of his life he'll never get back. How do I learn to live with that? How do I begin to make it up to him?

"Not your fault," Deck says reading my mind. "Auggie's."

I face him. There are other amends I need to make. "I'm sorry I didn't believe you when you said someone was setting you up."

Decks shrugs. "Hell, wouldn't have been the first time I made that claim. Psycho brother drugging me to get the rest of our family back to town? Yeah, it's a stretch." He looks back at the greenhouse. "No. If anything, this has given me more reason to get myself right. All this time, I've been running from the fear that I'm gonna end up like Kathy. Turns out, she's not so bad."

I wrap my arm around him. "No, she's not. She promised me she won't go off the meds again once she's stable, whatever Harry argues."

Deck offers a skeptical brow. "And you believe that?"

I shrug. "Time will tell."

He looks thoughtful. "I'm gonna go away for a bit, too."

I squint, surprised. "Where?"

"I'm gonna take a chance on that place in Arizona Mark keeps talking about. If I'm gonna do this, and actually do it this time, I need to be removed from all the noise." He smiles. "Besides, those ninety-day inpatient places come with around-the-clock therapy, which, after all this, I could use a shit ton of."

"Is that your way of asking me to fork over my checkbook?"

Deck hugs me tighter. "Nah. Let's put it on Marky this go-around. It's his turn."

I laugh, not thinking I was capable of it any longer, and we stare up at the copper dome of the greenhouse for a while. It's a closure of sorts. For all of the rest of my life, I will never step foot in it again. I know that for certain.

*   *   *

Auggie couldn't have known it at the time, but his confession on the troller set multiple things into motion. Within two days, the entire Pacific Lake is dredged and the bodies of Adrian Bennet, along with five other women missing over the last decade, are surfaced. It breaks like wildfire across the news, reaching national coverage that the man convicted for the Pacific Lake murders in 1997, Harold Weaver, had been innocent. His son, local Pacific contractor and known family man, August Weaver, was the true culprit, having been preying upon women along the Gulf of Mexico for the last nine years since. His final victim was his pregnant wife Bridget Weaver, found strangled to death in their honeymoon suite later that same day. This final revelation devastates me. Poor Bridget, who did nothing wrong other than love the wrong guy.

Auggie's face has become the news' symbol for a monster. A testament to violence and activists' preaching that white men are the ones committing the true, heinous mass murders in America. My brother is being compared to Ted Bundy, the Zodiac Killer, Hannibal Lecter. His face has become a warning sound for overprotective mothers across the South to tell their daughters not to trust the boy with the pretty face—he could be an August Weaver. It destroys me a bit to see his image used like that. The contradiction is eating me alive: the brother I loved and the brother the killer. Where did one end and the other begin? Or had it all been an act, his love for me another lie he told to convince himself he was human?

We have his body cremated. That isn't even debated. Deck makes a crack about the lightning having half finished the job already, and receives a slap to the head from Mark.

When the day comes, none of my siblings want to say goodbye to him. The three of them are a rainbow of grief and rage. I don't push them. Something about me doing this alone feels right. I'm not in black; this isn't a funeral march. But I do feel the weight of carrying Auggie in my hands as I make my way out onto the community dock at Barker's Point. I'm alone, the shoreline around me stitched in by woods.

It's a long walk to the end, the longest of my life, but I do it in steadying steps, the rickety beams shifting beneath me. I think of all the times I've walked these same planks with him when we came out here to swim. At the end, I clutch the box to my chest. It's coarse, the wood unpolished and simple. I feel a splinter dig into my thumb.

I've been humming. It isn't something I'm conscious of until now. It's a melody I have never written and will never write—the story of my brother and the lake. Of Harry and

Kathy. Of May and those women. Of my living siblings and me. I close my eyes and I take it all in. The sounds of Pacific Lake: the birds whistling from the trees, the ripples of faraway boat motors whipping across the water, the smell of the muddy sand and beach. This is my one gift to Auggie—the brother I thought he was.

Maybe for some people, grief is black and white, but I learned a long time ago how to mourn the gray. People in reality, and the people we believe them to be.

I open my eyes, release the lid, and flip the contents of ash into the water. It's not goodbye or good riddance. It feels more like an apostrophe, an incomplete. There will never be closure for me and Auggie. I turn away before I can watch what is left of him be eaten by sunfish or wash up on the shore. That moment is for the killer.

When I climb the wooden stairs to the road that leads the half mile up to the cemetery, I'm surprised to find Gabe leaning against his truck. He's a spark of light, in all ways. His smile alone cuts through the bleak.

We haven't had a chance to talk since that day on the shore. Gabe came to the hospital, but was told to go home once he answered the detectives' questions. This last week since has been a blur.

"Hey," I say.

"Daniela called me from the diner. Said y'all were heading here. Where are your siblings?"

I nod up the hill. "At the cemetery. Visiting May."

"You want a ride?"

I remember the first time he asked me that. How different nine years make.

I stop in front of him, place my hands in my back pockets. "Nah. They're coming to grab me."

"Right. I just wanted to make sure you were all right." He runs a hand through his hair. "I feel terrible that I let you go back into that house alone. I wish I'd gotten to you sooner."

I touch his shoulder. "I never would have figured out any of this if it wasn't for you. And it turns out April has a bit of a hidden savior complex, so it worked out."

"You saved her, too," he says. "You distracted him."

"Maybe." I'll never feel like that did much, and I'll always wonder if I'd made another choice—if I hadn't knocked Auggie into the water, if I hadn't left him there to drown—what if? But then again, if I hadn't, I might be dead or living as a captive now. Auggie would be killing more women. He would have hurt April.

"So, what now?" Gabe asks.

"Deck's off to Arizona for his program. Mark's going back to New York to be with his wife. And April's coming with me."

April's decision to move to Nashville for her senior year shocked us all. Mark and I had given her the option to live with either of us or remain with Kathy in Pacific. But my little sister wants nothing more to do with this town or our family legacy. Probably best, with the influx of death threats we're receiving via phone and mail on a daily basis again. I can't imagine how she'd be treated in school. And now that it's looking like Colton Davidson's about to win the mayoral race, Connor has conveniently disappeared from April's life entirely.

I don't know how I'm going to make up the last near decade to my sister, or ever get her to trust anyone again after Auggie, but we'll figure that out together.

Gabe inhales. "So, I guess this is it, then."

I still love Gabe Santana. There's a piece of me that I don't think ever stopped.

"You know," I say, "there's a good art scene in Nashville. Antique furniture, galleries. Probably be a good business decision to come check it out."

Gabe raises a brow. "Is that right?"

"Might even be enough business that you're forced to spend a whole lot more time there. If that's something you'd be interested in, that is."

He smiles small. "I'd be willing to consider it."

I grin ear to ear. "That's a relief. Because if I'm going to start writing music that's half decent again, I'm going to need someone around to tell me how it measures up to my earlier stuff."

He comes forward and kisses me, once, short, sweet. Not a promise of forever, but a promise of maybe.

Mark's rental truck comes down the hill then and pulls to a stop behind Gabe's. He gets out. "Santana."

Gabe nods, no sign of malice toward him. "Weaver."

Mark shifts on his heels. "Sorry about the whole reporting you to the cops thing."

I about fall over. I don't know if I've ever heard the word *sorry* come out of my middle brother's mouth before.

"Not a problem," Gabe says.

Mark nods back up the road. "April and Deck were still cleaning up May's tombstone." He yells in that direction, "Children, move your asses! I don't want to be late." He looks back to Gabe and me inquisitively. "Is it possible to be late to prison?"

I look at my watch. "We might find out."

Gabe offers me a final look, the absurdity of my family making us both laugh. "See you soon," he mouths and then he is in his truck, pulling out.

I feel emptier when he's gone. But it doesn't feel like an end. Only another apostrophe.

April and Deck appear in unison down the hill, our brother bounding like a child and our sister following slowly after him, clearly questioning the other's sanity.

"I'm flying!" he yells leaping up a tire and over into the bed of the truck.

"We're going on a major highway," Mark says.

Deck sits down. "Just until we cross the town line then. April?"

"Hell, no," Mark says.

To my surprise, April looks to me expectantly.

"You want to?" I ask.

She shrugs. "You were all gone. I never got to try it."

"Come on, guys!" Deck says.

Mark and I exchange glances.

"We can't judge her for being stupid when we did the same thing at her age," I say.

"I've never been stupid," Mark grumbles, but rounds the truck to the driver's side without further protest.

I shrug and April takes that as confirmation to climb up. She takes a seat across from Deck, with her back to a tire.

I point to Deck. "Listen. You wait until we are all the way down the hill, you hear me? And the moment we get to the town line, you won't argue when Mark stops the car and orders you both inside."

Deck holds up his hands. "Whatever, Kathy."

I shoot him the bird, close the tailgate, and climb into the cabin to slide in beside Mark.

As we descend the hill, I stare out at Pacific Lake twisting past us. I wonder if I will ever be able to see it and not think about all of them, of how my past is so intricately woven to those dead women. To Auggie and May.

"I talked to Kathy on the phone this morning," says Mark. "She sounds better than she has in years."

"She does."

I'd been talking to our mother, too. We're bringing her home from the hospital tomorrow. Insurance kicking her out and all. She wanted to come today, but we didn't have enough room in the truck.

Mark stares out the back window at our two youngest siblings. "He's going to get them both killed."

"Probably," I admit.

Deck moves to stand up in the bed. I open my window and listen as he holds a hand out to April. She hesitates, but only for a second. Deck helps her up. The truck picks up speed as Mark turns onto the main road.

And I watch them. It's unspoken between Mark and me that I'm on younger sibling duty. If one's about to go down, I'm the safety net.

"The trick is to stay close to the hood and hold on with one hand!" Deck yells. "If you get too close to the back, you'll get whipped off! Got it?"

"Got it!" April yells through the wind.

I smile small, remembering. It's also accompanied by pain.

But there's still some joy left in my little sister. I can see it. She's not hollering and hooting like Deck is. But I can feel her faint smile every whip and turn, her red hair billowing into her eyes.

We'll find a way to be happy. I silently promise her that. Or at the very least, all of us will find something close.

*   *   *

"And you were worried we'd be late," Deck says to Mark.

Deck and April are sitting on the tailgate facing Mark, while I'm pacing the lot. We've been waiting what feels like an hour.

"It's prison," Mark says. "There's a lot of paperwork."

"You're sure he wanted all of us to come?" April asks.

It's a squeak. She doesn't remember Harry like the rest of us do. It'll be like meeting a half stranger.

"That's what he told me on the phone," I say. "He wants us all here."

I walk to the edge of the parking lot, looping my fingers through the barbed wire fence. It's sunny today, the lawn that hugs the prison grounds decayed brown with early fall. But it's still humid. Georgia humid.

I'm nervous. I keep stretching my knuckles through the wire, blocking my siblings' voices out behind me. I don't know what I'll say to Harry when I see him free for the first time in nearly a decade. I don't know where to begin making amends for my part in him being here.

It isn't lost on me that I'm like that little girl again, the one who lingered at the end of the dock night after night, watching the lake for that same speck of dust to appear.

The prison gate opens. I suck in a deep breath.

A figure appears on the horizon: Harry.

And here I wait, his Livewire. I wait to welcome my father home. I can't help but start counting in my head.

One Mississippi. Two Mississippi. Three . . .

ACKNOWLEDGMENTS

To my incredible literary agent/advocate/part-time therapist, James McGowan—I will forever owe you the moon for taking a chance on my writing. I hope this is just the start for our partnership. Many thanks also to Bookends Literary Agency for being downright amazing.

To my editor, Sara J. Henry, thank you for seeing this story about a quirky, beautifully damaged family for everything I wanted it to be and fighting to make it ours. To Matthew Martz, Rebecca Nelson, Madeline Rathle, Dulce Botello, Thai Perez, Holly Ingraham, Jess Verdi, Laura Apperson, Doug White, Stephanie Manova, and the entire team at Crooked Lane, thank you for taking a chance on this book and for everything you did to make it better in every way.

To my thesis advisors, Stephanie Grant and Dolen Perkins-Valdez, I wrote the first hundred pages of this novel to impress you—I hope it worked. So much of this book and every word I write is influenced by what I learned in your classrooms. Special thanks also to Marianne Noble, Rachel Louise Snyder, Kyle Dargan, Tyrese Coleman, and the rest of the faculty in American University's Department of Literature for their wisdom and encouragement. The same goes for Benjamin Truax, Cara Racin, Ricardo Kimbers Jr., Dara

Feldman, Will Schick, Vic Ruble, Jefferson Thomas, Akash Vasishtha, Austine Model, Cristi Donoso, and everyone else a part of my AU Creative Writing MFA cohort.

As for my family and friends—you all know who you are—I am here because of you. But especially to my brothers Tyler and Grey, my person Jessie, my stepmom Julie, my mentor Michele, my grandparents Ellie and George, and my aunt Julie and uncle Paul, I love you all fiercely.

To my mom, Mary—God, how I miss you in these moments and can picture you jumping up and down right now. So much of this book is a love letter to grief and therefore a love letter to you. I think of you every time I see a butterfly.

Finally, to my dad, Dave, my best friend and man in the arena—there will never be enough words for all that we have been through together, so I'll settle for thank you and I love you. I couldn't have done this without you.